An Accidental Affair

Book 1 in the Liliana Batchelor Series

Holly Blackstone

Copyright

An Accidental Affair

First Edition - Revised

e-pub ISBN: 978-0-9891912-0-3

Hardback edition (September 2014): 978-0-9891912-5-8

Hardback edition- cover revision (March 2016): 978-0-9891912-5-8

Cover art

Notice:

This book contains explicit language and descriptions of sex and includes some instances of BDSM play. If any of this sounds offensive to you, please do not continue reading. This book is not meant to encourage or instruct the reader concerning a BDSM relationship, and is for entertainment purposes only.

Acknowledgements

For Mr. Man, who has been unerringly supportive.

Special thanks to Meetra for her patience.

In Memoriam: W.S.A. – if only someone had been there.

Introduction

"…and when one of them meets with his other half, the actual half of himself… the pair are lost in an amazement of love and friendship and intimacy and one will not be out of the other's sight even for a moment..."

— Plato's Symposium

Chapter 1

Lily sighs as she slips her car into drive and manoeuvres out of the parking lot. It's Friday evening and she has just spent the last several hours doing some research for her Master's thesis. She put it off as long as she could, but now it's time to face the drive back to her townhouse and another supper alone.

You have no one to blame but yourself, her snarky inner voice pipes up. There's some truth to that; she worked full time supporting herself while going to school and that hadn't left much time for a social life. What little free time she had carved out had been punctuated by a string of failed relationships, each more disappointing than the last.

Lily will be 28 in December. Most of her friends are married or in serious relationships that will soon turn permanent, whereas she hasn't had a serious boyfriend in… years. There must be something about her that just doesn't work in a relationship she reasons, as all hers have been short. Sometimes there had been good, perhaps even great sex; several times there had seemed to be a real connexion, but all had managed to fizzle out by the nine month mark.

She turns on her blinker and slows for the stop sign. How many times has she driven this same path? Out of the lot to the gate; left at the entrance to the university and down to Pacific and Montlake. Depending on her mood, she will select either I-90 or side roads and meander through streets to her development; the dark windows of her quiet home are a stark contrast to the bustling, brightly lit houses of her neighbours.

Tesla and Fermi will be there; they are always happy to see her, at least. Their purrs and rubs will go some way towards alleviating the loneliness that is now a permanent fixture in her life. Still, they are no replacement for a lover - someone she can confide in, enjoy life with.

Almost too late she remembers that she needs to stop by the store. At the bottom of the hill she turns left instead of going straight and heads towards the strip mall that houses the local liquor and grocery stores.

It's quiet for a Friday; *everyone is inside or where they need to be*, she thinks. Lily remembers calling her best friend Janet earlier in the week to see if she and her beau Louis wanted to do anything to-night. It took a few minutes to weasel the story out of Janet; they were throwing a supper party for couples and Janet hadn't wanted to hurt Lily's feelings by mentioning it.

So tonight, instead of spending time at her best friend's house as part of a couple whiling the night away, she spent hours in the library at the U (again), requesting books for her thesis project and otherwise wasting time.

As she coasts to the intersection, the bells for the railroad crossing ahead begin to clang and the striped gate starts to lower slowly. She rolls her eyes and shakes her head - what luck. Well, she needs too much from the store to just turn around and she is already here. Might as well wait it out; Lily has nowhere else to be except home.

She notices a car on the opposite side of the tracks in the dim light. *Wow. A Porsche Panamera.* She looks covetously at it. Someone at work has one and she drives by slowly and gazes at it longingly if she happens to pass by - the sleek styling makes it look fast just standing still. A friend has an old Boxster and Lily has driven it a few times; it handles like it is on rails, whipping around corners effortlessly. *One day, maybe.*

The gate is nearly down and she watches a set of headlights come up rather swiftly on the Panamera from behind. *Oh my God,* she thinks. *It's going to hit!*

She watches in horror as the car smashes into the Panamera behind and off centre, pushing it hard enough forward that it slides under the nearly closed railroad gate and up to the tracks. The car backs up and speeds away, leaving the Panamera and its driver in harm's way.

Lily is out of the car and stepping across the tracks before she realises it. *Whoa, when did I decide this?* She hadn't consciously commanded it, but of course there had been no time to think. From her vantage she can see the bright speck of the train's headlights far down the tracks. No one has budged from the car, which means someone is wounded or unconscious.

Perhaps it is the memory of her uncle's advice - who had tried to be a stand in father to her after her own had died - and his words to 'always be ready to help another in need' that has awakened her subconscious to action. Whatever the impetus, she rushes across the tracks as carefully and quickly as she dares. She doesn't want to be a witness to a terrible accident, to death like this.

She steps to the car; the driver's door is unlocked and she yanks it open. The limp form of a man pressing against his seatbelt now leans out of the car. He is obviously unconscious and airbags are deployed but even, so he is bleeding from his head.

Lily can see in her peripheral vision that the train light is brighter - a lot brighter. She hesitates only a second before reaching across him to the buckle. She feels the dead weight of his body press against her as she releases the seat belt and the suddenness of it nearly knocks her off her feet. She regains her footing and puts her hands underneath his armpits and pulls him from the seat.

She nearly stumbles as she steps backwards. *Please body, please, just work, be co-ordinated*, she begs. The train is close enough to see the car; its horn blasts in warning. She tugs and the man doesn't move - he's caught, and he is slipping from her arms.

Do it! She commands herself and tightens her grip and pulls with the strength of fear, of endorphins, of will. He breaks free from the car and she drags him down and away from the tracks. The brakes of the train are squealing, and still she tugs at him; he is tall - close to six and a half feet she guesses. Lily summons all the stubbornness in her and gives another yank.

She is exhausted and collapses on the pavement, his head in her lap, as she watches the train clip the front edge of the Panamera and crush it. The car spins around and the driver's side smashes into the engine. She reaches into her pocket and grabs her cell phone, calls 911 and informs them of the accident.

****

The flashing lights of aid vehicles seem to take forever to appear. She gently lays the mystery man flat on the road and places his head on her windbreaker. She is able to get a better look at him now that she has a minute to check him over. He has dark hair that is somewhat short and spiky, a button down shirt, leather pants and dark boots. He looks like the stereotype of a rock star and she idly wonders if he is. His pulse is a little weak and the blood on his head is troubling, but at least it has stopped. She took First Aid training and does the best she can to make him comfortable, hoping that the rough tugs to free him from the car haven't injured him further.

Lily talks to him, not sure if he can register the words. She knows they comfort her some, as she has begun to shake now that the situation has sunk in; she could have been killed along with this mystery man.

"You were in an accident. I've called paramedics. Please just be calm; it will be okay." At one point he moans and she gently places a hand on his brow and shushes him.

She is grateful the train didn't derail. A few moments after it comes to a stop she can make out a dark figure walking alongside the tracks. Finally she is able to discern details; it must be the train engineer.

"Did you…", he begins. She can smell grease and exhaust on his clothes.

"I already called 911", she answers.

The engineer nods. "I'm Joe. I was relieved to see no one was in the car. What happened?"

She can just begin to make out the sound of sirens in the distance. She relates the story as best she can; her voice sounds shaky to her. Joe however just looks at her, his expressive brown eyes wide.

"That was VERY brave", he says, awe in his voice.

"Could have been very stupid", Lily mumbles, the darkness hiding the blush that has crept into her cheeks. She realises she still has a calming hand on the unconscious stranger's forehead and makes a motion to remove it and he begins to moan, so she lightly strokes the side of his forehead that isn't caked in blood.

"But it wasn't. It was brave", Joe says before turning to answer his chirping walkie-talkie.

She looks down at the bloodied and bruised face of the stranger she is comforting. His car must have been hit pretty hard to push it near the tracks. Will he be okay? Who is he? Where was he on his way to when he stopped at the tracks? And who would slam into a car like that and leave someone in danger? It seemed to Lily that he would have died had she not rushed to help, and the thought makes her tremble all over again. If something had happened to him - if she hadn't tried to help, how could she have lived with herself after that? *But that's not what happened. You've done something you always wanted to do – you've made a difference.*

She somehow feels bonded to this man now, whoever he is. His face looks young; he can't be more than thirty. He seems fit; when she heaved him out of the car she felt muscles through his shirt. *Hey, he's an accident victim, not someone to lust over,* the snide part of her consciousness chimes in. The sirens are close now -and she had thought it was going to be another dull Friday night.

Lily watches as an ambulance turns onto the road and races towards them. Behind are two police cars and the effect is startling. The yellow light of the headlights and Joe's flashlight are augmented with a kaleidoscope of flashing colours. She whispers some more encouragement to the Mystery Man as all at once figures rush towards them. "The paramedics are here. You're in good hands."

"Please step back, ma'am", one of the EMTs cautions her as they approach. She gives Mystery Man (or MM as she thinks of him now), one more reassuring pat and stands up and steps away. She realises now how achy she is, how weak her knees are from squatting on the asphalt trying to comfort MM, not wanting to leave his side. A hand reaches out to steady her.

"Are you all right, miss?" Lily turns; it is one of the officers. "Were you hurt? I'm Officer Patterson. Can you tell us what happened?" He gently guides her away from the paramedics who are examining MM.

"I'm… fine. Just a little shaken up, I think." She relates what happened, one ear cocked as she tries in vain to hear what the paramedics are saying. She is still trembling a little. *Stop it*, she tells herself. *He was hurt, you weren't. Don't be weak*. Gosh, that inner voice even sometimes sounds like her mom's - chiding her, always critical.

She is surrounded by four police officers now, listening intently to her story. When she finishes they look at one another in silence. One of them steps away and towards a paramedic to exchange words while the other EMT is going to the back of the ambulance, more than likely to retrieve a stretcher.

Officer Patterson speaks. "That was one gutsy move, miss. You saved his life." He beckons to what used to be MM's beautiful Panamera.

“I… um.”, she doesn’t know what to say when put as bluntly as that. “I just wanted to help”, she offers, as if that is sufficient explanation.

Officer Patterson puts his arm around her shoulders and steers her towards the waiting police car. He nods at the two remaining officers and they head towards the smashed remains of the vehicle and Joe, who is standing nearby looking at it forlornly. She can barely make out his voice. “That was a damn nice car…”

Chapter 2

She didn't want to go to the hospital. Officer Patterson – Fred, as he insisted on being called – hadn't listened to any of her objections. He'd been gentle in questioning her - taking down the pertinent information in a professional manner and his voice had been kind, sympathetic. When she balks at the ride to the hospital, he becomes firm.

He overrides all her objections. Her car is on the other side of the tracks. Officer Friendly (yes, that is his name and she chuckles at that), will drive it to the hospital for her. If she gets a clean bill of health, she can drive it home from there. She hasn't been in an impact, Lily points out. Fred counters that no, she has just dragged a grown man more than half a foot taller than her out of a car and several yards to safety. Besides, she has a cut on her arm. She looks down and sure enough a several inch gash is on her left forearm - dry blood is caked around the wound. She must have gotten it when she dragged MM out of the car, but she hadn't felt it. *That explains the tear in your windbreaker you were so baffled by*, her inner voice observes sarcastically. Fred points out that if she hasn't been aware of that cut, it is possible she sustained other injuries.

So the end result was that she reluctantly climbed into the ambulance and is now sitting next to the stretcher that contains MM. He is in a neck brace, an IV line is in him, and Geoff, one of the paramedics, is monitoring his vitals. Despite the gash and blood, it's clear that he's an incredibly handsome man.

She knows they probably won't tell her – patient confidentiality and all that, she reasons – but she asks anyway. Will he be okay? Geoff hesitates only briefly. "Current assessment is that none of his injuries are life threatening." Lily breathes a sigh of relief.

It has been a while since the excitement of the rescue wore off and she becomes more aware of discomfort in her body. Her left shoulder is incredibly painful and she winces whenever the ambulance hits a bump. Her knees ache and she feels 'tired to the bone', as her grandpa used to say. All she wants to do is go home, take a shower and crawl between some clean sheets. But God is she hungry! It is now approaching 11 and she hasn't eaten anything but a granola bar since noon, almost 12 hours prior.

They pull up to the hospital and she watches sadly as MM is hurriedly wheeled down the hall. She is taken to a large room with several beds and steered towards a gurney. The nurse follows her in and pulls the curtain along tracks until they are blocked from the view of other patients; the pervasive smell of antiseptic makes Lily's nose twitch.

Temperature, questions, a quick look at her arm and the nurse puts a dressing gown on the bed and asks Lily to change into it. She then excuses herself and returns a few moments later with a doctor. He's middle age with salt and pepper hair, bright brown eyes and a nice smile. He introduces himself as Dr. Chong and sets to work.

Lily endures more questions and this time, prodding. After he examines her shoulder he frowns, his expressive eyes worried.

"You may have torn a ligament in your shoulder. It could be a sprain, but…", he palpates the area and rotates her shoulder. An involuntary yelp escapes her lips.

"We'll send you to x-ray just to be safe", he says, his brow creasing in thought. "I didn't like the sound or feel of that. By the way", he puts his hand on her good shoulder and looks her square in the face. "We all heard what you did, and what would have happened. Crossing the tracks to help… that was amazing. We'll take good care of him." She just nods, too tired to protest that anybody else would have done the same thing, that it could have been the wrong choice, or any of the hundred other excuses that minimize what she did.

It's nearly two hours later before she is discharged. Lily's left arm is in a sling and she has a bottle of oxycodone in her pocket along with folded up instructions. Her forearm tingles from the topical anaesthetic they used when they stitched up the cut there. Officer Fred Patterson stopped by just before she left; her car is in the hospital lot now and they discovered what had probably cut her. The remains of a plastic insulated mug were scattered around in MM's car.

"It was pretty well smashed", says Fred. "It's hard to know which impact shattered the container, but it seems like a reasonable assumption." He smiles at her and looks her in the eye. "Let me give you an escort home tonight", he says and she agrees. She wants to know about MM but is too nervous to ask; it will probably be in the papers or on Northwest Cable News, she rationalises. Lily wonders who he is and whether the authorities have made contact with his family yet. As far as she's concerned, everyone has been incredibly nice - prompt in looking after her and very kind, so she knows MM is in good hands.

The splint-sling combination they have her in is unwieldy. When she finally makes it home, she is greeted by insistent mewling and massive leg rubbing. She's seldom out this late and 'the Boys' - as she refers to her cats - are reacting to the upset in the schedule.

Rather awkwardly she opens some cans of wet food for them and, too tired to do anything else, she undresses and tumbles into bed.

****

It is the fourth time that morning that she gets a phone call; *I'm normally never this popular*, Lily thinks. She reaches for the phone, fumbles with the base, and turns the ringer off. Her shoulder hurts as if it has been hit with a baseball bat; she can see it is swollen and black and blue. Her forearm throbs as her immune system pumps antibodies and anything else it can find into the gash in her arm and the rest of her body doesn't feel so great either. It's sort of a hangover without any of the fun stuff up front.

You're 5'8" and 154 lbs and yanked a flour sack weighing over 200 lbs across the road. How do you think you'd feel?, comes the sarcastic observation. She realises she probably won't be getting much peace until she quiets the growling in her stomach, so she decides to hunt up something to eat.

When she's in the kitchen she remembers the reason for all the excitement last night – the trip to the grocery store that had been necessarily aborted. Sighing, she returns to the bedroom and gingerly dresses, her shoulder seeming even more achy than it was last night. *The old twenty-four hour rule – it always feels worse the day after.* Her intention was to be productive to-day around the house but dealing with her arm this morning makes her recognise the need to change plans; best to just head out, grab a bite and take it from there. It's difficult to think on an empty stomach.

It is Saturday and predictably Denny's is crowded, even though it is nearly noon. Lily waits for a little while before being led to a seat. She sits down and doesn't even bother opening the menu, ordering a Diet Coke to start off with. Suddenly she's aware that her phone is ringing and she fumbles while pulling it out of her pocket. *Janet.* She sighs and answers it.

"OH MY GOD!", she squeals as soon as she hears Lily's voice. "Why didn't you call and tell me?"

Lily is baffled. "What did I do now?"

"Your name and picture are all over the local news! The accident! Have they interviewed you yet?"

Lily rolls her eyes. "What do the articles say?"

"Just that Lily Batchelor is a certifiable hero. You dragged a guy from a car that was about to be hit by a TRAIN. That is SO James Bond!"

Lily sees out of the corner of her eye a patron next to her reading the *Seattle Times*. She can make out part of the headline, 'Heroine saves unconscious man…'. She groans. She now notices her waitress at the soda dispenser is pointing at her and talking in whispers to the hostess. An uneasy tingling begins in her spine, and dread settles in her stomach.

"They have my picture?", she asks with trepidation.

"Yeah, the one from the state science awards ceremony." *Someone must have worked overtime to dig that one up*, Lily thinks.

She notices the man reading the newspaper has begun to look at her out of the corner of his eye. Lily's waitress has returned with the glass of Diet Coke, and several other servers follow her, crowding the table.

"We were just wondering… were you in the paper?"

Lily's eyes widen, and she grabs at the loose dollars in her jeans pocket, throwing several down next to the glass of soda. "I… won't be needing a table", she explains and grabbing her purse, she stands and weaves her way to the front door.

"What was that?", Janet asks.

"I was at Denny's getting breakfast and someone started to look at me and the waitress asked if I was in the paper", Lily replies. She was just trying to help a guy in need; she hadn't counted on this - she hates fuss.

"Come by, I'll make breakfast for you, brunch… whatever you want. Louis is dying to hear the details!"

"Janet, I'm really beat. I was on my way to get groceries when it happened because I didn't have much of anything in my house; all I really want to do is sleep. I dislocated my shoulder trying to pull the MM… er, Mystery Man out of the car. I'm just not up for much."

"Mystery Man", Janet repeats, a hint of awe in her voice.

"So, who is he?", Lily asks casually, her heart beating faster at the thought of him.

"You don't know?!", asks Janet, incredulous.

"No, he was dressed like a rock star though, leather pants. C'mon Janet. Don't tease." Lily already is back in her car and carefully pulls the seatbelt across her lap and shoulder.

"Well that's funny", says Janet. "This is what it says: 'The victim, who is in stable condition, could not be identified pending notification of family.' So, still a mystery - how exciting!"

Lily wraps up her call with Janet as quickly as she can and heads to the grocery store. *Better stock up for the next few days and hunker down,* she thinks. She hadn't anticipated this and wonders how the news agencies have gotten a hold of it – she hadn't seen any reporters on the scene. *Funny they got my name but not MM's,* she thinks and frowns. *It's not like I gave anyone permission to tell the world.* Her stomach is now in open rebellion and demands satisfaction, its growling clearly audible.

She makes it into Safeway and is back out in record time. She doesn't usually shop at this hour on a Saturday, so fortunately none of the checkers she chats with are there. They would definitely have asked about her shoulder and what would she have said? She could either have lied, which wasn't her style, or… *I plucked a man from a smashed car and saved him from certain death,* her voice chimes in. Gosh, that sounds so arrogant, so superior.

She pays for her groceries and accepts help out to her car. Her shoulder is incredibly painful now and she needs to get home, ice it, eat and take something for the pain. She told herself she would resist the urge to take the oxycodone, knowing it would make her feel dopey, but her shoulder is crying out for mercy. She looks down when a passerby does a double take at her. *Please just get me out of here!* She can't leave quickly enough.

At home, Lily puts away her groceries while a bagel toasts. A nice layer of cream cheese on the bagel, the whole thing washed down with some apple juice, and her stomach finally begins to forgive her. She hesitates before actually taking one of the pills – she is worried they will make her too groggy and she'll sleep the day away – and then realises she isn't going to be going anywhere anyway. She makes her way to the bedroom, closes the curtains and heads back to bed.

Chapter 3

"Ah. There you are George."

George hesitates only a moment before closing the door behind him and walking towards the figure on the bed.

"You look much better this afternoon, sir", George says, a note of relief in his voice.

The figure on the bed inclines his head an inch in acknowledgement and then winces at the discomfort. "Still feel rather… well, I've been better." He says, flashing a bright, if brief, smile. "But yes, it's an improvement from this morning. Did you do as I asked?"

"Yes, Mr. Watson. I didn't find out much yet – not enough time to obtain a lot of detail. Just wanted to inform you of what has been gathered so far."

Stuart Watson reaches out with his left hand for the papers; his right forearm is in a cast and even a slight movement causes it to ache. It takes great effort to concentrate, what with the drugs they've plied him with.

George steps forward while opening a brown attaché case. He places a file folder into Stuart's outstretched hand while meeting his eyes. They are as crisp as they always are; a mix of gunmetal grey and blue skies and only slightly unfocused from the effects of the painkillers.

Stuart looks up at George. "I'll read them over later. Summary?"

"Liliana Batchelor, most often goes by Lily. She's 28, a graduate student in Materials Engineering at the University."

Stuart cocks a well formed eyebrow. "You don't say…"

"Yes sir. Single, lives alone it appears, near Woodinville. Works at NewTech Materials Labs."

"Has my name appeared in the paper?", Stuart interrupts. Placing the folder down, he runs his left hand through his hair, avoiding the butterfly bandages that hold the gash in his scalp closed. Being restricted to bed rest is frustrating him.

"No sir. As you asked, we were able to withhold that, but just."

"Well done", says Stuart. An acknowledgment in the form of a fleeting smile passes over George's lips.

"I want to see her, George. What is the likelihood that she knows who I am?"

"I don't believe she does, sir. Your picture is not often in the paper, and the officer who took her statement said she didn't appear to have any idea as to your identity."

"Good. We'll just go by first names then, obviously no references that would give it away."

"Yes sir. When would you like to see her?"

"This evening, if possible. Well it's almost that already, so whenever you can fetch her. Inform me if there is a problem."

George tips his head in agreement and heads to the door.

Stuart lies back on the pillow. The throbbing in his head, the pain in his arm and the purported internal bruising have left him weak and spent. This feeling of being incapacitated isn't a sensation he is accustomed to, nor one that he likes.

He closes his eyes and he can nearly make out her voice so exactly it is almost as if she is in the room.

"You've been in an accident, but you'll be fine." "Help is on the way." "The paramedics are here, don't worry." Her words of comfort had seeped into his subconscious; it was almost as if they were burned into his brain. Her voice had been calm and low, a constant reminder that she held vigil while he was unconscious. When he had heard about what had happened, he was stunned; a stranger had raced across the tracks to pull him out of his car, the train barely missing both of them. He HAD to meet the woman who had risked her own life to save his.

He doesn't want her to know who he is, not yet, and this… he looks around in frustration at the IV in his left arm and at the cast on his right. It puts him at a disadvantage.

He is curious; what will she look like? Is she the mousy engineering type? Her voice had a sultry edge to it that haunts him, and he remembers a touch - soft and tentative, yet it eased his mind. Odd, how the impression was so powerful that it penetrated through the pain and injuries and lingers still.

****

Lily briefly turns her phone on mid Saturday afternoon only to turn it off again. Reporters call, asking for her story; the local news wants her on the evening broadcast. Her doorbell rings twice and through the chain bolt she declines both requests for an interview. It's now early evening and she is glad that she managed to grab groceries before the story took off. Strangers invading her privacy, investigating her, trying to get background information to flesh out their stories and scrutinizing her life? *No thank you.*

Friends call as well, basking in the reflected glow of her newfound celebrity and she begs off as soon as she can. Her mom calls, and she ignores it. She didn't run across the tracks and help MM because she thought it would bring her fame or attention; it had been instinct, a sudden reaction to a crisis that was unfolding in front of her. Because it hadn't been a conscious decision that she had reached, she doesn't feel as if she can take any credit for it, accept any accolades - she wasn't a hero. Not that she regretted it - she didn't - and had she been given time to consider it she would have done the same thing, but that hadn't been the case. Her body knew what to do before it really registered in her brain - it was that simple.

Her shoulder still throbs and she is considering supper prospects when her doorbell rings again. She growls, scattering the cats. Lily thinks about not answering, but worries it will be another persistent reporter ringing incessantly when she just wants peace and quiet.

She opens the door the generous inch the chain allows. "Can I help you?"

A gentleman with broad shoulders stands in the doorway; he has an ex-military air about him, and is probably in his mid-40's. *He doesn't look like a reporter - insurance investigator?*, she muses. He's well dressed, but doesn't hold any papers or a folio, as she would expect an adjuster to have.

"Are you Miss Batchelor?" His accent is British, Welsh perhaps?

"Yes, I am, and I'm afraid I…", she stops mid-sentence, as the man holds up his palm.

"Please, Miss Batchelor. My name is George. I'm an… a friend of the man you saved last night. He would very much like to meet you." George smiles.

Lily looks at him and then back down at herself. She hasn't showered and is dressed in sweatpants and a t-shirt. She NEVER ventures outside dressed like this.

"I… I'm afraid George that I'm not very presentable right now. And please, if this is for some sort of… photo op or whatever, I really don't want any of that." Her tone is pleading. What is unsaid is that she would very much like to meet MM; she was just hoping the circumstances would be different.

"No, Miss Batchelor; Stuart would just like to thank you in person - no press, no fuss. You will be escorted discreetly in and out of hospital."

She helplessly points to her attire.

"I would be glad to wait downstairs for you. Please, no rush."

"How do I know you are who you say you are?", she asks cautiously.

"Well. I see." He pauses for a moment. "Since a description hasn't been posted in the press, I'll describe him to you. He is six foot four inches tall, with short dark brown hair and blue eyes, but you wouldn't know that last bit since he never was conscious at the accident site. He was wearing leather trousers and a black and white patterned shirt."

"Alright.", Lily concedes. "I believe you."

"Do take your time, Miss Batchelor; it's quite all right. I will be waiting for you in the black Suburban in front." He makes a short bow, turns and leaves.

Lily closes the door and places her back on it. Stuart. His name is Stuart. It is a good name, one that suits him. *You haven't even seen him with his eyes open, how do you know?* Her inner voice is in rare form tonight. Lily pulls herself up, annoyed at the nattering that is going on in her head, but otherwise intrigued.

It's true she is a bit fixated on him; why is that so terrible? She roughly pulls her shirt off and her shoulder flares up. She quickly undresses and runs the water; luckily, as a habitual late sleeper, she is the queen of the five minute shower and is out in no time. Brushing her hair is a bit difficult to do almost one handed, as is pulling on jeans and buttoning them. Her shoulder complains loudly at that, but she manages to get herself together and looking presentable in just over twenty minutes, even if her hair is still wet. The cats eye her warily, surprised at her sudden energy.

She laces up her brown chukkas, grabs her purse and tosses a quick goodbye to the Boys as she hurries to the door. She feels guilty keeping George waiting but at the same time, would have liked more time to primp. *It's not a date*, her voice reminds her in its most withering tone, but she ignores it and makes her way down the stairs to the waiting car.

Chapter 4

"If you'll wait out here for a moment, Miss Batchelor, I'll just check on Stuart."

She takes a seat on one of the chairs outside Room 309. She can hear the whispered conversation of two nurses who walk past. "That's her", Lily hears one say, and the other nurse turns to look. She will be glad when this fades from the headlines; she wonders how many more days it will take.

She looks up at the sound of the door opening. "Stuart would like to see you now." Odd, how George's mannerisms seem to indicate more of a servant than a friend. She gets up awkwardly, the sling still immobilizing her left arm and throwing her sense of balance slightly off. Her stomach is wiggling inside; tense, then relaxed, only to knot up again. She knows her pulse is racing - she can feel it throbbing against her skin. In mere seconds she will see 'Stuart', the man she saved (yes, she'll finally admit it to herself) - MM revealed. She takes a breath and walks through the door George is holding open for her.

It is a private room; a radio is playing music, but it is very quiet, and she can barely pick out the strains. Rachmaninoff? *Focus, Lily.*

Tentatively, she enters the room, taking one step then another, and approaches the waiting chair that has been staged for the meeting. *Just relax,* she tells herself, and tries to push the anxiety down; it's easier said than done. She smiles and walks to the edge of the bed.

He is sitting up, carefully watching her approach, studying her. She is fairly tall; her blonde hair looks damp and hangs in loose waves past her shoulders. Stuart frowns when he sees her left arm; long fingers delicately poke out of a black sling that holds her arm across her chest.

The feeling in the room changed when she walked in. There is an undercurrent of energy now that hadn't been there before. As she approaches he can see the pale green of her eyes and warm rosiness of her lips as they spread into a smile. She is more than he had bargained for.

Lily walks up to the side of the bed and holds out her right hand to him; she is surprised to see that it isn't shaking, as she is positive that she must be trembling all over. He is no longer the bloody and unconscious accident victim, but a calm and composed figure observing her from a distance with penetrating blue eyes. It seems as if he is watching her intently, carefully examining her movements, gauging her reaction. She can see the sinewy muscles in his arm as he raises it to grasp her hand. She looks up and their eyes meet, and it seems as if all at once her breath is knocked out of her and her legs feel unsteady underneath her. There is a fierce intelligence and personality behind those eyes that stun her. *Wow,* is all her brain can muster.

"I'm glad to meet you, Stuart", she says. His left hand grasps her outstretched one tightly and she squeezes back in greeting.

"Please, Liliana, or do you prefer Lily…?" He releases her hand to motion towards the waiting chair. "Have a seat."

Even lying in a hospital bed he seems commanding, the strength of his personality clearly evident. She smiles at him again and sits, stunned by the feeling of power and confidence he exudes. She realises he has asked her a question, and she's sitting there dumbly.

She gingerly eases back into the seat before answering.

"Either." She says and tentatively looks into his face, worried she'll be captivated once again by his eyes. "Which ever you prefer."

Lily feels almost as if she is speaking to a prospective employer or someone in a position of authority, and yet there's no question that he's incredibly attractive. She has to fight the urge to study his handsome face – the high cheekbones and strong jaw with a smattering of stubble; he has thrown her off balance. *What did you expect?* Her sarcastic voice has broken out of its thrall. *A weepy declaration of gratitude? A meek man?*

"I quite like Liliana, but Lily is pretty as well." She feels her cheeks grow hot "One day you'll have to tell me the origin of your unusual – and charming – name."

"The accent… are you Scots?" she says, trying to change the topic away from her.

He raises an eyebrow. "Yes, as a matter of fact I am- I was born in Scotland. Many people make the mistake of thinking I'm English. Have you ever been to Scotland, Lily?"

If he is trying to put her at ease, it isn't working. She feels as if his eyes could penetrate the very depths of her being,understand her in ways she doesn't yet acknowledge herself.

"I…", she takes a deep breath to regain her composure. "Once. I went to England and took a train to Scotland. I enjoy reading history, particularly Elizabethan, and I wanted to see Linlithgow Palace, Edinburgh Castle, Dunbar. I'll be going to Scotland again in a few weeks – for work this time - and I'm taking an extra ten days to see the countryside." That was better – a fairly neutral topic that bordered on his heritage. She smiles at him.

He watches her mouth as she speaks, mesmerized by her lips. Her bottom lip is more full, with a slight dimple perfectly bisecting it, adding to the appearance of lushness. Her top lip is slightly thinner, with a well defined Cupid's bow giving way to soft curves.

"Why did you want to visit Dunbar, Liliana?" She stirs at the sudden switch to her given name. *It sounds wonderful coming out of his mouth.*

"Well, because that's where the Earl of Bothwell took Mary Queen of Scots, and well…"

"Ravished her."

"Yes", Lily looks down for a moment. *Keep it together, why the fidgeting?* "Some say her behaviour towards the Earl afterwards caused her to lose her remaining hold on the crown. The location… it looked like it would be a wild spot, exposed to the weather."

"What did you find?" His Scottish accent is carrying her along on the memories of that trip.

"The coast there *is* wild, to say the least", she sighs, and allows herself a soft laugh. "It was terribly windy when I went. I wish I had seen the castle in its glory, perched like a stone bird roosting on those enormous rocks. The arches that hopped from one crag to another - imagining them holding up this fortress…", her hand comes up and follows the curve of the stone buttress she remembers. "It must have been magnificent, to stand there, the water swirling below you, the sea in front of you spread out like that. It was beautiful, even in its ruined state." She flushes, a little embarrassed by how caught up she was in remembering the ruins.

"I like the way you describe it", Stuart says. She turns at the sound of his voice, to find a wistful look is in his eyes. "I can almost imagine it as it was then from listening to you." The barest hint of a smile touches his lips and she really blushes this time. "What conference are you attending?"

"International Society of Materials Engineers in Edinburgh. Pretty banal, I know", she says apologetically.

"Are you a materials engineer?"

"I have a Bachelor of Science and am working on my Masters now."

"Ah. Quite." He shifts himself in the bed to get more comfortable and pauses for a moment. "Not to interrupt this topic – I could listen to you talk of Scotland all day", Lily smiles at this, "but I want to hear what happened. From your lips."

The last sentence makes her stomach twist into a knot all over again.

"Okay", she concentrates on recalling as much in the way of details as possible. "I was on my way to the store. When the crossing lights came on, I stopped. I saw you pull up and ogled your car, so I saw the vehicle behind you approach."

He looks at her curiously. "Why did you ogle my car?"

"Because it was so obviously a Porsche Panamera and they are BEAUTIFUL." The sigh comes out before she can stop it. "Whoops." She's momentarily embarrassed.

Amused now and thoroughly charmed, he waves his hand. "Continue."

"The other car was obviously going too fast…", she says and relates the entire event as honestly and truthfully as she can.

"Did you notice anything that might help identify the vehicle at all? The beautiful car is totaled after the train impact, making it all a bit more difficult to sort out."

"Well, it was a truck."

"A truck? How do you know?", he watches her carefully.

"It could be an SUV. The height of the lights, for one thing. It was dark, but based on the configuration of the headlamps, I'd say perhaps an Expedition or a Super-Duty truck, about five model years ago."

"How can you be so certain?" Stuart looks dubious.

"My uncle is a mechanic. We would play all sorts of games related to cars when I was growing up. I notice them, even to-day."

Stuart nods. "Any colour?"

"It was dark behind you", she reminds him apologetically.

"I appreciate the information", he says. "And I appreciate you saving my life. I'm probably not the first person to tell you this, but what you did was brave, incredibly so." This time she can't help but look at his eyes. They are sincere, warm and full of genuine appreciation. She has to look away after only a moment; his gaze is too penetrating… too captivating.

"I just wanted to …"

"…help. Yes, I know. From what I have heard you seem quite reluctant to accept any accolades for what you did. Why is that?"

She can feel his eyes on her, watching intently. "I'm uncomfortable with the praise", she admits finally to Stuart and herself, as her right hand closes and opens nervously. "I don't like the attention, the sudden invasion of my privacy - newspapermen calling me incessantly, coming to my door. And I was brought up to try and be gracious when someone compliments you. I just reacted, I didn't really think about it, so it doesn't feel right to accept the kudos." *Wow, you really unloaded there, sister.*

Cautiously she looks up, and he is studying her, as if trying to understand her words, or decide something about her. "I think I can appreciate all of that", he replies, "but that doesn't make what you did any less impressive. Many people wouldn't have done what you did - many don't have the innate instinct to help that you obviously have, or your ability to assess and react quickly." His tone softens. "I wouldn't be alive here if it wasn't for that instinct, so you'll have to pardon me if I'm quite fond of it." She steals a look at him under her lashes. Even in his battered state there is something absolute mesmerizing about him, and she feels this surge of happiness at his words.

"I… thank you Stuart. I'm glad I was there to help however I could."

His mouth curls up in a wry smile. "Was that so difficult?"

"Yes!", she laughs, and Stuart's lips break into a genuine smile. *Wow, it's dazzling.*

"Once I'm given the all clear and released, I would like to show you my appreciation by taking you out to supper", he says. Stuart watches her carefully, hoping she will say yes, careful to observe any signs she's not interested.

Instead, Lily is flustered. "That's quite kind of you, but really unnecessary…"

He raises a brow and levels his eyes at her. "What were we just saying about accepting gratitude? Besides, I have a debt I feel I should repay. Allow me to make a gesture and tip the scales, even just a little. Surely you can grant a wish to the man whose life you saved."

Oh boy. When you put it that way… "Hmm", she bites her lip. "Alright." She stands up.

"What happened to your shoulder?" His brow furrows at her obvious discomfort when she moves.

"Oh", she's flustered again. "When I couldn't get you out easily, I really had to tug…", she absently moves her right hand to touch her left arm. "It was slightly dislocated, torn ligament. Not too bad, though. Small price to pay." She smiles down at him and she feels self-conscious once again, the colour rising in her cheeks. *Could you be any more obvious? You might as well shout at him that he's gorgeous.*

"Can you make sure George has your information?"

She nods and turns to go.

"Thank you, Liliana. And good night."

George is waiting at the door. "I'll take you home".

The entire ride home she is haunted by the memory of his eyes.

George walks her to her front door and reaches out to shake her hand. "Thank you for saving his life", he says, his voice tinged with emotion. Then he bows and is gone.

She unlocks her door in a daze and walks in. *My God,* she realises, *I don't even know his last name.*

Lily heats up some frozen pizza and enjoys a lazy supper with her Nook rereading Alison Weir's '*The Life of Elizabeth I*'. There are several times when she has to go back over a passage because she realises her mind is wandering. Knowing Stuart's name and speaking with him hasn't made him any less of a mystery - far from it.

A Scotsman who dresses in leather pants like a rock star but has the demeanor of a world class executive and a look that seems to go through my soul. She hadn't expected him to exude sensuality even from a hospital bed. The thought pesters her throughout the remainder of her evening until too tired, she finally goes to bed.

Sunday her shoulder feels a little better. She is grateful that her body responded when she need it to, even if it did result in an injury. At least the shoulder would heal and the scar on her forearm won't be bad if she keeps it out of the sun - not difficult to do in the Pacific Northwest.

The next day her co-workers present her with a cake at lunch. She blushes, but accepts it gracefully. Even her boss Nathan - who normally can only find opportunities to criticize – has some nice things to say. She's been somewhat unhappy and unsatisfied with her job, so this surprise is a nice change of pace.

Lily's talk with Stuart has made her think more about the accident. She isn't trying to leverage what happened and she is genuinely touched when someone makes a gesture of appreciation. Through this experience she has learned how to accept gratitude a little more readily, although it does remain difficult. *Just don't get a big head about it,* her voice warns.

****

The sling comes off just before the trip to Edinburgh for the conference, thank God; it is still a bit tender and feels different, but there is definite improvement. She wonders when Stuart was released from the hospital. As time went on, Lily realised that he would probably never call and she tried to make peace with herself about it. *I would have liked to have a normal conversation with him,* she thinks for about the hundredth time. *Talk more about Scotland. In the end though, it's probably better this way; if you don't start on a path you can't get disappointed.* It's easier to let it go now than it would be if they had spent more time together.

It was only after her visit that she really appreciated chatting with him, and recalled things. She can almost remember the way his hand felt in hers - close her eyes and visualise the blue depths of his eyes, see his mouth curl in the corner as he listened. At the time it had been a whirlwind and she hadn't really enjoyed it or been in the moment; she wished she'd been more present. *And I make things more difficult each time I think about that meeting.*

Should she have done more to make contact? The ball was in his court, she felt pretty sure of that. She had given George her phone numbers and email, and been especially good about checking her voicemail so she knows he didn't try to call. Every day she checks her inboxes at work and home, and she even paid special attention to her Junk Mail folders in case an email from Stuart got misdirected, but there was nothing. If it hadn't been for her shoulder injury and the gash on her forearm, she would have thought it was a dream conjured up by her overactive imagination. *There would only be heartache down that road*, her voice reassures her.

Finally it is the day of departure. Janet and Louis drive her to the airport and promise to visit Lily's cats every other day. As she sits at the window watching the plane push away from the gate she wonders if Stuart will call when she is on her trip, or whether it had all been just words. Why can't she just get him out of her mind? The farther away from their meeting in the hospital, the more he keeps clinging to her thoughts.

You're really good at hoping against hope, when the signs point otherwise. You know it's been your downfall before. She sighs. Why would he call, especially if he hasn't done so by now? She consoles herself with the knowledge that she helped a fellow human and that should be enough. Time to focus on work and then vacation, where perhaps she'll get some perspective and root her feet to the ground once more.

****

Ugh. Jet lag. Lily forgot how bad it was when she visited Scotland years ago; at least she was smart enough to fly in a day early, she thinks as she disembarks. Granted, she'll have to pay for the extra night in the hotel whereas NewTech, her employers, were partly subsidizing the remainder of the trip. They had come to an agreement about it, in any event. NewTech had wanted a representative there but were reluctant to foot the entire bill. A week in Edinburgh at a conference including hotel and airfare was expensive for a smallish company. Lily wanted to go and suggested she pay for part of it; that way she could tack on an extra week at her expense and use up her vacation before it expired. She rarely had the money – or time – for a vacation, but this seemed like a perfect arrangement. She saved her aunt and uncle's graduation present, (a generous cheque), and the pressure from graduate school was not bad right now, so Lily felt she could finally get away. She checks into the hotel without incident and has a quiet night before retiring.

The first day of the conference is a bit intimidating since she's there by herself. She knows some of the other attendees, if only in name or through email correspondence, but none very well. She's here to take in all she can and provide a presence for NewTech. Sometimes these seminars can be extremely dull; Lily hopes that's not the case here.

First off there is orientation; luckily it doesn't drag on too long and starts at 10. Since she is still fighting a bit of jet lag, Lily's grateful for a little later start; then, miraculously, an early lunch. *Whoever planned this schedule had a heart of gold, taking pity on those of us who flew in,* she thinks. She enjoys the afternoon talks which end a little early, as there is a mixer in the evening that everyone leaves to get ready for.

There is just enough time for her to shower and change. She has brought a black pencil skirt, heels and a purple silk blouse with a ruffled and slightly plunging neckline for the occasion. Lily definitely has curves but they look good for her shape and height. She has sort of made peace with the fact that she isn't ever going to be a skinny supermodel and now accepts her large breasts and slightly curvy hips. Her green eyes and full lips are compelling features, and when she decides to clean up she does so nicely, although she'd be loath to admit it.

Not bad, her voice concedes. *They are all geeky engineers for the most part though, so your effort is a bit wasted.* This isn't entirely true, but it's true enough to sting.

She grabs her black clutch and throws money, ID, credit card, room key, lipstick and powder into it. After one more quick check in the mirror she walks out of her room, pulling the door shut behind her. Feeling a little self conscious as she always does when she is dressed up, Lily heads towards the elevators at the end of the hall.

She planned her arrival so that the reception would already have begun; she didn't want to stand out or feel too awkward if the crowd was thin, as it would tend to be early on. She timed her entrance well because when the elevator doors open and she makes her way to the ballroom, she can see there is already a good sized group inside.

A server approaches and offers her champagne, which she accepts gratefully. She couldn't help but notice during the lectures that she was one of the youngest present in the thin ranks of females in attendance. Her entrance has already garnered a few appreciative stares from those already assembled; she will need all the fortification she can get, and quickly finishes what remains in her glass. Lily has a love-hate relationship with men; she enjoys the attention like any woman her age would, but wants to find a good match and her prior experience tells her it probably won't happen.

Another server meanders by and Lily exchanges her empty glass for a full one. She brushes her tongue against the rim to reduce the lipstick on her glass and takes a sip. Wow. She hasn't had champagne in a while, and likes how the tiny bubbles tickle her nose; this glass she promises to sip and savour, unlike the last one. She lowers her lids for a moment and appreciates the biscuit bouquet, the clean, crisp taste and the brightness on her tongue. *People are probably looking*, her voice reminds her and she looks up. To her embarrassment, several men nearby who had been in conversation have stopped talking and are observing her. She tosses a quick smile at them and blushing, turns away.

She makes her way further into the room and snags an appetizer from a passing waiter. *Why are you down here? You hardly know anyone.* Her social life at home is lacking, and here is an opportunity to get out, enjoy some alcohol, maybe engage in intelligent conversation and participate in a bit of harmless flirting.

So you just want to play dress up? Her self-doubts always flare up at times like this. Was she dressed appropriately? Did she look okay? Would her peers perhaps not take her seriously? She accepts another canapé from a passing waiter. *Oh!* She simply has to close her eyes for a second and savour this one; smoked salmon with crème fraiche, caviar and a sprig of chervil. Perfect with the champagne… actually it is divine. She sighs and opens her eyes.

Lily has the presence of mind to make sure she doesn't gape, but she does gasp.

Striding towards her is Stuart. He is dressed in a charcoal suit that fits him perfectly. He seems in his element here and his movements are purposeful, confident. The corner of his mouth is turned up in an amused, wry smile, his sensual lips now framed by a Van Dyke - and he is looking straight at her.

Chapter 5

She barely has time to compose her thoughts before he closes the distance. Her stomach has that gnawing, achy emptiness to it - a telltale sign that she is attracted to him. She is completely floored seeing him here.

Even with her nearly three and a half inch heels he is still over four inches taller by her estimation. She looks up into his bright blue eyes as he steps close.

"Liliana, an absolute pleasure", he says, taking her right hand and bringing it to his lips. She nearly swoons from the contact; it is so unexpected and intimate, and his lips are soft against the top of her hand. He holds on a moment and releases his grasp and her arm floats down to her side. Lily feels as if she must be levitating off the ground.

"Stuart… My goodness", is all she can muster. He smiles a little at having rendered her practically speechless.

His eyes carefully play over her body. "If I may say so, you look lovely this evening." God, but his Scots accent is sexy; not too overpowering, but the trilled r's are hot.

"Thank you. I'm glad to see you up and around." *Couldn't think of anything better to say?*

"Yes, almost as good as new, except for a little residual soreness." He holds up his right hand.

"How did you get out of that cast so quickly? I thought you tore a tendon or something."

"Reconstructive surgery, physical therapy."

"But still, that should have taken months."

"I can be very determined", he says in a meaningful way, staring straight at her.

Lily inwardly gulps. "Apparently." Luckily she is saved by a passing waiter proffering more champagne. Stuart removes the near empty glass from Lily's hand, puts it on the tray and retrieves two glasses, handing her one.

He holds out his hand and tips the glass until it touches hers. "To finally meeting under auspicious circumstances", he says and drinks. She pauses a moment and then raises the glass to her lips and takes a sip. Suddenly, everything has changed; how did this happen? He walks into a room and she becomes flustered, nervous, flushed.

"Stuart, I'm surprised to see you here." He raises an eyebrow quizzically, his eyes dancing playfully. "I'm glad", she hurriedly adds, "but surprised."

"I still spend a fair amount of time in Scotland. I had some… business to take care of locally and hoped you wouldn't mind if I dropped in, knowing you would be here. You don't mind, do you?"

It is wholly unfair. He has surprised her, has a definite advantage and they both know it.

He had been watching her from the moment she entered the ballroom, waiting for an opportune moment, studying her. When she had walked into his hospital room there seemed to be a sensual air about her, but he tried to pass it off as the drugs, circumstances.

Watching her move, sip her champagne and savour the food, he realised it hadn't been the circumstances at all; it was her, and what made it even more powerful was that it wasn't forced. It was simply who she was, and she exuded it from her pores; it was in all she did. From the way her long fingers found the stem of her glass to the way her lips parted, it was wired into her and he found it incredibly sexy, utterly irresistible.

Her slight nervous discomfort at being caught off guard seems to increase her sensuality as she fidgets, playing her fingers along her glass, her lips pursing slightly as she tries to regain her composure.

Stuart's gaze is intense and Lily feels a little flustered, and has a hard time meeting it; no man has ever affected her like this.

"What business are you in?" she asks, her hand nearly trembling as she lifts the glass to her lips and steals a look at him over the rim. She loves the Van Dyke; it makes his lips look even more sensual… as if he needs that. The neatly trimmed mustache accentuating the line of his top lip, then curling down to meet the goatee on his chin - the dark patch underneath his mouth makes his slightly fuller bottom lip appear more pronounced. She inwardly sighs; what a perfect mouth.

"I run my own business", he says. "My father and his friend started it." He knows others are staring at her. "Why don't we find a quiet corner to talk?"

Her eyes get wide – she can't help it – and she nods. He reaches out his left hand and cups her elbow and gestures to the far corner of the room. "Shall we?" Her body drinks in the sensation, his touch sparking a craving for more contact.

The combination of his well educated diction and slightly rough Scots enunciation is heady. He manages to seem intelligent yet a little dangerous at the same time. *He was dressed like a rock star when you found him*, her voice chimes in. *Most powerful business owners don't do that.*

As they approach the table, Stuart lets go of her arm and pulls the chair out for her. She places her glass on the table, and smoothes her skirt as she sits, while Stuart pulls out another chair and sits kitty-corner to her. Lily crosses her legs; she's grateful she packed something nice for tonight, and thank goodness she went downstairs. Take that, troublesome voice.

"Are you enjoying the conference?", he asks, taking another sip. She has a weakness for hands and his are strong, with long masculine fingers; she notices a Breitling watch around his wrist. *Wow.*

"Well, it just started to-day", she says, finally overcoming a bit of her surprise and managing more sustained looks into his face. He is gorgeous; she doesn't want to stare, but she could look at him all day. Here, in close proximity, she feels that hum of electricity around them like a cocoon. "But so far, yes."

She takes another sip as he speaks. "I believe you said you were going to take a holiday afterwards?"

"Good memory", she smiles, a little embarrassed. "I… thought with the injuries and drugs you probably hadn't…"

"Remembered much? Remembered our conversation?", the tone is playfully accusatory. "Oh, I remember it very well, Liliana."

She finds herself blushing a little and takes another sip of champagne. *Be careful, you haven't had much to eat all day.*

"Not many people call you Liliana, do you mind?", he asks suddenly, softly. "Liliana just sort of rolls off the tongue, and it's unique. I like it."

Why did such a simple sentiment make her heart feel like it was trying to break out of her chest? Her mouth suddenly is dry.

"When are you going to tell me the rest of YOUR name?", she blurts out boldly.

"Soon. I'm just a bit… cautious." Who was this man? A politician? No, he said he owned a business… why so cagey?

"Tell me what types of places you're interested in visiting while here in my beautiful homeland, and I'll be happy to offer suggestions."

She takes a deep breath. Wow, his intensity – he just seems to exude power and confidence – nearly takes her breath away. She would never have guessed this when she was trying to comfort his unconscious form as he lay on the asphalt.

"Well, to be honest I haven't made much in the way of plans. I anticipated doing a bit of research beforehand, but with the…", she fidgets, "… accident and all, and the bustle afterwards, well." She feels like a schoolgirl with all the flushing and fidgeting.

He nods as she continues. "I do know generalities though." Talking makes her feel a little more calm, although she worries about prattling on too much.

He looks amused, the corner of his mouth curled up and his lips slightly parted. *Oh God, PLEASE don't do that.* She wonders what his lips would feel like on hers; they felt nice against the back of her hand. She shakes her head to clear her mind.

"What is it, Lily?", he leans forward and reaches out a hand to touch her arm; desire shoots through her body. "Is anything wrong?"

"No!", she says hastily. "Nothing is wrong. Where was I? Oh yes, places in Scotland…", she nervously catches her lower lip with her teeth and touches her tongue to her top lip, her mind churning.

He watches her mouth and then raises his eyes to hers. They are smoldering, full of desire. *Oh my God, he's attracted to me.* If she had been standing she would have had to sit. Her insides are turned topsy turvy.

Her voice cracks slightly. "I'd like to visit some distilleries. Go see the rockiness of northern Scotland, perhaps the isle of Skye, or Islay. Ruins…" her voice almost falters again; he hasn't taken his eyes off of her, and the words are fleeing her as she is caught up in his gaze. "I love old ruins. Manor houses, castles…" It's difficult to continue; she feels hypnotized by him, completely disoriented.

She is aware of a voice. "May I get either of you anything else to drink?" She shakes her head; the thrall he had over her broken. It seems like she is taking a breath for the first time in minutes. She should leave; Stuart is dangerous, being around him is too heady, distracting. She stands up to go. "I'm a bit tired, actually. I was thinking of heading out", she uncharacteristically lies.

He puts his hand on her arm and she finds herself sinking slowly moving back into her seat. *How did he do that?* His touch is like life spreading through her body, all she wants is more.

"Surely you can spare a few more minutes Liliana?", he says her name as if he is making love to it, rolling it around in his mouth, tasting it. She sits, and he turns to the waiter.

"A bottle of La Grande Dame unopened, two glasses, and an assortment of the canapés would be perfect." He makes it a request, but something in his tone lets you know he fully expects you to deliver. *What company does he own?,* she wonders, not for the first time. *He's not arrogant, but you don't want to disappoint him. He must be difficult to negotiate with.*

The waiter nods in assent and leaves. Stuart turns his piercing eyes to her and smiles amiably. "Now, where were we?"

Chapter 6

Stuart can tell Lily is nervous around him; she should be. The things that cross his mind while he watches her are rather indecent. Her scent teases his nostrils - orange peel with perhaps a bit of clove and honeysuckle; crisp and spicy, but with a lingering hint of sweetness. It's exhilarating.

The champagne has loaned her cheeks a little bit of an extra flush, and remnants of her lipstick still cling to her full lips, giving them a warm, rosy hue that makes him want to nibble on them. He can see now that her eyes are a pale, mossy green, unlike anything he's seen before. How different this is from when they first met. Then he had drifted in and out of awareness; he wishes he could remember the crash, her pulling him from his car, but he can only recall the softness of her voice urging him to be calm. Now they are on more even footing, or perhaps uneven in some ways. She is definitely flustered around him, and their chemistry is unmistakable.

The waiter returns with a tray and puts it on an adjoining empty table. He places the ice bucket with champagne in front of Stuart and arranges a large plate of appetizers between them. Next he produces the place settings, napkins and the glasses. Stuart signs a receipt for the champagne, folds a bill, and hands it to the waiter who accepts it with a look of surprise and then hastily retreats.

Stuart reaches for the champagne and his lithe fingers began to untwist the wire around the neck. "Have you ever had La Grande Dame before?"

"Once", she says. "My uncle and aunt took me to the Herbfarm when I graduated college. I had it there."

"Lovely restaurant", he murmurs, as he reaches for one of the cloth napkins. He places it over the top of the bottle and using his left hand twists it slowly until the cork pops; Lily has never seen anyone do it so elegantly and expertly.

He switches the bottle to his right hand and begins to pour. "Your hand must be bothering you a bit, since you opened the champagne with your left." Anything to move the conversation to him; he is still Mystery Man to her in most ways. And she wants to gather any clues she can.

"Interesting you would observe that, but I'm actually ambidextrous", he says, "Although my right hand is slightly more dominant." Was it just her or did he stress that last word?

He smiles at her, one of his wry, slightly amused smiles. "Are you generally very observant? The car headlights, what hand I pour with…", he moves to top their glasses.

Lily's lips purse in thought; she can see his eyes narrow and focus on her mouth.

"I never thought of myself that way before."

"What way DO you think of yourself?" She gasps. How was the topic back to her again? He is both disarming with his warmth and yet still businesslike; she's never met anyone like him before.

"I…", she flushes. She really needs to get herself together and not let him affect her like this. It has been so long since she's been really attracted to a man, since she's BEEN with a man, and she has never felt this type of almost magnetic pull to someone before. She both likes it and hates it. The sensations are delicious but the effect is disorienting; she feels socially clumsy.

"Well?", he prompts. Why does he look so amused? She turns to the food, drapes a napkin over her legs and busies herself filling a plate. Perhaps not looking at him would help.

"That's a bit of a big topic, isn't it? Very wide open." She feels her insides squirm at that phrase. "I know so little about you and yet I already feel you know so much about me."

He can't argue with that, considering there is a rather full dossier on her up in his room.

She continues. "Since you are so guarded about your business, why don't you tell me about when you came to America and where you grew up?"

Lily chances a look at him - it is almost her ruin. He is sitting reclined in the chair, his left arm flung nonchalantly over the back. His right arm rests on the chair, the stem of his glass captured between his thumb and forefinger, its foot perched on the wood newel at the end of the armrest. His left ankle rests casually on top of his right leg, as if he is relaxing at home. He has unbuttoned his jacket and it shows an expanse of crisp white shirt that is opened at the top, revealing a sculpted collarbone and muscular neck.

She involuntarily sucks her breath in between her teeth. He exudes sex appeal; his body seems to be calling out to her.

"Is something the matter?" That is the SECOND time he's has to call her back to earth. She must seem incredibly obvious *and incredibly desperate.*

"No, I'm fine." She says with a smile. The tingling warmth between her legs continues to grow.

"Good." He smiles unabashedly for the first time that evening and it is like being struck by lightning. *I forgot how amazing his smile is.*

He reaches for the champagne and fills their glasses as he begins. "I was born near Glasgow, and we lived there until I was sixteen. My father had always dreamed of coming to America and starting his own business, so we pulled up roots and moved."

"Do you have any brothers or sisters?"

"Three; one brother and two sisters." He leans forward and plucks some canapés from the platter, puts them on his plate and sits back. She catches a whiff of his scent; manly and erotic, with a hint of something exotic like cinnamon.

"What's your favourite book?" She asks.

"Hmm", he leans back, perches the plate on his thigh and drapes himself over the chair again, obviously at ease with his body. *Take a deep breath, count to ten…* Her heart is racing.

"Currently *The Count of Monte Cristo*", he nods. "Although I am partial to Shakespeare as well. Classical education and all that."

His phone rings. He hesitates before answering. "Excuse me", he says and takes the call. Lily acts busy and moves a bunch of grapes to her plate.

"Yes?", his tone is all business. "Now is not a good time." He glances over at Lily; she's eating grapes in the most sensual manner he can imagine. She plucks one from the stem and just as it presses against her lips, they open; he can see the pink of her tongue as it curls to accept the grape. She's doing this absently - it's just the way she eats grapes - but he feels himself stiffen and has to suppress a strong desire to drop the phone and kiss her.

"I'll be in my room in fifteen minutes. Set up the call for then." He hangs up. His face as it turns to Lily is once again sensual, placid. She smiles at him.

"I have some important business I need to take care of via conference call. I'll probably be a half hour. Would you care to come up to my suite for a cocktail then?"

He stands up and shakes his pant leg down. She looks up at him, his glacier blue eyes making her pulse throb in her head.

"I… shouldn't."

A slight look of frustration passes over his face. "Why?"

"I should probably head to my room for the evening." She stands up and now their bodies are so close she can almost feel the heat radiating from his.

He looks down at her, his mouth slightly parts. "Why?" he asks again slowly, his hand reaching up and grazing her arm.

"Conference to-morrow?" she offers tentatively. She wants him so badly it hurts to say no, but this is so out of left field; she needs time to sort things out.

She hears the phone buzz in his pocket again and it makes him annoyed. "It has been a very nice evening with you, Liliana. I will see you again… soon", he promises, turns on his heel, and strides to the exit.

After he leaves it's as if a miasma has been lifted from around her. *Whoa, he really has an effect on me.* Lily pours the remaining champagne into her glass and sips it slowly.

Stuart makes his way to the elevators and to his room. He's greeted at the door to his suite by George and his personal assistant Ava. Ava is in her 50's, with cropped salt and pepper hair and an efficient attitude. She hands him a short stack of papers. "These came through Telex; I've already recorded them", she says and veers off.

George takes Stuart's coat from his hands.

"Is it a development?", he asks.

"Not sure, Mr. Watson."

Stuart turns left and walks briskly to the office and closes the door behind him. He sits down at the desk, logs in, grabs the earphones there and puts them on. He just begins flipping through the papers Ava gave him when Skype notifies him there is an incoming call.

"Stuart Watson."

"Mr. Watson. Dana Millner here." The voice is rough, thoroughly masculine.

"Yes, Dana. You have something for me?"

"I believe I do, yes."

Stuart leans back and pushes his lips together before answering. "Go ahead."

"I tracked down that expert and had him look at the tyre track fragments that the police obtained from the scene. There is a very good likelihood that they are from either of the vehicles you mentioned; a large SUV or a truck. This is based on the…"

"Send the technical items."

"Very well sir. I did pursue this further. I did locate a man – an employee of a nursery that grows stock in greenhouses nearby. He says that in the week prior to your accident, there was a large dark coloured SUV parked in the gravel lot by the road; he noticed it several times. The rest of the staff leave by five, and he is one of only two evening employees. Finally he decided to investigate and when he began to approach the vehicle it took off. He doesn't recall a licence number."

"Footage", says Stuart.

"Not of the lot. Only pointed at the greenhouses and front entrance."

"Anything else?"

"Yes sir. I was able to confirm that Lily Batchelor is in fact estranged from her mother and stepfather. She still does have some contact with her step sister, however."

"Leads on the possible corporate espionage situation I mentioned?"

"None yet Mr. Watson."

"Alright. Thank you for the update Dana, keep me posted and as always, the company issues are for my eyes only; not Ava or George. No one. Other items can come in so they can see and evaluate. This issue, absolutely not."

"Yes sir. I'll keep you posted."

Chapter 7

"So the bartender says all this stuff, and Argon *doesn't react*!" They all join in her laughter.

Lily is standing by a sparsely populated table, a glass of nearly empty champagne in her hand. Her hair is now slightly tousled and her lips are red from the flush of alcohol. Around her are several fellow engineers and they have just been swapping 'geek jokes'. She's a bit less self-conscious with the extra distraction of Stuart removed.

Jon, a youthful 40-something from Germany begins. "So I guess it's my turn", he says in slightly broken English to peals of laughter, as he shakes his head, trying to recall a suitable joke. Most of them are slightly soused, if not more. The ballroom crowd has thinned out a bit, and those that are left are in clusters.

Lily glances at the time. "I should be going", she says to no one in particular, and bids them all goodnight as they try to derail Jon from his joke.

She walks through the ballroom and heads to the exit and the elevators. Suddenly a voice breaks the relative quiet.

"I thought you were going to bed."

The voice gives her goosebumps - Stuart. She turns and he saunters towards her, jacket gone, his lean yet strong physique now obvious through his shirt.

Her smile is wiped off her face instantly. She feels guilty for turning him down earlier, and he seems annoyed that she lingered at the reception rather than visiting with him.

"It was my intent at the time", she says defiantly.

"Well, since you're still awake…", he walks past her and presses the elevator button. "…we'll go to my suite and continue the conversation." He takes her elbow and steers her to the open door. She's in that intoxicating bubble again; his touch is exciting and his assurance is overpowering. Nearly.

"No, I don't think so", she says, and presses the button marked '6'.

Stuart presses the Penthouse level button, but she ignores this. "Is there a reason?", he asks. The doors close.

"Because I really am tired now, and sessions start at nine to-morrow." She says determinedly.

The floors begin to tick by. "But you don't have to attend every session. No one ever does at these things."

"That's not the point." she says. The number five ticks by on the floor display.

He turns her around so she is facing him. His touch seems to melt her will. "I almost think you're avoiding me." The bells sound and the doors open behind her. Lily casts her eyes over her shoulder and down the hallway to her room. Stuart is still holding onto her arms and she isn't trying to pull away.

She turns to look him in the eyes as the doors begin to close behind her.

"Why?" she asks in a whisper, searching his face, wishing she had more willpower.

He lifts a hand and caresses the side of her face and her breath intakes sharply at his touch. "I want to get to know you", he says softly and continues to stroke her hair. There is a chime and the door opens.

He turns her around and places his arm across her back as they exit the elevator.

The Penthouse lobby is small and leads to a hallway. There is one door along each side and another one at the far end that says, 'Hotel Staff Only'. Stuart walks towards the door on the right, and the attendant standing discreetly in the lobby rushes to catch up to him.

"Good evening, Mr…", but Stuart quiets him with a shake of his head. The door opens and Stuart ushers Lily inside and after a professional 'Good Evening', the attendant closes the door after them. Lily hears Stuart lock it and there is now a lump in her throat.

“You know”, she begins nervously, “I’m here for the next few days, we could do this another night.” Being alone with him is daunting - a mixture of trepidation and desire.

“Come. I’ll make you a drink.”

“I think I’ve probably had enough for the night…”

“I was just going to have a wee nip”, he says in his incredibly sexy accent as he walks to the wet bar tucked into the right of the living room.

“Okay, fine, but just a little”, she cautions. She steps towards the windows that fill the wall in front of her.

“This is AMAZING”, she says emphatically as she turns her head to Stuart. The wide eyes and smile on her face are enough to make him break into a grin.

“It is at that”, he walks around the bar, a glass in each hand. He narrows his eyes at her. “How do you like your scotch?”, he asks playfully.

“Neat!”, she says without hesitation and he hands the drink over.

“Liliana”, he says softly and she looks up at the sound of her name. Their eyes lock and he raises his glass.

“Thank you”, he says, and the tone is so tender and earnest it nearly brings tears to her eyes.“Thank you for saving my life.” He reaches his left hand up and his finger tips touch her cheek lightly. Lily lowers her lids, relishing the sensation, trying to burn the feeling and the words into her head.

She opens her eyes to see him watching her. She raises her glass and clinks with his and takes a sip.

“Mmmm”. The strong taste of iodine and the smokiness of the peat fill her mouth, and her lips and tongue begin to tingle. The scotch warms a path to her stomach and leaves her with a contented feeling. “Perfect.”

Stuart is still lightly touching her cheek and moves his fingers to her lips, watching her reaction intently. She doesn’t move as his thumb brushes against her mouth, and then he slides his hand and is cupping her cheek. She hears the clank of his tumbler as it touches the tabletop and he removes her glass from her hand.

He leans forward into her; she can smell the scotch on his breath as he slowly moves his lips to hers. Lily's breath catches in her throat, her pulse is racing, and she feels her stomach twist expectantly.

He pauses; their mouths are a hairsbreadth apart, and she realises he's prolonging it, relishing this moment of anticipation. A burning desire for him has taken up residence in her abdomen; she longs for his kiss and leans forward but he maintains the distance.

"Is this what you were afraid of?", his voice is sexy - low and rough. His breath envelops her like a shroud of silk - seductive, soft.

"Yes", she gasps out.

His mouth parts in a brief smile and then his lips are on hers, as soft and sensual as she feared. His hand at her cheek urges her mouth open and he plunges his tongue into her, mingling with the remnants of the scotch, tickling her tongue while his right hands rests on her hip. He is overwhelming; she has never been kissed like this, forcefully and passionately.

Her left hand comes up and touches his face and he melts into her palm, their bodies pressed against one another, their mouths still joined.

Finally, reluctantly, he pulls away.

"Was that so terrible?", he growls.

She nods. "It was everything I feared." His mouth turns up in a smile and he reaches for his glass and takes another sip of scotch.

"When do you need to be at your first seminar?", he says and trails his fingers along the edge of the table in front of the window. He stares at her as she's seen predators eye prey.

"I should be there at nine, Stuart", she replies and takes another sip from her glass. What is wrong with her? She craves him like a thirsty man would yearn for water and yet she's trying to find excuses to leave.

You fear his intensity. That much is true. She turns to look out the magnificent windows; Edinburgh Castle is in the distance, lights marking angles into sharp relief.

He's behind her now, and uses the most delicate of touches to brush her hair aside. He leans down towards her ear and whispers. "What if I asked you to stay?" Her knees weaken and he puts an arm around her waist, pulling her to him. She can feel his erection pressing against her back and moistness is pooling between her legs.

He begins to kiss her hair. "Stay", he says as he drinks in the scent of her hair and the faint aroma of her arousal. It's more intoxicating than anything he's had to drink that night.

"Stuart…", she wants to protest. *He's so sexy and I do want him so terribly, terribly bad.*

There is the distant clacking of heels and then Lily hears a throat clear. "Mister… Sir, there has been a break-in."

He turns his head, his arm still firmly around Lily's waist. She can feel the strength in his muscles, the hardness of his chest against her back.

"When?"

"Just now."

He turns Lily around so she is facing him. "I need to, I HAVE to deal with this. Please. Just give me a short while."

He takes her head in his hands and kisses her forehead before turning to follow Ava. Lily can hear the clack of footsteps receding into the distance. As quickly and quietly as she can manage, she picks up her purse and heads to the front doors. She nods to the attendant, calls the elevator and takes it down to her floor.

She is exhausted – emotionally wrung out. She closes the curtains, locks the door and readies for bed in record time. She sets her alarm and turns off the ringer on her phone. Tonight was completely unexpected; what would to-morrow bring?

Chapter 8

She dragged herself out of bed in time for the 9AM seminar the following morning. *You just have to prove something*, came the admonishment. She was too tired to argue; besides, it was a correct assessment.

The only way she could justify slipping out of Stuart's suite is if she attended the early session and, as if the Fates were punishing her, the talk was boring and the speaker could induce narcolepsy in someone who was an insomniac.

It is about to run over time too, so she packs up and moves to her next seminar choice, about carbon fibre nanotubes. It is one of the sessions she is the most excited about. Dr. Paulo Antonini, one of the field's leaders, is on the panel. She has followed his career with interest and is excited at the opportunity to hear him speak and perhaps meet him. *You're such a science groupie*, her inner voice chuckles.

She manages to get a seat near the aisle a few rows back. This auditorium is nicer than the previous one; the rows are a long contiguous desk with seats placed evenly apart. There are personal lights and electrical outlets. *Too bad my adapter is in my room* she thinks as she gazes at the odd plugs.

She grabbed a handout when she entered the room. Besides Dr. Antonini, there are researchers from Eberline in Germany and Watson & Dickson in the Pacific Northwest. *Ah, my dream job*, she sighs inwardly. She doesn't quite have the courage to send them her resume, afraid of rejection as she is. Referred to as 'W and D' most commonly or 'Wats and Dicks' by people trying to be humourous, they are a mid size company doing some fantastic research. Their lab is much better equipped than NewTech, and they are one of the top companies to work for in Washington state. *Big enough to have the cool toys, small enough so you don't get lost*, she thinks. Perhaps when she heads back home she'll pluck up the courage to send them her resume.

She feels a presence to her right and turns towards the aisle. A hotel employee is standing there, an envelope in his hand. "Miss Batchelor?", he asks in a tentative whisper. The panelists are slowly filing onto the dais. She nods and he hands her the envelope, tips his head and retreats.

She opens the envelope, which is hotel stationary, and unfolds the enclosed paper. On it, written in masculine script with what appears to be a fountain pen, is the following:

> I'm having supper for us delivered to my suite at 7:30. Hope you will join me for cocktails at 7.
>
> -Stuart.

She tears off a piece of engineering paper from her pad and replies in her elegant handwriting:

> Thank you very much for the kind invitation but I'm afraid I'll have to decline - I already have dinner arrangements. A well respected expert I admire, Dr. Antonini, may attend.
>
> -Liliana

Ducking out again I see, comes the observation as she leaves her seat and makes her way to the back of the auditorium. She quickly threads her way to the front desk, requests an envelope and addresses it:

> Stuart, Presidential Suite, Penthouse floor

She doesn't know how else to route it. She flags the clerk over, and requests it be delivered. She hurriedly returns to her seat, and sits just as introductions are beginning.

The panel is great, and more than makes up for the 9AM bore. She is excited at the prospect of Dr. Antonini being at dinner that evening. Three of the engineers from the mixer last night approached her that morning and told her about supper and asked her if she'd like to attend. "Nothing confirmed but old Antonini might be there", Jon had said. That had clinched it, although he could hardly be called 'old'; he was just over forty, if that.

The panel runs late but since lunch is next, she doesn't budge. *So a mixture of boring and interesting thus far; typical seminar,*she thinks as she gathers her belongings once the session finally ends.

She is packing her leather rucksack when Fox Blankenship approaches; he is one of the seminar organisers and a lecturer at Cambridge.

"Lily, isn't it?", he asks and smiles. He is in his late 50's and looks every inch the tenured professor, with a shock of unruly, greying hair and careful air about him.

"Yes", she smiles back at him.

"Paulo – Dr. Antonini – would like to meet you."

She nearly drops the rucksack. "He does?" She frowns. How could he know her? They've had no contact, have no mutual connexions that she knows of.

"Yes, please, this way", and he motions for her to follow.

Dr. Blankenship leads her to the front of the lecture auditorium and into a side room. Dr.Antonini is busy speaking on his phone, but ends his call as she enters. Fox nods to him and leaves, closing the door behind him.

Antonini is fairly tall, *not as tall as Stuart,* with sandy hair and pale brown eyes. He extends a hand and takes hers, a smile spreading across his broad face.

"Lily Batchelor, I presume? Paulo Antonini, pleasure to meet you." She was already prepared for his soft Italian accent after the panel.

She shakes his hand in awed silence. "Not to be rude, Doctor…"

"Paulo."

"Paulo…", she smiles, "but how do you know me?"

He laughs, perhaps better described as a roar. "We have a… mutual friend who has spoken highly of you, who said you would like to meet me. Well…", he spreads his hands wide, "here I am!" He laughs again.

Grateful merely for the opportunity, she doesn't want to press further. She spends the next hour and a half – the lunch break and then some – chatting with Paulo. He is charming and intelligent, and grills Lily about her work at NewTech as well as her Master's work thus far. By the time Paulo leaves, she has his card clutched tightly in her hand and he expresses a desire to collaborate with her on a paper and serve as an unofficial advisor on her thesis.

No one at work will believe this, except I have the card to prove it, along with his personal email, she thinks to herself as she makes her way to the back of the lecture hall in a daze.

She decides to skip the next session and grabs a bite in the hotel's restaurant. She orders a side Caesar and half a roast beef sandwich. She is almost too excited to eat, except that her stomach is making pointed complaints about its empty state.

She's just pulled out her Blackberry and is about to check her mail when the shadow of a figure falls across her table. It is one of the clerks, and after confirming her identity he hands his charge over to her and leaves.

She puts her phone down and rips open the envelope. *What's with the nearly archaic method of communication?* It's charming, but she's embarrassed that clerks have to hunt her down.

She looks down at the clean script:

> I believe you are now free for supper this evening. Seven o'clock.
>
> -Stuart.

She is so annoyed she almost involuntarily crumples the paper. So he arranged the meeting with Paulo and she finds this out now, when she can't ask him anything about Stuart.

"Grr…", she can't resist venting her frustration, and the woman at the adjoining table looks over at her in alarm.

Get it under control, Lily. He did say in the hospital he owed you dinner. Stuart is in control, she muses, and he likes it. If she is honest with herself, she'll have to admit how exciting it is that he is pursuing her so persistently.

She retrieves her engineer's pad from her rucksack to write a response.

> Stuart-
>
> I did make an engagement to have supper with several of the other attendees, and while Paulo's potential attendance provided impetus, it would be impolite to bail on the dinner arrangement simply because I've had a personal chat with him (thank you for that).

-Liliana

She finishes her lunch, leaves a tip and retrieves her belongings. She approaches the front desk, addresses another envelope and after apologizing profusely, asks for it to be delivered.

She is almost twenty minutes early for the session at 3, but snares a seat in the same lecture room Paulo's session had been in earlier. She pulls out her Nook and opens her current read, *Surely You're Joking, Mr. Feynman.* She enjoyed it before, and it was one of the staples she went back to when she hit a period of indecision about what to read next.

People start filing in, and she retrieves her Blackberry hastily, remembering that she had been interrupted when she wanted to check her email earlier.

Her inbox holds the usual suspects, as well as a text.

Liliana-

Paul will be attending the supper to-night, and I am sure he can keep the party occupied. I, on the other hand, will notice your absence. I did promise to buy you supper. I intend to dress for dinner.

-Stuart.

He is too persistent for her and at least it's a text this time, but how did he find her number…? Probably Paulo – she gave her cell number to him. *He won't stop until you say yes. You're just afraid.*

She sighs and replies.

Fine. 7 o'clock.

She hits send and tries to concentrate on the lecture.

Chapter 9

Lily hoped to enjoy supper at some fine restaurants during her vacation, so fortunately she packed several changes of nice clothes. She skips out of the lecture a little early so she can nap before taking a shower. She is worn out from the previous late evening, a lingering bit of jet lag and the crazy day. *Well, you hoped it wouldn't be boring,* her inner voice chimes in. *You got your wish.*

She selects her black pencil skirt with a slit again, and a black camisole with spaghetti straps underneath a gauzy shirt with a leopard pattern on it. She showers lazily, enjoying the feeling of the warm water hitting her skin - she didn't realise how tense she was until then.

After toweling off she grabs her favourite set of lingerie; a reddish purple bra and matching panties with embroidered green ivy. She is careful not to push a nail through her black lace top stockings and finally slips on her black heels.

She looks at herself in the full length bathroom mirror. Her thighs could be a little more toned and her breasts are on the large size, but she has a curvy waist and only the barest hint of belly. *All in all though, not too bad I guess.*

She applies foundation, powder and blush and sets to work on her eyes. 'Purple brings out green', a Sephora saleswoman had told her and so she decides on that. The gold highlight goes nicely with the taupe part of her shirt, and the purple makes her green eyes pop.

Will I sleep with him? I never got off the Pill. She pauses applying her lip liner to look at her eyes reflected in the mirror. She has no idea who he is, really. He's a wealthy business owner who keeps things close and his name is Stuart. Hard to say yes when that's all you know.

He's pursuing me ardently. That's true, but it could be some misplaced feeling of gratitude. After all, he is a young, devastatingly attractive man; she is fairly intelligent and not bad looking but come on… women must throw themselves at him constantly. She feels this incredible, inexorable pull to him and other women must as well; he's just too beautiful, too strong to resist.

Does every man have to have long term potential? That was the problem, wasn't it? She'd like to have a long term relationship once, even if it ended up fizzling out eventually. She has had one date and a little bit of making out since her last boyfriend dumped her, a year and a half ago. She always falls too fast, or trusts too much and ends up getting hurt in the end - sometimes horribly hurt. It's not easy for her to do the casual thing; she's a passionate person and can easily see that wanting a little bit of Stuart would mean wanting all of him.

She slides her arms into her shirt and carefully buttons it, leaving the top two undone to show the lace of her camisole. She checks her reflection; her hair hangs in shaggy waves around her face, her burgundy lips shimmer from the gloss, and her green eyes are vibrant, almost glittering. *If you're not trying to drive him mad or get him to fuck you, I don't know what you're doing.*

She brushes the thought aside and grabs her purse and heads to the elevators. It takes them a moment to open and when they do, she finds the car pretty packed. Conference attendees are going to freshen up before supper and tourists are returning to do likewise before their evening out in Edinburgh.

She can see in the elevator's mirrors that several men give her a full appraisal, and all of them seem to approve.

By the time the last passenger leaves the elevator, Lily is feeling quite nervous. She had psyched herself up and the constant stops mean she rode out her words of self encouragement long before the elevator stopped at the penthouse.

There is a clerk at the lobby again, and she has to supply her name before he allows her to pass. She reaches the door of the suite and uses the knocker – once, twice – and somehow manages to suppress the urge to turn and run. It is just after 7 PM.

The door is opened by the woman from the previous evening, who introduces herself as Ava and leads Lily to the living room she was in the night before. The memory of Stuart's arm around her waist is enough to make her weak kneed and wonder all over again why she said yes to supper tonight; she's just setting herself up for a fall.

"Stuart will be with you momentarily", Ava promises and turns to leave. Drawn again to the view, this time with the sky lit up from the sunset, she walks to the wall of windows. The stones of Edinburgh Castle glow with a kaleidoscope of purple and vermillion hues, the shadows a dark Payne's Grey. *It would be fun to try and paint,* she thinks, to capture the colour and movement. The castle looks otherworldly, sitting on the hilltop with the dwindling rays of the day dancing across it.

Lily senses a presence behind her, and before she can turn she feels an arm slip around her waist and warm breath is in her ear.

"I'm so pleased you're here", Stuart says huskily, his arm tightening, pulling her against his body. He kisses her hair, drinking in the subtle scents that waft off of her.

She is speechless; once again she is spellbound simply by sharing a room with him. She doesn't needed to see his eyes; his sultry voice, accent and the warmth of his arm around her instantly make Lily feel wobbly, as if her will is being sapped, as if nothing else matters but that she's here with him.

"It's beautiful", she says softly, glad he is there to enjoy the majestic colour, the fiery clouds, the corona of darkness pushing down towards the horizon. It is one of the most gorgeous sights she has ever seen.

"It's nearly as beautiful as you", he whispers it so quietly she isn't sure she heard it. Things have moved, this declaration was a surprise. *Probably just gratitude,* she reminds herself.

"You didn't need to invite me to supper." She says, still watching the light show outside. "You don't owe me anything."

His arm tightens around her. "Is that what you think? The invitation was out of gratitude for what you've done?" God, how that sounded like the very thing she had been thinking.

She doesn't know what to say. "Answer me", he demands, and turns her around to face him.

Stuart's eyes are ablaze. *How they can be blue but still fiery I don't know,* she thinks as she looks into them and then scans the rest of him. The tailored navy suit hangs off him flawlessly and his tie is the colour of his eyes. *My God… what a perfect man,* she thinks before crashing back to reality.

She can feel his annoyance. "You said you'd invite me to dinner as a thank you… when we talked in the hospital, the note", she reminds him. "I just assumed…"

"I kissed you last night", he sounds incredulous. He doesn't understand how Lily could think this way. He steps closer and looks down at her. "I think you enjoyed it."

"I…", she has to look away. Liliana knows what is in her eyes; that she craved more but the desire frightens her.

"Did you Lily?", his hand moves to her face and turns it back to his. "Look at me. Did you enjoy it?" She tries to turn her head again but he holds it firm, his fingers curled around her chin.

She feels cornered. "What do you want from me?" she pleads, her eyes looking at his mouth, no, not his mouth, not his eyes…

He moves his right hand and cups her face in his palms and forces it upwards - she has no choice. Their eyes meet and it is like falling into an abyss with walls of sheer blue ice on either side; nothing else is real but those impossible eyes.

"I want the truth, Liliana", he says her name as if it is a caress. "I can see it in your eyes regardless. But I want to hear it. Did you enjoy it when I kissed you?"

"Yes", it is almost inaudible.

"Why are you struggling against me so?", his thumbs are stroking her cheeks.

"Who are you?", she asks, her voice tinged in wonderment.

"You'll find out to-morrow." She hears a distant bell. "That will be supper. Come." He offers his arm to her.

They walk into the dining room, her hand perched on the crook of his arm. She recognizes the maitre'd, Saul, from the French restaurant in the hotel's lobby. Stuart walks Lily to her chair and pulls it out for her and then Saul helps Stuart into his.

The room shares the same wall as the living room so she can still enjoy the sunset. They sit at right angles to each other, so close they can easily touch. Candles are on the table and oil lamps and tea lights are tucked into shelves in the wall. They, and the sunset outside, provide the only illumination in the room. It is terribly romantic, something out of a fantasy.

Saul pours some champagne and then serves the appetizers- blini with caviar and shrimp butter canapés. Saul retreats outside as Stuart raises his glass.

"To many more such evenings", he says and clinks her glass before she can say anything. *Oh… my… God… this just doesn't happen to me.* She recovers and smiles at him before taking a sip.

It takes serious self control, but Lily is finally able to overcome her nervousness. She finds her groove and loosens up and really begins to enjoy herself. Stuart is incredibly charming and obviously wicked smart, besides being handsome enough to grace a billboard in Times Square. Conversation touches on everything from Scottish history to the National Ignition Facility in California.

It's difficult to not be intimidated by him, she thinks to herself as they pause to allow Saul to serve them their main course - Wagyu prime rib with smashed Yukon gold potatoes and sautéed squash. *He exudes confidence in everything he does, from the way he walks to the way he interacts with everyone. It's just heady being around someone like him.*

They are working on their desserts – he has strawberry sorbet and she tries the tiramisu, which is divine – before she feels relaxed enough to ask him something that has been bothering her. *The wine helped, I'm sure.* Her inner voice has thankfully been quiet throughout the meal.

"Stuart", she says slowly.

"Mmm, I like the way my name sounds, coming from your lips", he says; his voice is languid and sensual.

"I was wondering why, if you're a businessman, you were dressed like someone out of a rock video, all leather pants and open shirt." She peers at him over the glass of Vin Santo she is enjoying.

"Well…", he says and looks at her considering. "Try this sorbetto first."

He scoops some with his spoon and she reaches her hand up to take it. "No", he shakes his head gently and she lowers her hand as he moves the utensil towards her mouth.

She watches his eyes look at her mouth as he slides the sorbet laden spoon between her parted lips. A low groan of arousal escapes his mouth, and he retrieves the spoon. His eyes are smoldering; the desire in his body reflected in them clearly for her to see.

She enjoys the sensation of the confection melting on her tongue. "It's divine", she finally murmurs, squirming under his intense gaze.

He leans forward and slides his hand to her neck, guiding her mouth to his. She opens her lips and his tongue slips into her mouth, enjoying the remnants of the gelato mingled with her taste; his lips are pressing hard against hers.

Finally he pulls away, and rests his forehead against hers. Both their breaths come in rasps and the area between her thighs is hot with desire.

Stuart brushes softly against her lips and sits back, looking at her for a moment. She knows her mouth is red and swollen from his kiss, and feels herself blush as he admires her; his gaze is so wanton and lustful she almost doubts it can be for her.

After what seems like an eternity, he speaks. "I was dressed as I was that evening because I enjoy going out to hear live music; I was going to a concert."

"Listening to Beethoven while dressed in leather. WOW", Lily teases as he lets out a low chuckle and screws his lips in amusement.

"I do enjoy Beethoven, but not dressed like that. I… was in a band in my teens, and I rather enjoy good music."

She takes a bite of tiramisu. "Who were you going to see?"

"Atomic Playboy", he says. "Well, they weren't the headliner, but they're the ones I wanted to see."

"Interesting", she says, finishing the last of the dessert and pushing her plate away. "What instrument did you play?"

"Guitar." She can't take her eyes off him as he licks his spoon lazily. *Oh my God. To be that spoon.*

"Did supper meet with your approval?", he says, a note of amusement in his voice.

"Yes. It was lovely." He motions for Saul to remove their plates. He waits until they are cleared and Saul has left the room with his trolley to lean forward. With a quick movement Stuart grabs her right hand in his and brings it to his lips. The unexpected contact makes her shiver with excitement.

"Are you alright, Lily?" he says, looking at her intently.

Not really, your touch just drives me crazy. "Yes Stuart, I'm fine."

"Your hand is shaking." She tries to pull it away but he hangs on more tightly. "You didn't answer my question before; why do you keep fighting me?"

"I'm not really…", she struggles for words. "Am I?" *What a direct question to ask.* "I'm just being cautious."

He pulls back, releasing her hand as he remembers his own words from the previous night. "I wanted to spend some time with you first, Lily. I wanted to… test the waters as it were. Are you seeing someone, is that it?"

"No", she looks down at her hands briefly and shakes her head before tossing it back and looking him straight in the eye. "No, there's no one. I could ask you the same thing. I know nothing about you, as I've said before. Are you with someone?"

"Not right now, no. I am divorced, however."

Wow, one more whole data point. "Why do you want time with me 'first'? Time with me before what?"

"I just want to see what you're like, who you really are."

"I'm not hiding anything, Stuart." *Well, except for the bits about being so madly attracted to you I don't I feel I can trust myself and well, I'm terribly afraid of being hurt.*

"I don't feel you've let your guard down, Liliana. Am I right?"

She's frustrated; perhaps it is the wine or fear or a little of both. "I nearly saw you smashed to bits and that one act of mine has sent my life in a direction I don't fully understand yet. This isn't something I expected when I pulled you from that car."

"What did you expect?" Now it is Stuart's turn to be annoyed. "Is this not to your liking? Do I offend you?"

Lily looks at him, shocked. "Good God Stuart, no. Not at all."

"Then what is the difficulty here?" *Corporate President mode – watch out!*

"I don't want you to feel that you owe me anything." She finally blurts out. "And I worry that's what this is."

"Is that all?", he looks at her warily. *How does he know?*

Rather than lie she just toys with her empty wine glass. She stares at it, mouth pursed, her fingers lightly trailing up and down the stem, almost as if she is fondling it.

"Please!", Stuart says after watching her for a moment. "Don't do that."

"Sorry.", she says and puts her hands on the tabletop and pushes her seat back. "I've had a lovely time. I'm sorry about this… misunderstanding." She stands.

"So quick to try and bolt off. I don't want the night to be over, Liliana", he stands up and faces her.

"Stuart, I don't think you appreciate the position I'm in."

"What does it matter who I am, what my name is? Do you like what you know of me thus far?" He steps closer and takes her hand, once more bringing it to his lips and kissing it slowly. He makes the chaste nature of the gesture intensely erotic. *How does he do that?*

"It's not that simple…", she says slowly, obviously not entirely convinced herself.

"Isn't it?"

"Addressing those notes back to you – you're the mysterious 'Stuart' in the nice suite. When I pulled you from the car I thought of you as the 'Mystery Man'. I don't feel I know you much better now than I did then."

"I'm surprised you say that. We've spent a bit of time talking these past two days…"

"But the substantive things – who you are, what you do – I have no clue. You could be a cartel kingpin for all I know." She recalls the time she dated a man and accidentally found out he was a drug runner for the mob; she made excuses and drifted out of his life as quickly as she could. Not something she wanted to repeat.

"But I'm not."

"It's just good to know basic things, before…" *Almost slipped there, sister.*

"Before what?" He still holds onto her hand, and begins to lean towards her.

"…before… before…" His lips are so close; his breath still smells of strawberries.

"Before getting in too deep", she finally answers. *Before sleeping with you? Before falling in love with you? Before investing my heart and soul in you just so you can trample them into the dust?*

He hovers over her slightly parted mouth; she can feel her lips tremble at the prospect of another kiss.

"I think we're already in quite deep, don't you?"

How can he influence me this way? I want him to touch me so badly. I'm like an addict who hasn't had her drug; I'm shaking from want. So soon, TOO soon to feel this way…

And then their lips touch; it's the barest of kisses, just a brush of his sensual mouth on hers. She gasps as desire shoots through her body, like a match touched to too dry tinder.

"I thought so", and there's a note of triumph in his voice as he says it. "I know you, Liliana", he continues as he wraps his arm around her waist and brings his hand to her face. "I understand better than you think." His fingers lightly trace down her face across her jaw to her mouth. He runs his index finger lightly over her lips.

"Your delicious mouth", he says and she gasps. All she wants is more of him. He leans down and nips her bottom lip, pulling on it slightly, making it swell. She can't help it and sighs.

He puts his mouth by her ear. "You are so incredibly sensual; so responsive. I like watching you", he says and nibbles at her ear as she moans. "I watch your every move; your graceful fingers, your lovely mouth." He feels her sway under him as he leans down and kisses the side of her neck. "I know you."

"Please Stuart…", she's begging him, unsure if it's to continue or show her mercy and desist.

"Mmmm, I do like it when you beg me. What do you want, Liliana, hmm?"

He runs his lips along her jaw line. Her breath is coming in pants; her whole body is tingling with passion.

"Perhaps this", and he nuzzles at the front of her neck, pushes her chin up and begins to lick and kiss the front of her throat.

Lily's hands clutch at his arms for support; she can feel the taut muscles of his body through the jacket.

"Perhaps something else", he whispers and trails his lips down to her collar bone, kissing the exposed skin at the top of her blouse.

"Please…"

"You want something, but for some reason you can't tell me". Dear God, but he's enjoying this. He can feel her shaking; every kiss, every lick brings on another tremor. How can he know this about her, sense what turns her on?

"I think perhaps I've given you something to think about", he says, his face buried in her hair. He brushes the side of her neck, then brings his lips to hers and kisses her tenderly.

"I know you have an early morning. I'll see you later tomorrow", he whispers and leans back to look at her.

"That is incredibly…", she begins, her voice hoarse and staccato.

"…cruel? No. Think about it - what it means, what it says about us. About what I want and perhaps, about what you want."

He offers her his arm and she takes it reluctantly, her insides roiling with conflicting emotions. Anger? Humiliation? Desire? Oh yes, plenty of that, so much it

threatens to spill out of her. She knows what she wants; she's just terrified of it and he's made her face it. The bastard.

Chapter 10

She makes it to her room and locks the door behind her before letting out a large sob.

He's right; it is making me think about what I want. I want a relationship, I want passion. Just so many unknowns, and all so fast, so unexpected. Didn't have time to protect myself…

It's too late; she knew it the moment she saw him yesterday striding towards her - Lily hadn't been prepared, didn't see the signs. Oh, she knew she was attracted to him, but didn't anticipate that somehow she was already deeply connected to him and felt this intimate thread of attachment.

Now he knows it; he has put that knowledge on display for her with painful clarity, held up a mirror to her.

She removes her clothes and stumbles into the bathroom in a fog, brushing her teeth mechanically, removing her makeup, putting on her moisturizer. All the while it plays over in her head. 'Think about it', he said. What should she do?

Mercifully, she dozes off easily, into almost a trance like sleep.

The next morning the apprehension kicks in again. *How am I supposed to concentrate?* It's the last day of the conference, and there's an awards ceremony in the evening. *I can't skip out to vacation early; everyone at NewTech will want to know about the banquet.* The thought of not having to face the truth is comforting, but his cryptic promise that she'll know who he is to-day haunts the recesses of her mind.

She dresses in a burgundy oxford, jeans and her beloved boots. She's feeling the need to be comforted and these familiar northwest togs fit the bill. She slings her indigo Tom Bihn rucksack over her shoulder and with as positive an attitude as she can muster, heads out.

Her mind isn't fully in it, but she manages to concentrate enough to take down some interesting notes from the sessions she attends.

The day breaks early again so everyone can prepare for the awards ceremony that night. She's puzzled but somewhat relieved she hasn't heard from Stuart; he said he would see her to-day. Lily retreats back to her room to prepare for the ceremony.

She grabs her red panty and low back bra set with black lace trim and slips them on. She brought a special dress for tonight- a long deep purple chiffon sheath with silver beaded accents, a thigh high slit and a cut panel that leaves most of her back exposed. Perhaps it's a bit too fancy for tonight but then this is THE important awards ceremony of the most pre-eminent organisation in her chosen field. It doesn't get any more impressive than this, so if she's going to go all out, to-night is the night.

She slides on shimmery thigh high stockings and then a pair of silver, strappy Jimmy Choo heels - a rare clothing splurge of hers. She twists her hair up carelessly; languid curls snake down and tickle her neck. She finds her silver clutch, loads it with necessities, and heads downstairs.

She's gratified to see most of her fellow male attendees are in tuxedos and the women are in evening wear as well. She is too occupied thinking about Stuart to notice the scores of appreciative stares she is getting. The simple fact is, Lily looks beautiful tonight. Whether it's the attire or the newfound passion in her life, she exudes sexuality and the fact that she is nearly oblivious to the potential of her own charms makes her even more desirable.

She looks at the placards and finds her table assignment; lucky her, it's one in front of the stage, to the right. There are a few familiar faces she knows, and soon she is in animated conversation. Stuart is not quite forgotten, but the current company is pleasant and she's soon laughing and enjoying herself.

The supper is lovely - wonderful appetizers, a rich crab bisque, chicken Lyonnaise with accompaniments, petit fours as dessert and some nicely paired wines.

Soon Fox is at the podium for the award presentations. Lily sits back with some port and a cup of Earl Gray tea. *What a lovely evening* she muses, sipping her drink contentedly. She claps at appropriate intervals, laughs along with everyone else at Fox's attempts at jokes, and feels herself relax.

"The last award of the evening", Fox says, "is given to the organisation or individual that the society feels has made the most significant advancement in materials science this year.

"It was a very difficult decision this time around, I'll admit. Arton, among others, were top contenders." Fox motions to Henri Arton, who is sitting at the next table.

"However, when we considered all factors, it became clear to us that one breakthrough had the potential to revolutionise materials - medicine in particular - in a way like nothing before had.

"This year, the Fourier Engineering Advancement Award goes to Watson & Dickson Materials and Manufacturing for NexSkin. Here to accept the award, President Stuart Watson." There's clapping and movement in front as a figure approaches the stage; people begin to stand and cheer. Lily hears a whisper from one of the ladies near her, 'He's my dream date, no doubt', and an answer, 'I'll fight you for him'.

Lily now has a clear view as a man approaches the podium and it feels as if all the blood is leaving her body and she's left weakened. *Jesus Christ. It's Stuart.* She grips the table for support as the full impact of his words from last night kick in. 'You'll know who I am to-morrow', he'd said.

Somehow she manages to command her body to stand and clap. She read about NexSkin, and based on the response – in particular by Henri Arton – there are no hard feelings. Finally the crowd quiets and returns to their seats, their eyes focused on the stage.

Stuart looks breathtakingly gorgeous. She's never seen a tuxedo fit a man so well; he is in his element here, fully the corporate executive and a great representative of the company.

"On behalf of the employees who worked so diligently on NexSkin, I want to thank you for this generous acknowledgement of their efforts. There was wonderful progress made this year in the field of materials engineering, and we are humbled to have been chosen as the recipient of the Fourier Award from amongst all of them." Many begin to applaud again. After a polite interval, Stuart holds up a hand and when there is silence, continues.

"I couldn't be more proud of us as a community. We have pushed at the bounds of possibility, and I'm excited to see what the coming year holds. I know there is a great deal of excitement about projects that are in work, both at Watson & Dickson and elsewhere. It's my belief we are entering a Golden Age in materials science - one that will make the Alchemist's dream of a Philosopher's Stone seem like the plans of a tyro." This brings some cheers from the audience. "There has never been a more exciting time to be in materials, nor a better group of scientists devoted to it.

"On a personal note, I want to thank you for the support you gave me after my accident several weeks ago. Were it not for the heroic actions of a Good Samaritan, I would not be here to-night to accept this award. And by sheer coincidence or providence - whichever you believe - she is here amongst us tonight. Lily, would you please come up?"

Stuart stands back from the microphone and begins to clap. Everyone at her table turns to look at her in shock before rising and clapping. She steels herself, stands, and walks to the side of the stage and up the stairs to join Stuart. By the time she reaches the podium, her face is composed, and she's managed a shy smile. The entire auditorium is standing and applauding; some are also cheering and whistling.

Stuart waits a moment and watches her. She's overwhelmed at first then, placing her hands on her thighs, bows in acknowledgement. Stuart raises his hand to quiet the audience and begins to speak.

"Lily saw that a vehicle had been smashed on the opposite side of the railroad tracks, rushed across and dragged me from my car mere seconds before we both would have been killed by the train's impact, and she injured herself in the process. I have since learned that she would prefer to stay out of the spotlight, but I think you will all agree with me that it's fitting to give credit to one of our own for such a selfless deed.

"Once again, you have my gratitude for your kindness during my recovery and thank you from the employees of Watson & Dickson for this generous recognition."

There is another large round of applause and Stuart walks towards her, puts his hand on her exposed back and ushers her off the stage. He continues to steer her to the far back of the room, as Fox makes some last remarks to draw the conference to a close.

Stuart is clutching the award in one hand as he turns to her near the entrance to the auditorium.

He leans in to her, "You are the most beautiful woman I've ever seen, and it's taking all of my will…" he lets it hang, but the tension is palpable in his voice. His presence is even more magnetic, more powerful than it was last night.

She begins to walk back to her table but he grabs her arm. "Where are you going?"

She manages to blurt out, "My purse".

"Hurry", he says as she pulls free and quickly makes her way to the table, snatches her purse and walks to the back of the auditorium. Stuart meets her at the exit and holds the door open for her before catching up and putting his free hand against her back again; the steady warmth from his touch makes her ache with longing.

She doesn't know whether to be angry at him or thankful for blurting out her role in his accident. In some ways it felt… cathartic. She stops and turns to him. "Where are we going?"

"To my suite", he says and taking her elbow, steers her to the elevator.

They manage to get a car to themselves and as it ascends he steps closer to her. "Please, Liliana - don't fight it anymore." His tone is gentle and earnest and she looks at the floor nervously as he continues. "You feel it, I feel it; anyone who spends a moment with us will sense it. It's… palpable."

The elevator stops and they are at the penthouse. He takes her hand firmly in his and leads them to his suite and on in. He places the award on the console table in the entry and turns to her. His eyes are full of lust.

"Why didn't you tell me?", she whispers as he draws near.

"I'm a cautious man, and the past few years have been tumultuous to say the least." He's standing in front of her and reaches up to loosen his bow tie. "I wanted to know who you were before I let you see who I am. Maybe you can understand some of that now." He throws his tuxedo jacket on the table.

Rumours of a hostile takeover attempt last year come back to her now, other things she can't remember... something personal, perhaps. He loosens the top button on his shirt. Her insides are quavering; she's alone again with him, and the sexual tension between them is growing exponentially.

He steps closer to her and she fights the urge to step back. He reaches a hand out and gently strokes her cheek with his knuckles.

"Did you think about what happened between us last night?" His tone is one of a teacher asking a student. Her teeth graze her lip and she nods.

"Unless you want me to start things right here in the foyer, I would advise you to not draw more attention to your mouth. I already find it almost irresistible", he says softly, but it's a promise. He pushes a strand of hair away from her face. "What conclusion did you come to?"

Part of her wants to just surrender right there to him, but there is still too great a fearful part of her.

"Can we proceed slowly?", she asks, both hopeful and nervous at the same time.

He steps a little closer. "Still a bit skittish? I'd like to know what you're so afraid of Liliana." He wraps his left arm around her and traces circles on the skin of her bare back.

Just the smallest of his touches are enough to make her stomach somersault, and there's the all too familiar burning desire between her thighs.

"It's difficult to explain", her voice is breathy.

"I like the effect I have on you", he says and looks down at her, an amused smile on his face. "I also love this dress. You're beautiful in your jeans and shirts, but so incredibly sexy when you dress up - the plunging neck in front, and the surprise in back that shows your soft skin." His hand is still absently tracing designs on her back.

"Shall we have a nightcap to celebrate?", he says and clutches her hand. They walk towards the living room and wall of windows.

Chapter 11

Lily sits at the bar as he walks around the back of it and begins preparations for what looks like…

"Gin martini?", he asks and she nods.

"Sure".

"Liliana, you're terribly quiet", Stuart observes.

It's so difficult to manage these competing urges. One of them is to flee, avoid the possibility of being hurt but also leave behind the chance for something she desperately wants. *But you'd probably be disappointed anyway. He's so perfect, how could it last?*

The other urge is to throw herself at his feet, plead with him to do whatever he wants to her, anything at all.

"I'm trying to find some middle ground", she says truthfully.

"Hmm." He considers it. "Two conflicting impulses. Am I really that bad?" He says it lightly, amused.

"No", she says it emphatically.

"Good", he smiles, and a playful look passes across his face. "I'd like to understand a little more of what goes on in that beautiful, intelligent head of yours, sweetheart."

Her heart skips a beat at the word. My God, he is serious. Is he really making all this effort just to woo me for one night? *Maybe he likes conquests.* Her inner voice has been unnaturally quiet as of late.

He places a filled, cold martini glass in front of her. "Shall we go and look at Edinburgh?", he asks as he comes around the bar holding his drink.

She notices a love seat turned so it faces the windows. It is flanked with end tables.

"I don't remember this being here last night."

"You are observant and correct" he says, and waits for her to sit, a real gentleman. *Hopefully not entirely a gentleman.*

"I was hoping you would join me after the ceremony, and I know how much you love this view."

Lily crosses her legs and her skirt slips, the slit showing an impressive amount of thigh as well as the top of her stocking.

He looks down at her leg and then raises his eyes to hers; they're smoldering windows of desire. "You are stretching every bit of my self control", he says huskily, his accent almost making it menacing.

He reaches his right hand out and slips his fingers underneath the lace top of her stocking and slowly runs them back and forth.

"To a bit faster than 'slowly'", Stuart says, raising his glass and drinking. She takes a healthy sip, then another. The gin burns a delicious path right to her stomach. His fingers are still stroking her skin underneath the lace top of her stockings.

"Mmm, jet fuel", she says and rests the martini glass on the end table; her fingers are still lazily caressing the stem. She leans her head back and rests it on the cushions behind her and closes her eyes.

"Feels good?", his voice is soft but she can hear the checked passion in it.

"Yes", she says, beginning to surrender. The gin feels good, his hand, his touch… oh yes, VERY good.

He pushes his fingers deeper under her stocking, so his palm is now on her thigh. She can feel him move nearer; sense the closeness of his body even with her eyes closed.

The hand on her leg is now moving up, circling her upper thigh. The warmth between her legs grows with every pass of his hand, her breathing more ragged.

"Open your mouth", he says, and she can feel him lean over her. She obeys.

Suddenly his lips are on hers and her mouth is filled with ice cold gin and his tongue swirling around, dancing with hers. She feels the rasp of his goatee against her skin and it's a sensual combination - the languid warmth of his tongue and the pricks from his facial hair.

Lily's hand leaves her glass and she brings it up to his face; the first time she's ever really touched him, more than just in passing. Her hand tangles in his thick hair, the fingers of her left hand curl over his arm. She can feel a thick cord of muscles through his shirt, and she presses her lips against his mouth harder, suddenly overcome by how much she wants him, how sexy he is.

His lips pull away for an instant. "That's it", he urges, and once again his mouth covers hers, his right hand still on her leg, squeezing her thigh, his left hand now in her hair, pushing her against his mouth.

He is an exquisite kisser; his tongue sensually explores her mouth, and his lips are soft yet strong against her. Intoxication consumes her; his heady scent, his urgency and the gin still warming her throat overwhelm her. He releases a pin from her hair and she can feel it fall gently against her shoulders. His fingers find the remaining pins and her hair tumbles down around her face.

He pulls back to look at her and she opens her eyes. She's completely drunk on the feelings he evokes; the magnetism between them is powerful and undeniable. He reaches both his hands up to her cheeks and holds her face in his hands.

"I'm so grateful you fell into my life", Stuart says, and her eyes widen. "I don't care how", he kisses her lips tenderly, "but I'm grateful."

She blushes, but moves her right hand to his mouth and lets her fingers brush against his lips. He kisses them, and grabs her arm. He slides his lips down and back up the inside of her forearm and murmurs. "You have such delicate wrists and hands." He begins to kiss her palm and it feels very erotic.

"God, Stuart", she gasps. "You're the most sensual man I've ever met." It comes out as an earnest whisper, an unchecked admission of just how badly she wants him.

"Mmm. You bring it out in me", he says and reaches for her glass and holds it to her lips. She takes a sip obediently and then he brings the glass to his lips and takes a drink. She watches his mouth and wonders what it would feel like trailing over her body, down her abdomen… she licks her lips.

"What *are* you thinking about? Your eyes just flashed", he says and offers her another drink. She takes a sip and shakes her head.

The alcohol is definitely going straight to her brain - the wine from supper and now gin. She feels relaxed, and that pleasant lightheaded feeling is creeping into her body. She shakes her head again.

He raises an eyebrow and puts the glass down. "You won't tell me?" A glint of wickedness passes over his eyes; Lily musters as innocent a look as she can. He leans down towards her, puts his mouth by her ear. "I'm good at playing this game, and I like it."

He trails his lips to below her ear and plants the softest of kisses there. She feels her body stiffen with arousal. "Yes…", he whispers, and his Van Dyke tickles the soft skin of her neck. He nips at where her throat meets her shoulder and she gasps loudly and wraps her arms around his shoulders, pushing him to her. She can feel the muscles of his back tight under her touch.

She throws her head back again, baring her neck, and he growls at the act of submission. He trails his lips towards her mouth, just stopping shy of it, his hand stroking her throat.

"What were you thinking about", he says, the words dripping sensually from his mouth.

She has no choice. "You, Stuart. I was thinking about you."

He kisses her on the side of her mouth - a reward. She feels herself melt under him.

"Hmm. What exactly?" She pauses and his fingers on her throat trail electricity down to her collar bone. "I can do this all night."

The teasing is delicious; she's never been so thoroughly seduced in her life, and every part of her is screaming for him now. She's sure it's just what he wanted - her body's absolute allegiance to him so the mind has no choice.

"I was thinking about your mouth", she betrays herself. "How good it feels, how good it would feel…", her voice seems to beg.

"I'm just following orders. You said slowly, Liliana. You did say slowly, remember?" His lips find her chin and he trails hungry kisses along her jaw. His erection is a throbbing presence against her thigh.

"Oh God, I think I'm going to die", she whimpers, almost pleading.

"I'm afraid not, Liliana. I'm not letting you off that easily", he says, and his mouth covers hers and he's pressed so hard against her it's almost suffocating, but the sensation of him around her, enveloping her, is heavenly.

Her hands untuck the back of his shirt, and she slides her palms against his skin and she can feel the muscles ripple underneath her fingers. Stuart's mouth is at her throat, licking and nipping and she can't resist and digs her fingernails into his back.

He moans. "You like that?" he whispers hoarsely, before his lips continue to consume hers. Lily's only answer is another moan as she pushes her body against his.

He pulls away and jerks her up with him and she stumbles against his chest. He tugs her to the windows and pushes her down onto the rug in front of them. In an instant he's kneeling over her, straddling her. Her hands move to his chest.

"Still want slow, Liliana?", he's panting.

She searches his eyes; her body is screaming for him so loudly he must be able to hear.

"Your eyes, hmm. Not quite there, are you?" Stuart observes.

"No, I mean yes. PLEASE…"

"I want you when you're ready to surrender everything, Liliana; willing to give it all up. Your body is ready…" He trails a hand along her side, following her curves. "But your mind… no it's not there yet."

Lily's body is still screaming, but now at her mind, the traitor, denying her what she needs. "Please Stuart, anything…", she can't believe what's coming from her mouth. She squirms underneath him, ready to give him what he wants, even if it's just one time.

"How you tempt me", he says and leans over and kisses her cheek. Amazingly, the chasteness of it makes her tremble with even more passion. Stuart's hands move to the closure at her mid back and he unfastens the clasp there and slides her arms out of the straps. She's plaint, her body absolutely under his control.

He grabs her wrists and puts them above her head. She's never been able to come without direct stimulation before, but she's so close she almost thinks she can and pushes her hips up against him, hoping, hoping for release…

"Not yet", he says and her yell is animalistic, raw. She's almost at her limit.

He whips the bow tie from around his neck and ties her wrists tightly together above her head.

He stands up, his erection pressing hard against his pants. He finishes untucking his rumpled shirt and begins to unbutton it as he gazes down on her figure.

"Please", her mouth forms the word, but no sound comes out; she looks into his eyes, her desperation manifest.

Stuart pulls his shirt off and tosses it aside. The sight of his bare torso with its short dusting of hair makes her squirm more. His chest is perfect, his abdominals exquisitely toned, his shoulders broad and strong. He kneels astride her again and her bound hands come up and run down his chest; she closes her eyes as her fingers explore his skin and then start to move towards his face, but he stays them.

"I like you like this", his voice is hoarse.

"Like what", she whispers.

"Wrists tied, squirming, begging for me", she feels his breath on her face just before his lips meet hers. One hand pushes her arms above her head again while the other pulls down the front of her dress; their lips part.

His breath is a sharp intake between his teeth as he gazes at her bra, the red a striking contrast against her creamy skin. His hands slip underneath her and he unfastens the clasps and slides if off her.

Her breasts are exposed, her erect nipples plain to see on her full, rounded breasts. Stuart growls and moves off her, sliding her dress down until it's resting on the ground next to her.

Lily feels so vulnerable, dressed only in her thin red panties, stockings and shoes.

"My God", he whispers as he drinks her in, her body still heaving, wanting more than anything else for him to touch her.

"Please Stuart", she whimpers as he moves to straddle her again. His hand lightly plays on her skin, his fingers tugging on the ring in her belly button, then moving back up her body.

He lies on top of her, his face nestled in her neck, languidly kissing her. She arches her back, pushing against him. The bare skin of his chest is rubbing against her exposed areolas, torturing her. He trails his lips along her body to her right breast and her breathing accelerates in anticipation of his mouth. He slides a hand to her left breast and begins to cup it, pinching and pulling on her nipple.

"Anything", she promises again, as his mouth claims her right breast, sucking on her nipple, rolling it between his teeth until she is bucking underneath him.

"Is this what you were thinking about?", he asks, his voice lusty.

"Oh God Stuart, yes." She's gasping, finding it hard to breathe. Lily can feel her clit exposed and swollen between her nether lips, pulsing, impatient.

His mouth moves off her breast and his other hand comes up and he continues to pinch and tug on her nipples while his mouth trails down her abdomen.

"Oh!", she's yelling, encouraging him, coaxing him to move lower.

"I can smell your arousal", he says and his voice is raw, primal sounding.

His mouth is at the top of her panties; he kisses her mound, nibbling it through the mesh.

Lily begins to whimper again. "Take me, Stuart. Anything, anything", she's nearly crying, her arousal so acute it hurts.

He strips her underwear off in one swift movement and is between her legs, his right hand trailing down her abdomen to the soft tangle of neat hair between her thighs. She bucks her hips to meet his hand, her pulse throbbing in her ears, her breath coming in pants.

He slides his fingers between her lips and gasps. "You're so wet."

"Yes", Lily's body is undulating, pulsing under his touch. His left hand pulls on her nipple as Stuart slides a finger into her, brushing against her clitoris. His touch goes through her body like a shot, making her moan. Slowly she opens her legs for him and he nibbles on her lower lips.

"Good girl", he encourages and she throws her head back and sighs as his finger slides in and out of her. He flicks his tongue between her engorged lips, grazing her clitoris and she pushes against his mouth, eager for more. She's utterly broken, completely under his spell, her body willing to do whatever he wants of it.

He slides another finger inside her, and begins to stroke her g-spot. His tongue continues to tease her clit, alternating between roughly lapping it and tenderly nipping it. His left hand is still on her breast pulling on her nipple, pinching it.

"Have mercy", her voice is desperate.

Stuart pushes his tongue between the folds of skin and licks her, pulling her bud into his mouth and caressing it with his tongue; his Van Dyke feels rough and good against her sensitive, swollen lips and he feels her tense underneath him.

"Oh my God!" Lily's voice is almost spent, her body tightening around her, and every bit of her feels pulled into a knot.

He plunges a third finger into her as he licks her clit and she explodes, screaming, her body twisting underneath him, her moistness covering his mouth and chin.

Still he laps and strokes and Lily cries out again and again as her body heaves, her channel clamping down on his fingers.

Stuart kisses her swollen lips and slowly pulls out his fingers, his left hand gently rubbing her breast.

She nearly blacked out from the pleasure of it - stars float in front of her eyes, her body hums with aftershocks.

He sits back, grabs his shirt and wipes his face with it before tossing it aside.

"Let me", her voice falters in her throat. "Let me taste you." Her eyes are glassy from the orgasm, her body trembling below him and it's almost too much. He wants to take her now, claim Lily as his own.

Stuart stands up, pulls off his shoes and socks and slowly strips off his pants, sliding them over his hips. She can see the dimple of his muscles as they glide over his pelvis, and the thin trail of hair below his belly button. He's wearing boxers that barely contain his erection; they look like dark blue silk and he steps out of them.

He's gloriously naked, bathed in the sodium glow of Edinburgh below. He's as perfect as a Greek statue, tall and chiseled except for the eyes; the unearthly, luminous eyes that she's positive can see into the deepest parts of her soul.

She looks at him hungrily. A glistening tip emerges from his foreskin, his thick, long shaft incredibly powerful and masculine.

He steps to her so he's standing over her chest, then reaches down and grabs her bound arms and lifts so she's standing. Lily can barely manage it, her legs nearly giving out, and he pulls her to him, the skin of their bodies touching, wanting desperately to merge.

He guides them to the loveseat and he collapses on it, thrusting his hips forward. Stuart's eyes are blue flames of lust as he watches her sink to her knees in front of him.

She kisses the inside of his knees and he spreads them open for her as he moves towards the edge of the couch. She sits up and takes his cock in her hands and strokes the underside of her tongue along his tip. He shudders and sighs, relaxing back into the seat.

She tugs on his balls and moves her mouth to his right pelvis, enjoying the feel of his skin underneath her lips, raking her teeth over the curve of his hips, allowing her tongue to trace the lines of his muscles as they plunge down to his crotch.

Lily bites at the soft skin just above his shaft and his hips thrust involuntarily and he growls, a low guttural noise. His head is thrown back, his lips slightly parted, his breathing heavy. Stuart moves his hands to her head and his fingers massage her scalp, losing themselves in the fine strands of her silky hair.

She runs her tongue around the base of his shaft, his skin and hair there musky, erotic. She opens her lips and slips her mouth along his thick length to his tip and circles the head, her tongue flicking at the underside of his cock, enjoying the moans that come from his mouth, as she feels his fingers tighten against her head.

Her teeth just barely graze his head as she plunges it into her mouth and he jerks, a loud groan escaping his lips. Lily takes him in to the back of her throat and still there's more; Stuart is filling her mouth and her senses are assailed by his heady scent, the saltiness of his skin.

She wraps her lips around his cock and works up and down his length, her tongue periodically laving the underside of his shaft before curling around the end and bathing his head.

Her mouth on his shaft feels so incredibly good it takes all Stuart's will to restrain his body from coming quickly. He wants to enjoy the sensations for as long as he can as she teases and torments his cock. Her tongue is at once soft and unforgiving, caressing him then probing his length, while her hands cup and tug at his balls, sending thrills of pleasure throughout his body.

His orgasm is building quickly as her mouth explores his length and all too soon he feels the tingling in his hands and feet, and his entire body becomes taut.

Lily senses he's on the brink and curls her tongue under his head, caressing the sensitive spot she knows is there. With a loud moan he suddenly explodes in her and she's taking him in as quickly as she can, but he's pouring himself into her and she can feel his seed trickle from between her lips. Stuart's cock pulses against the roof of her mouth and then finally he is spent and collapses back into the cushions.

With her bound hands she wipes her lips and leans her head against the inside of his thigh. His right hand absently caresses her head, traces the shape of her ear. A soft sigh of contentment escapes her lips.

Her pulse has finally slowed from racing, yet still she wants him. She can taste him in her mouth and relishes it, knowing she pleased him. Stuart stirs and sighs above her.

His hands take hers and he pulls her on the seat next to him and his fingers undo the bow tie around her wrists.

"I felt you come in my mouth", he says, incredulous. "This surge of warmth against my face, like nectar. Has that ever happened before?"

She opens her mouth and closes it before answering. "Once", she says softly.

"Thank you. That was…", he sighs, "incredible." The attraction there is greater than before, now that they've begun to explore one another.

"I really enjoyed it too", Lily flushes at the admission. He puts an arm around her shoulders and pulls her to him; sitting nearly naked next to him feels oddly normal.

"The other time you came, was it from something similar?"

She blanches and feels her body tense. "Um, sort of", she says slowly. "Why?"

"I've never met a woman who could do that. It's rare."

"Well, it rarely happens", she says.

"I like the way you taste", Stuart rolls his tongue inside his mouth. "Citrusy but sweet. Mmm", he closes his eyes.

"Stuart – what did you mean when you said my body was ready but my mind wasn't?"

He kisses her hair. "I can sense your body wants mine. Even now, I can feel it pulling on me." It's true; curling up against his side with a shattering orgasm behind her, she still wants more from him.

"But your mind… well, I can see in your eyes some hesitancy."

"Why is that so bad?"

"I just want all of you", he says as a matter of fact. "I want you to be mine, utterly, without reservations."

"Surrender…", she whispers.

"In some ways, yes", he says, his fingers caressing her shoulders, the warmth between her legs growing again. "I want to possess you. When you give yourself to me, I want your longing for it complete, irrevocable."

Lily gulps.

"When I desire something - truly desire something - I'm not satisfied with half measures", Stuart says, looking down at her. "I'm persistent, as you've learned."

He is in such command of himself it is difficult to not be swept up in it.

"Have you made reservations for your trip yet?" he asks, leaning his head against hers.

She closes her eyes. "Just a car rental. I bought some maps to-day during lunchtime."

"Give me the rental information. George will cancel the car."

"But Stuart…"

"I have several cars here; we'll use one of my Range Rovers."

"We?", she is still processing what just happened. He pulls back so he can watch her reaction.

"Yes. If you're up for it, I would rather enjoy showing you around Scotland. I have a manor house in Aberdeenshire that we can use as a base of operations."

"I suspected George wasn't a friend."

"Well, he's an employee and friend. So you'll give him the information?"

"I'm sure you have better things to do than play tour guide."

Stuart turns to Lily and places his hands on her shoulders. "Allow me to be the judge of my obligations", he says a bit sternly. "I often spend weeks at a time away, and I am adept at handling things remotely."

There isn't a chance in hell of saying no to him when he is in this mode.

"Okay", she says. *Why the hesitancy? Because you're afraid this will just disappear like so many other relationships and admit it; you were attracted to him from the second you saw him in that car.*

"Good", he kisses her forehead. "We're going to have a wonderful time. We'll need to leave a bit early in order to make some stops I have in mind along the way."

She trails a finger along the side of his face to his Van Dyke and traces its outline with her thumb.

He closes his eyes. "I like it when you touch me", he murmurs.

"I like this", she says, enjoying the feel of the hair under her fingertips. "You have a sensual mouth, and this frames it perfectly."

He opens his eyes and looks at her in surprise. *Progress - she's not quite so guarded now.* He looks into her eyes as he brings his mouth close to hers; she doesn't break contact until his lips touch hers in a lingering kiss. She moves her hands to the back of his head and pulls him to her, opening her mouth to him, wanting to feel his tongue.

Stuart can't resist; his tongue darts into her mouth and tangles with hers. He can taste the residual saltiness of his own come just as surely as she can taste the musky spice of her arousal.

Lily pushes her bare breasts against his chest, craving the skin to skin contact, feeling the bristle of hair against her sensitive nipples and she moans into him, while his greedy mouth consumes her lips.

His hand moves to her back gently and she shivers into him, causing him to smile; she's so responsive. His hand cups her arse, pushing her further against him. Desire is quickly rising in him; his cock is already stiff, pressing against her belly.

It's all he can do to push away from her. He looks into her eyes, feeling her body tremble in his hands from desire.

"You should get some sleep", his voice is filled with need.

"Haven't you just had partners, to see where it would go?", she says, disappointment all over her face.

"Yes, but that's not what I want from you. Is it what you want?" He reaches a hand up and holds her face so she's forced to look into his eyes. "Do you just want me to fuck you?" She's startled by the word, and her eyes widen. "Or do you want to belong to me?"

She doesn't say anything, but he knows her answer. "I would like nothing more than to you have you right this minute under me, my cock inside you and your body arching in pleasure." Moisture pools between her legs at the thought. "But I want all of you, Liliana. I want your trust, I want your mind and your body. I generally get what I want." He looks at her in his confident way and it gives her goose bumps.

He stands and pulls her up with him. "Pack your suitcase; George will take our luggage ahead to Cairness for us. Wear something durable. We're going to be making a little stop in the countryside." He plants a soft kiss on her lips.

Stuart watches her as she pulls her panties and bra on and slips the dress over her head; he moves around to fasten it for her and then quickly pulls his tuxedo pants on.

"I think we need to find another occasion for you to wear something like this", he says, kissing her neck. Lily leans back into him, enjoying the feeling of his warmth against her back.

"George will pop by around ten for your suitcase." He takes her elbow and escorts her to the door, the pants hanging off his hips seductively. He gives her one more kiss before opening the door and ushering her out. She's still in a daze as she takes the elevator to her floor and walks to her room.

This trip has suddenly become a lot more interesting, she admits as she locks the door for the night. Her heart begins to start thudding against her chest as she thinks about what to-morrow will hold. She ends up tossing and turning for at least half an hour before she can relax enough to sleep.

Chapter 12

She is restless that night, the chime on her Blackberry waking her from an unsatisfying slumber. *You have a man who desires you, what's the problem?*

Abandonment, that's the problem. She yawns, slips out of bed and makes her way to the bathroom. He simply seems too good to be true and well, the power he has over her and how her body just craves him, is alarming.

But pleasurable. I'll never know unless I surrender.

As usual she's running a little behind schedule and has to rush in order to be packed in time. George is predictably punctual and takes her suitcase. She's taking one more cursory look around the room when she hears a knock and Stuart steps in the half opened door.

Her stomach instantly tightens when she looks at him. He's wearing faded blue 501's that hang on his body perfectly, a pair of Doc Martens, a button down shirt and a leather jacket. His hair is still damp and his hands are shoved in his pockets. He looks like a working class man rather than the president of one of the world's top materials engineering companies and by God is he gorgeous. She sighs.

"Ready?" his eyes are clear and crisp; he must have had a good night's sleep. He leans down and kisses her. "How did you sleep, hmm?" He puts his hand on her back and she grabs her purse from the bed.

"Fitfully", she says honestly.

"I guess I didn't tire you out sufficiently", he says kissing her hair. He's so willingly affectionate it begins to put her at ease.

They walk to the front desk so she can check out and collect her receipt; they then make their way to the front doors.

A brand new black Range Rover sits nearby. Stuart pulls keys from his pocket and unlocks it. He holds the door open for her before walking around to the right side of the car, taking off his jacket and getting in.

"It's so odd to be sitting on this side without a steering wheel!", she laughs.

Stuart grins and starts the car. "I like it when you're smiling like this", he says, leans over and plants a kiss on her temple.

He shifts and pulls away from the kerb; she lets out a deep breath.

"How are you feeling?"

"Nervous, a bit", she says, still smiling. "I'm not sure what to expect and I'm not quite sure that I shouldn't be worried."

"Honesty this morning", he observes. "I like that too. I want to know what you're thinking – be open with me." He shifts and she watches his hand, his long fingers curled on the knob of the shifter. He's so utterly at ease with himself; it's refreshing and very sexy.

"Where did you go to school?", Lily asks and gets the rundown. Texas A&M, then Cambridge for his doctorate, presidency of W & D at 27. Lily does the math – *wow, he doesn't look 34, more like 24.*

"Texas? Wow, I'm imagining your accent among a bunch of Texas ones." She chuckles.

"I enjoyed my time there, to be honest", he says. They're on the A90 heading north. "Texans are quite direct and no-nonsense. They have an excellent Materials department. Where did you complete your undergraduate?"

She tells him about her last two years the University of Idaho, and moves on to her experiences so far at the University of Washington. They merge onto M90, still heading north.

"You told me you like ruins. Why?", he says, his right elbow resting on the door, his fingers lightly guiding the steering wheel. She can see a small pink scar on his wrist.

"Hmm." She narrows her eyes as she thinks. "I like the loneliness of them. Cities can be wonderful - art and museums, restaurants and all that. But there's something beautiful about the countryside. I remember driving to Linlithgow Palace; there was some fortification on a hill I could see from the road and I meandered my way up there. It was a tall red brick tower, in good repair, still in use in some capacity, it seemed. Near it were some tan stones - the remains of some larger house and a wall - and it must have been an older house by the looks of it. Near the remnants of the wall was a tree; it was the only large tree on that hillock, and it was all so lonely. I could feel it here", she motions to her chest, "that it was an old place; that humans had been there in some capacity for a long time. This thread... a connexion to the past through that place, and the valley below laid out so prettily. I thought, '*I* would want to build a house here, I understand why.' I felt it." She laughs and looks over at Stuart. "It probably doesn't make sense."

He takes his eyes off the road a moment to look at her. "I understand too", he says quietly and smiles before turning his eyes back to the motorway.

"And there's something else – the effort. It took a great deal of effort to build these castles and manors and yet they built them so spectacularly! Some of them like Dunbar must have been engineering marvels, others are so old and beautiful and the stones so well fitted, you wonder what hands laid them there, and whether they knew it would stand the test of time."

A90 turns towards the northeast. The countryside begins to change - the bustle of Edinburgh and Dundee give way to a freeway running near smaller towns. They turn off near Oathlaw to find a pub to have lunch.

The Rover crawls through town until they spy a prime candidate, The Twisted Bramble pub house.

They clamber out of the car and put their jackets on. The sky is overcast and a cool wind whips through the town. Stuart holds out a hand and Lily takes it and smiles, enjoying how natural it all feels, how normal. His hand is strong and she remembers how delicate a touch it can be too and blushes.

He opens the door and ushers her inside. A small table is nestled in a corner near the lit fireplace. She sits down, rubbing her hands against the cold as Stuart pulls a chair around to sit next to her.

"You seem so much more at ease to-day; I can't get over it", he says, his eyes glowing in the light of the fire. He reaches a hand to tuck a tendril of her hair behind her ear. "I can't tell you how much it pleases me."

"I'm on vacation, and I like this", she looks around at the warm wood beams that crisscross the ceiling, the old, worn tables. "This feels good". She smiles unreservedly and it's contagious. Stuart laughs.

"I could get used to being around you like this. Your wonderment and joy are really amazing to behold."

"Well, the world can be a pretty amazing place. This is a really unique opportunity for me, a trip I've definitely been looking forward to."

Just then a barmaid comes over to take their orders. "Two Belhaven, two fish and chips". She takes it down and walks off; Stuart's also in his element here.

"I understand the leather pants now.", she says and he throws his head back to laugh.

"Do tell more."

Lily watches him, mirthful and enjoying himself. "I could get used to you laughing like that too, although hopefully not at me", she says. Did last night break the ice? She feels so comfortable around him today - she's been yearning for a relationship like this. "You blend in here with your faded jeans and Scots accent. You're obviously very good at your job, but I can see the need for something different - an escape, an outlet."

The barmaid comes back with coasters and two tall pint glasses of beer and retreats.

Stuart lifts his glass. "To a wonderful vacation." She nods and their glasses touch.

The beer is so cold and refreshing - a counterpoint to the hot fried fish their server returns with.

"Hard to go wrong with beer and fried fish", says Stuart as he tears into a piece, releasing a small cloud of steam along with heavenly aromas.

Lily tries to coax their destination out of him, but he refuses. Her playfulness to-day is disarming, and he is utterly taken with her - her wit, her charm, her innate sensuality, her ready smile.

After finishing the fish and another pint each, they head back to the Rover. Lily is enjoying that relaxed feeling again from the alcohol and ambiance, and her appetite is sated from the excellent fish.

While Stuart's driving she takes the time to watch the countryside go by. It's September, and patches of heather dot the tops of hillsides. It's nice that the silence between them is comfortable; there's no need to fill the space with chatter. It's quite peaceful.

"What are you thinking, Lily?" Stuart asks softly after a long silence, the gentle bumps of the drive nearly lulling her into a trance like state, his voice like a soothing breeze around her.

"I was looking at the heather, at how vibrant it is against the greens and browns of the hillside. And I was glad to discover that we do silence well." She turns from her window and smiles at him wistfully and his mouth curls up at the edges.

"We're about to make our turnoff", he says. The sky is blustery, angry. "It might shower on us", he observes.

Soon they're bumping along on a rough road; Lily has a hard time following the turns and suddenly they're at a small dirt parking lot. The wind whips her hair the moment she exits the car. Stuart admires her for a moment as she gauges her surroundings. Her blonde locks dancing animatedly about her head are a contrast to the serenity and peace on her face. She's completely non-plussed, despite being transported out to the middle of nowhere in the Scottish countryside, surrounded by hills of brilliant green and a darkening sky. Not for the first time Stuart thinks about what an incredible person he has found in her - so many contradictions and interests that blend smoothly somehow into Lily, this beautiful and intelligent woman who is so full of life.

The sky is stormy pink and blue and the leaves of the car park's trees are being tossed around. Stuart extends an arm to her and grasps her hand firmly in his. "I believe you said you liked wild weather", he says wryly and tugs on her hand.

They make their way to a rocky path and begin their ascent to the top of the hill. The sky grows more angry looking with each passing minute, and apart from them, there are no visitors.

The wind snatches her breath from her lips; it's a bit of a walk and up an incline. She's not in as good a shape as Stuart and his strides are long, so her progress is slower and she trails along slightly behind him, their fingers still tangled intimately.

He waits for her and they crest the summit at the same time.

They're standing on top of a hill that has a commanding view of the countryside in all directions. To the west, she can see a veil of rainclouds as they pass through a valley; below her to the east, a silvery stream winds in a canyon surrounded by lush green hills.

"My God", she whispers, overcome by the majesty and loneliness of the place.

Stuart steps behind her and puts his arms around her. "This is the White Caterthun. It's the remains of an old Pict fortification."

A trail of stones traces the shape of the hilltop like a crown. She walks near the edge and looks out - the view seems almost infinite. She completes a circuit of the top, walking around it slowly, trying to imagine the crumbling ruins as an indomitable fortification.

"This is beautiful, Stuart." A feeling of achy loneliness steals into her heart, oddly warming it. It has the air about it of an ancient place. She pulls out a pocket camera from the folds of her jacket and takes several snaps of the hillside and a few of Stuart before tucking it away.

He steps to her and turns Lily around to face him. Her hair is still whipping around her face and he grabs it in his fist, wrapping it around his hand. Slowly he pulls it until her head tilts back, and he brings his lips down to hers and kisses her hard on the wild hillside, the echoes of a long dead people all around them.

She runs her hands inside his jacket along his body to his back, pressing him against her; the leather smells so good mixed with his spicy scent. Being here amongst these ruins with him, feeling his strength underneath her hands along with the force of his personality excites her, and she moans into his mouth. He is as strong and indefatigable as the hillocks and mountains around them, and he feels almost as untamed. She would stand here forever with him, if he asked.

He pulls away to gaze at her. "What am I to do with you?", he asks simply, his eyes tender.

The first drops begin to fall then. Their eyes meet and they head for the path to the car park.

They are halfway down the hillside when the rain begins to pour in torrents, soaking them to the skin almost immediately. Lily skids, nearly sliding down the path, and Stuart grabs her hand tightly. They scramble into the car just as they hear the first distant rumble of thunder.

They turn to each other and laugh. Stuart slips the key in the ignition and points her to the heated seat control. "You'll be needing that before long. I'm afraid we'll have to skip the second stop of the day and head straight to Cairness."

"Cairness?", she can already feel a bit of cold creeping into her bones.

"My home. It's just over an hour's drive."

Stuart manoeuvres through the maze of farm roads and back to a main thoroughfare. Lily's grateful for the heated seats, especially since the driving rain slows them down. It's an hour and forty minutes later before Stuart says, "Nearly there" and turns down a drive.

They approach a set of gates and he enters a code at the keypad and they swing open.

"This is your home?" Lily gasps as a structure comes into view. "This is something out of Jane Eyre" she whispers, awed.

The house is large and in the style of late 18th century homes, with a gravel drive in front of the rectangular framed entrance.

The rain has abated some, and Lily exits the car and stares at the facade. *I don't belong here -this is surreal.* The contrast between Stuart in his tight, worn jeans and the elegance of the grounds is stark.

He's next to her, grabbing for her hand. "Let's get you out of those wet clothes", he says and looks down at her and smiles. At the look of discomfort on her

face the smile passes and he frowns. "Come on", he says and tugs her towards the entry.

Chapter 13

A butler greets them at the front door. "Mr. Watson. Miss." He bows to them.

"Thomas, this is Miss Batchelor. She is a very special guest; she's to have anything she wants." Thomas bows in understanding.

"Luggage is already in your room, sir."

Lily has little time to marvel at the entrance hall as Stuart is leading her to an alcove and staircase to the next floor. They ascend the stairs and at the top Stuart turns and faces her.

"I gave you a room next to mine. I didn't want to make any assumptions that would… overwhelm you. Just so you know." He smiles reassuringly at her.

"All right Stuart." She returns the smile as best she can. She's staggered by the place; after having read about old manor houses and day dreaming about them as a child, she's about to stay in one.

And it's your boyfriend's. Is he her boyfriend? Not lovers technically, no not yet. *And whose fault is that?*

He studies her a moment and adds, "Although you may want to use my bath; there's a large soaking tub in it."

She catches her lip with her teeth and there's a flash of desire in his eyes.

"Are you sure?", she asks, unsure herself.

"Yes, quite."

"I'll just go get a change of clothes", she says.

"Right here", he motions and steps ahead of her. The heater in the car might have partly dried their clothes, but her jeans are still damp and cling to her body, and tendrils of hair are sticking to her neck. It is hard for Stuart to concentrate on anything else; he really wants to peel her out of those jeans and…

He can't; not yet. But she is close, very close. He can sense a change in her even to-day. He can be a patient man when it means he will get what he wants, and right now he has never wanted anything or anyone more than he wants Lily – all of her.

He steps down the hall, opens a door on the right and motions her in.

Lily steps in and gulps. The room isn't overly large but it's still sizeable. The walls are a dark fawn colour, except for the wall with a fireplace, which is a purplish burgundy. An old looking tapestry hangs over the fireplace, which faces the foot of the bed. A small blaze burns in the grate.

The bed is a large four poster canopy, with carved wood newels. The bedding is nearly the same wine colour as the accent wall - it's beautiful.

"There's a private bath", Stuart says, "through this door".

She walks to the doorway and steps inside. The bathroom is almost more charming, with a claw footed tub and antique fixtures. The walls are an airy green and a small bronzed fixture hangs from the ceiling; it gives one the feeling of a tub in a garden.

Lily looks at Stuart; he's trying hard to hide the pride he feels. She looks around and is truly amazed by how beautiful it is. She knows W & D has grown under his leadership and now they have a prestigious award to add to their growing list of accomplishments. She's proud of him and knows firsthand how focused he can be, but she can't shake the feeling that she must be in a fairy tale of some sort.

"Is everything to your liking?"

Something she hasn't heard before; a tinge of apprehension in his voice. *He really wants me to like it here, be comfortable.*

"Yes, Stuart. This is a really lovely place, and this room is perfect. Thank you." Overcome by his kindness and concern, she impulsively plants a kiss on his cheek. He's startled at first and then breaks into a warm grin.

"Let's see about getting you a change of clothes and then bathed."

Rummaging around in her luggage, she finds clean jeans, a t-shirt, undergarments and snags her toiletries bag.

She experiences a fleeting moment of nervousness as she turns to follow Stuart from the room. "Are you sure you don't mind? I mean, the tub here looks wonderful. I don't want to inconvenience you."

"Not at all; I think you'll like my bath better."

They exit the room and Stuart walks to another door, nearly opposite the staircase. He opens the large wooden door and they enter. Lily nearly drops her clothes.

It's a thoroughly masculine room, and she whole heartedly approves. The walls are a rich red, with a cream chair rail running along the walls. The hearth and sides of the fireplace are white marble, and a tapestry that looks even older than the one in her room surmounts the mantel. The tapestry is of a forest glen, with ruins in the distance barely visible between two large trees in the foreground. The greens and reddish browns in the hanging are a perfect complement to the walls and dark wood of the king sized four poster bed that is at a right angle to the fireplace. As in her room, the fireplace is already lit.

"This is a gorgeous room, Stuart. It feels like you." She turns to look at him and he's smiling.

He playfully swats her on the bottom. "No more dilly-dallying! Time for your bath." He says it suggestively and her eyes widen. He puts a hand on her back. "This way."

He leads her to a door and into a smaller room. "This was another separate bedroom; it's now a study with a wardrobe as you can see."

They pass through another door and into a sumptuously appointed bath. It looks to be a shade smaller than hers, but against the foot of the tub is an obviously modern shower enclosure.

"These older manor homes rarely had wardrobes and no separate showers. This shower is the only change I made to the manor, and it was quite difficult to get permission for. In the end I exposed a secret door between two rooms and blocked – but did not remove –a second entrance to the bath. It can be easily returned to the original configuration."

Lily places her clothes on a chair set by the windows.

"So the choices are a steam shower, or large tub - whatever you prefer."

The tub is a big claw foot, roomy enough for two people; the steam shower has a large glass surround. There are two shower heads and several long vertical bars house jets.

"Wow, tough decision, what do you recommend?"

"The tub is nice since you can recline, but the steam shower is brilliant."

"What are you going to do?"

He raises an eyebrow. "I am going to wait outside."

"Oh", she says, disappointed. She hoped he would join her. *You're having trouble committing and he knows it, remember?*

Stuart kisses her forehead. "Enjoy your shower", he says and turns and exits, leaving the door open a crack.

He knows your body will sway your brain if he does this enough.

She sighs and begins undressing and turns the water in the shower on. It takes her a minute to get the hang of the controls, but soon the enclosure is filled with steam.

With one more quick glance at the cracked door, she steps up and inside and is immediately enveloped by warm vapour.

"Ohh…", a contended sigh escapes her lips, and she places her shampoo and conditioner on the low tile bench in the corner of the shower.

She steps underneath the showerhead and turns the jets on. She's immediately bombarded with thousands of tiny water-needles impacting her skin. It's almost painful yet incredibly erotic and relaxing at the same time. She reaches for the shampoo and massages it into her hair as the jets pound away at her skin; the combination is very sensual. She rinses her hair and puts conditioner in it, and searches for some soap.

She turns and the jets pummel her chest, stinging her nipples, making her gasp. *What has he done to me? I'd almost convinced myself that a relationship wasn't in the cards and now all I can think about is sex.* It was as if he'd flipped some sort of switch in her. *I wonder how these jets would feel elsewhere…* She looks down to her breasts and then the small tangle of hair between her legs.

Lily feels a hand on her shoulder and she lets out a yell and turns around.

"I wasn't doing anything…" she blurts out before she can stop herself, her guilty thoughts now confessed.

Stuart's blue eyes are like beacons in a fog. His lips curl in a sardonic smile. "What were you thinking about?"

All she can do is pant and look at him. *You know I want you Stuart, please, you can feel it.*

He looks at the jets and at Lily and his smile becomes a grin. "Enjoying the shower I see?" He reaches out a hand and cups her right breast, his thumb slowly circling her nipple. She feels her lids lower - the steam, his caress, the water all wash over her in sensual waves.

"Why do you torture me?", her voice is tight.

"I haven't *begun* to torture you, Liliana", he says and her eyes pop open as he moves his mouth to hers.

She can feel her lips trembling against his. His breath is cool against her face, his mouth just barely making contact with hers. "Tell me what you were thinking about, Lily." His voice is seductive.

"The jets felt good", he's trailing his mouth along her jaw line, barely skimming her skin. "Good on my breasts."

He raises his right hand and cups her breast while looking directly into her face. He pulls and pinches the nipple, then lightly strokes it. Between her legs is on fire with desire.

He turns her around and pushes her towards the jets, and brings his left hand up to her other breast. He molds himself against her and she can feel his thick, wide erection along her lower back.

He lifts her breasts in his hands and pinches her nipples hard, so she squirms against him and gasps. He alternates, first lining up one breast with the hard stream of water, then the other, kissing her neck as he does so. Her hands reach back and cling to his legs for support.

"I could take you here, now", he says, his voice full of lust.

"Yes, Stuart. Please." She rubs herself against his chest, the length of his shaft tucking into the crack between her ass cheeks. He moans.

"You are naughty", he says as a matter of fact, "As naughty as I'd hoped."

"Yes", she has abandoned any pretense of control.

He pulls her away from the shower, and sits, pulling her down with him onto the hard tile floor. He leans back against the bench and places her between his legs, his erection still a throbbing presence against her back.

"Put your hands around my neck." It takes a second to realise what he wants, but she rotates her shoulders back and rests her hands behind his neck, causing her back to arch and push her breasts out. Her forearms are resting on the top of the tile bench; it's a difficult position to maintain.

"Don't move them", he commands, and suddenly his hands are on her nipples and he begins to tug roughly on them, causing her to cry out. He places his feet on the inside of hers and spreads his legs, causing her to open hers.

He is so commanding and forceful and she is so turned on she begins to squirm and arches her back further against him and moans.

She tangles her hands in his hair and he pushes her head to the side and begins to nibble on her ear, causing her to lean into him even more. He slides his left hand down her abdomen to the slit between her legs. She is so open, so vulnerable; it's a sexy feeling.

He can feel the slickness sticking to her lips, different than water. He swirls around her clit with his index finger, pushing underneath it while he nips at her neck, his right hand still teasing her breast.

She tries to push her pelvis into his hand, she's desperate to come. It's as if she's been trained by his expert touch; he arouses her thoroughly and so quickly that it's overwhelming.

"Not so fast", he says, obviously enjoying teasing her. He sticks his finger in her and rests his thumb on her bud and she pushes against it, desperate for more stimulation.

"Yes, oh that feels so good."

"What do you want?", he voice is quiet, almost slightly menacing.

He lifts his thumb for a second and she pushes against him.

"To come."

"I think you need to ask." The finger inside of her is swirling, moving.

"Please Stuart. Please make me come." It vocalises as a gasp; she's writhing around on his finger, begging for release.

His thumb brushes against her clitoris and she leans into it; he pulls back.

"Please, let me come. Oh please."

"I'm not convinced."

She begins to move her right hand. "Don't", he warns and she moves her hand back into position.

"I want you so bad Stuart", she says as his finger again flicks across her sensitive clit, now swollen and fully exposed. She moans again and squirms, her movements pushing against his hard cock, stimulating him.

"Please let me come, please make me come." It's like a chant, a promise.

He swirls his thumb around her bud and her body begins to quiver. He strokes her and thrusts his finger inside her and she reaches her climax as her body is twisting in his arms. He bites at the base of her neck and she cries out and pushes against him, her screams of pleasure mingling with the steam.

Finally she is spent and collapses back onto him, her hands coming down to rest on her thighs. He kisses her neck and she whimpers softly, her body still reeling from the orgasm.

"I love it when you come", he says and nuzzles her hair. "I love that you're so loud."

"I can't help it". She can feel his hard cock twitch against her back. *I've been selfish.*

She untangles her legs and turns to face him. His sensual lips are parted; he's obviously very aroused. Pleasuring Lily is stronger than any aphrodisiac he could care for, an incredible high.

She can barely manage it, but she kneels between his legs and bends over, her arse in the air.

"Mmm", he says as he reaches and places a hand on one of her buttocks and begins to squeeze it.

She licks his shaft, lapping along its entire length, moving her left hand to his balls and stroking his cock with her right. She places her mouth over his tip and flicks her tongue at his head, causing him to groan and squeeze her arse hard. He moves his remaining hand to her other cheek and spreads them wide, massaging them. The water is beating on her back incessantly, the rhythm trance like, relentless.

She continues to caresses his cock with her mouth while moving her hand up and down, sometimes twisting, sometimes speeding up or slowing down. His left hand leaves her rump and then she feels it come down hard against her ass cheek.

Lily moans, his shaft in her mouth, her hands stroking and cupping him. He spanks her again, harder, and she feels the warmth between her legs again and pushes her bum up higher. *I'm such a hussy, I almost don't know myself.*

He moves a thumb to her rosebud and begins to circle it, making it pucker. She sucks harder, slightly tugging on his tip with her lips, swirling her tongue quickly around his head. She can feel the tension in his body, it is primed for release and she plunges him into her mouth just as he lays a hard swat on her ass and then he's coming, filling her, his cock pushed hard against the roof of her mouth, his hands grabbing tightly onto her buttocks.

His head is resting back on the top of the tile bench, eyes closed, chest heaving. She sits back and lets him slide out of her mouth and she kisses the hard muscles of his stomach, trailing her mouth to the curve of his hips and his body responds beneath her, enjoying the touch.

Stuart sits up and opens his eyes, and watches her as she kisses his body and he reaches out to touch her hair.

Lily looks up at him. "I thought showers were supposed to be clean places." She smirks up at him and his lips part in a smile.

"Come then. Let's get washed up."

****

Supper is a pretty simple affair that evening; Guinness stew with lamb, salad and homemade bread. Stuart has loaned her a pair of sweatpants which are too large, so she rolls the waist down. He looks incredibly sexy in a pair that hangs low off his hips and a dark t-shirt.

"Mrs. MacDonald makes the best Guinness stew on the planet", he says as she clears their plates. The housekeeper and cook chortles at him and potters around the room.

"She and her husband live here year round as caretakers", Stuart explains. She looks to be a jolly woman, with round cheeks and hips, her greying hair pulled back from her friendly face.

"I love soups and stews", Lily says. "And that was one of the best I've ever had. Thank you, Mrs. MacDonald."

"Ah t'was nothin", but she's clearly flushed with pride. "Glad ye like it as well. Is one of Mr. Watson's favourites, that", she says in her strong Glaswegian accent before making her way out to the hall and giving them privacy.

They ate supper in the breakfast room, a relatively unadorned place with a long wooden table in the centre and a cheery fire burning in the hearth.

"I love that every room here has a fireplace, and that you use them." She says wistfully. "It must be really cozy here with a blanket of snow outside and hearths lit."

"It's quite lovely, actually. You'd really enjoy it."

Lily looks over at Stuart and smiles. Their interlude in the shower has mostly sated her for the time being, yet always there's this tug on her. *Is this what he means when he says my body talks to him?*

He refills their glasses. "So. Why don't you tell me about that other time you had an orgasm and came as well?" He sits back.

She's midway to bringing the glass to her lips and stops, blushing.

"There's nothing to be ashamed of", he says. "We've explored one another have we not?"

She casts a quick look to the door Mrs. MacDonald had exited from.

"I… hum." What should she say? The fact that it happened is embarrassing to her.

"Well, I haven't told anyone about it before."

He leans back in his confident way and appraises her carefully. "I think you would find it impossible to shock me."

She takes another sip of wine. What could be the harm in telling him? *He might think you're a bit odd, but other than that…*

"I don't want you to get the wrong impression about me."

He raises his eyebrow. "Wrong impression or correct one?"

"You really think I…", she lowers her voice, "That I came."

"I know you did." He's confident. "I felt a rush of liquid against my lips, quite like I would imagine an ejaculation would feel like, although I have no firsthand knowledge."

"Why are you so curious?"

"Because it is rare and interesting, and I would like to make it happen again."

She gulps, takes another swallow of wine and closes her eyes for a moment and then opens them. "I had an ex, his name was Brett. He liked to do some alternative stuff."

"Such as?"

"Bondage", she can barely get the word out. Stuart smiles.

"So one time Brett finally talked me into letting him tie me up." *Phew.*

Stuart leans forward in his chair, now thoroughly interested. "Hmm, I'd like to know more."

She blanches, shocked at his lack of surprise.

He takes a sip of wine and looks directly into her eyes. "Actually, I want to know everything."

This is not what she expected.

He stands suddenly. "Come. Let's retire to the library."

She takes her wineglass and he grabs the bottle and his glass and they move to the hallway. Lily knows where they are headed, having been given a tour of the two main floors after their shower.

He ushers her ahead of him into the library. The walls are nearly the same red as his bedroom, and lined with shelves bursting with leather wrapped tomes.

She sits on the couch in front of the fire and tucks her feet under her, as Stuart closes the door behind them and sits next to her, turning so that his body faces hers.

"Tell me", he urges, his face a picture of calm interest.

Perhaps it's the result of their intimacy earlier, or the relaxing supper or both, but after a moment of hesitancy she begins.

"Well, Brett and I didn't date long, but I knew he was interested in BDSM beforehand – you know, bondage, domination, et cetera. He'd spoken to me several times about doing other things."

Stuart is paying rapt attention.

"So we agreed on some stuff and set a day and did it."

"Go on."

"I mean, I've done other positions besides just had missionary sex, but he really knew what he was doing. He tied me up well; he even had leather cuffs."

"And…?"

She can't look at Stuart, can't believe she's telling him this, but after all this time the need for it to come out is pressing. She doesn't want to seem like a whore or some sort of weirdo for being turned on by it, but Stuart seems surprisingly blasé so she continues.

"It was a rather long affair. A lot of teasing, and he blindfolded me so I couldn't see what was going on." Lily's really uncomfortable now. "I've never told another man I've been with about this."

"Interesting. Did you like it?"

"Like it?" Her face is flushed, and she brings her knees up and her fingers twist in her lap as she looks down at them.

"Like what he did to you; being tied up, submissive."

She's silent, and rests her head in her knees.

"In other words, yes, but it's embarrassing to admit."

"Perhaps", her answer is muffled.

"Look at me Liliana."

"I should never have said anything."

"Do you think it offends me? It doesn't; I'm not horrified by it, nor do I think the worse of you for it. And I did ask you, remember?"

"Yes, I remember." She chances a peek at him. His eyes are boring into her, and there's a raging erection in his pants.

"Oh", she says surprised.

"Quite."

"Have you ever done anything like that?" She ventures, but he just grins wickedly.

"Bastard."

"We'll see", he says and smiles a knowing smile. "But now it's bedtime - YOUR bedtime."

She looks confused.

"I need to stay up for some calls, finish some work."

"Ah." She says and stands, disappointed. *He's made it clear that until you commit totally there's going to be a barrier.*

"Good night Stuart." She turns to go but he stands up and pulls her into his arms and kisses her passionately, his erection pushing hard against her stomach as his lips consume hers and his tongue claims her mouth.

He releases her and she stands, dazed for a moment. *This must be what drugs are like,* she thinks as she walks to the door, opens it, and leaves.

Stuart watches her go, his desire for her even greater after she shared her story. She's so close to surrendering - just about ready to push her concerns aside and give herself over to him.

He shouldn't have joined her in the shower, but he needed her and her disappointment that he would wait in the other room was obvious.

He'd had several lovers since he'd divorced Megan; there was no short supply of beautiful women who threw themselves at him. He even dated Lina for several months.

But there wasn't anything compelling to keep him interested. They didn't have Lily's spunk, intelligence or vulnerability, and the fact that she was a materials engineer and not slutty, just sensual… it seemed like she had been custom ordered and personally assembled with him in mind. He didn't really want to waste time on shadows of a relationship, especially not after the crash - the night he cheated death because of Lily's intervention.

And then of course there were his interests; things he didn't always share. He craved Lily, wanted her for himself, and he was used to getting what he wanted - but he wouldn't share that private part of his life until she was his.

Chapter 14

Its 9:30 and Stuart is in front of the mirror in his bathroom, spitting into the sink. He's wearing navy blue brushed cotton pyjama bottoms that hang precipitously on his well formed hips; his dark hair is spiky and tousled.

Thomas knocks on the door and enters, prepared to take his breakfast order. Normally Stuart is up earlier than this, but he was on calls late and decided to sleep in.

"Is Lily awake yet, Thomas?" He rinses out his mouth.

"No sir."

"I'll wake her and phone down both our orders."

"Very good sir", Thomas murmurs and departs.

Stuart grabs the dark green silk robe hanging on the door hook and ties it as he wanders out of his rooms to Lily's nearby bedroom. He tries the door and it's unlocked, and he enters quietly.

Lily is lying in bed on her side, her blonde hair splayed against the pillow like a golden fan. In her arms is another pillow and she hangs onto it in sleep, as if it gives her a sense of comfort.

Stuart stands a minute, awed by how peaceful and vulnerable she looks. After committing her innocence to memory he walks to the side of the bed and kisses her softly on her exposed cheek, which elicits a sigh, but fails to wake her. He kisses her again, this time on her jaw, moving along its length, and caressing the back of her head. She lets out a soft moan and stirs, finally opening her eyes.

She sits up with a start, pulling the covers up with her as she does so. Stuart realises she's naked; her side is exposed, and he can see the soft curve that leads to her breast. His cock instantly starts to throb.

She runs a hand through her unruly hair. "Oh, God, Stuart. I'm sorry, did I sleep too long?" And suddenly it almost seems to him that he shouldn't have disturbed her; she looked so beautiful and helpless, like a maiden from a tale.

"It's 9:30", he sits on the edge of the bed and cups her bare shoulder in his hand, trailing down her arm. "I was going to have breakfast and hoped you would join me."

She nods sleepily. She's incredibly sexy in this state; lethargic and at ease, still trying to make her way out of the fog of drowsiness.

"What would you like for breakfast?" He's aroused and has to resist the urge to push her back onto the bed.

"What are you having?"

"Eggs, sausage, blood pudding, toast, oatmeal."

"Sounds lovely, but smaller portions for me. I'll need a moment…" She points to the door leading to the adjoining bathroom.

"Of course." He wants to linger but makes his way out and closes the door, and then heads down to the breakfast room.

After Stuart's gone, Lily makes her way to the washroom; it's difficult to wake up quickly, and Lily has always enjoyed lazing about in bed on holidays. It's an effort to put in her contacts, brush her teeth and dig around her suitcase for pyjamas.

Finally she's clad in a purple silk pair of drawstring pants, matching top and the woolen socks Stuart loaned her the previous evening.

She's still feeling the effect of sleep when she meanders into the breakfast room. Stuart is there reading a newspaper; the smell of eggs and sausage wafts into the room.

"Mmm", she sits down, bleary eyed, and yawns. "I liked the wake up call."

Stuart puts down the newspaper and looks at her and chuckles. "You're not a morning person, are you?"

"Not too much; can be if I need to be. Prefer nighttime; bed feels so good in the morning-cool and nice. You must be a morning person."

"I'm both, in a way", he says, picks up his cup and drinks. "Coffee or tea?"

"English Breakfast tea, please." He returns with a pot, teabag and a charger with cup, cream and sugar.

Lily dumps the teabag into the pot and pours cream into the cup. "This will help wake me up."

"Do you always sleep naked?", Stuart asks

"Yes. Your sheets are nice for it too. What's on the agenda for to-day?"

"Well, that depends. Do you have another nice dress like that purple one you wore to the banquet?"

"No. Just pencil skirts and professional shirts."

"Really? Doesn't have to be that fancy, just a little dressy."

"Nope."

The door opens and Mrs. MacDonald appears carrying a large tray, which she places on the sideboard. She serves them their plates, makes sure everything is in order, and then quietly departs.

"Why do you ask?" Lily pours some cream into her oatmeal.

"I'd like to take you out for supper to-night, and I'd like you to dress up."

"Oh. Well, I only brought that dress."

"We'll go down to Aberdeen to-day then and get you something."

Lily crosses her legs and tucks into her oatmeal. "Well, I suppose we could." She frowns. She hadn't budgeted for another expensive dress this year, and what are the chances she'd find something that would fit well?

"What's the matter? I'll take you down and Mrs. McCready will find you something terrific. I will take care of the bill."

She purses her lips. "Things don't always fit well with the… ahem." She points to her ample bosom. "You don't need to buy me anything."

"I'm sure she can find something. I know I don't have to, I want to."

"Where are we going for supper?"

He reaches his hand over and takes hers. "Someplace nice." His eyes twinkle mischievously. She rolls her eyes. "George will drive us, reservations are at 8."

She eats most of her breakfast, even part of the blood pudding, which impresses Stuart, and then they retire to their rooms to get dressed to go into town.

She finds a clean pair of jeans and a long sleeve t-shirt, guessing it's the easiest to get in and out of quickly. She meets Stuart downstairs in thirty minutes. He's dressed in another pair of faded 501's and a dark green v-neck sweater with a white t-shirt peeking out. He's an incredibly sexy man and he looks ready for anything.

"So are you going to wear your leather pants?", she asks as they clamber inside the Rover. It's a crisp day outside, definitely tinged with the approach of autumn.

He laughs. "Don't have a pair with me. I'll wear them for you sometime."

It's a forty-five minute drive to Aberdeen, and they pass the time comfortably, with Stuart pointing out various landmarks. It's nearly noon by the time they find a parking spot near Mrs.McCready's shop.

At the sound of the shop bell a middle aged lady turns to look; her face lights up when she sees Stuart.

"Mr. Watson, what a real pleasure!", she says and comes over, taking his hand.

"Mrs. McCready, this is Lily Batchelor. I'd like you to find something nice for her for this evening, as we'll be going to…", and he bends down and whispers in Mrs. McCready's ear.

"Heavens! Yes, something nice indeed, then. I have an idea of what you'd like."

"On my bill, shoes, purse, whatever she needs."

Lily is growing a little impatient and somewhat frustrated. *Dislike the fuss.*

Stuart turns to her. "Mrs. McCready will take wonderful care of you. I'll see you in about 3 hours. Mrs. McCready, I'll send something over to see the two of you are fed." He turns back to Lily and kisses her tenderly on the lips, the first time he's ever done that in public, and then he's gone.

"I hate shopping", Lily sighs.

"It won't be as bad as all that, dear. There's a few things I have in mind…"

Stuart exits, and makes his way down a few blocks and into a restaurant; the sign over it says 'Lumiere'.

The Maitre d' is about to wave him away and then recognition dawns and he bows.

"We received your request, Mr. Watson and accommodations have been made. Our most intimate table has been secured for you for this evening. The sommelier is reviewing your wine requests. Is there anything else?"

"No. Thank you, Pierre."

Stuart heads out and turns down the street towards his next destination. Normally these things are a bit tedious, but he's enjoying the prospect of surprising Lily to-night.

****

It's nearly two, and a deliveryman enters the shop with chicken salad sandwiches and crisps for them. Lily's lost count of how many dresses she's tried on. Mrs. McCready has made the experience interesting, perhaps a bit fun even. Lily's stomach is in knots as to where they are going and why Stuart has made such a fuss. *Must be a nice place.*

They finalise a dress shortly thereafter, although Lily has some reservations and feels it might be a bit too revealing, but Mrs. McCready is positive that it's perfect and takes the dress in back to make a tiny alteration. Lily was worried there wouldn't be anything that would fit properly, but this gown's bodice laces up the back, so problem solved. *How can people shop all day, I'm already tuckered out!*

Stuart arrives back at the shop at around 3:30, his hands empty, his smile wide. "How is everything?" Lily can just watch him all day, his charm is like a balm for the soul.

"Mrs. McCready's in back wrapping the dress." Lily answers trying to read something from his expression, but can't.

"Good, I don't want to see it. I've arranged for a stylist to come to Cairness in a few hours to assist you in getting ready."

She closes the distance and gazes into his eyes. "Stuart, you don't have to do these things. It's quite kind, but is it really necessary?"

"I've liked this little… project. I want you to be pampered and draped in luxury. Ah, here she is."

Mrs. McCready emerges from the back room holding a full length zipped garment bag. "It's a lovely dress."

"I'm sure it is; I can't wait to see it. Is she properly kitted out?"

"Yes, the whole bit; wrap, shoes and clutch", she says and hands a tan bag to Lily.

Stuart slides over a card, pays for the items and grabs the garment bag.

"Do take some snaps, dears, will you? I'd so love to see them!"

"Certainly, and thank you", Stuart answers. Lily thanks her and they're off.

"How are you doing?" he says.

"Pretty well, but trying on all those dresses is tiring. I've never spent so much time shopping in my life!"

Stuart laughs and unlocks the Rover. "I'd love to grab a pint here, but we should be getting back; you'll need to get ready soon."

"When is supper again?"

Stuart pulls out into traffic. "It's not until 8, but it's here in town, so quite a drive."

She looks at him warily. "Why all the fuss?"

"Because I like doing things for you, and I love you dressed up. You're positively stunning, and I can't wait to show you off."

"I think you have me confused with someone else."

"I wish you wouldn't say things like that", his brow furrows. "There's more to beauty than perfect symmetry and pencil thin legs. Actually, thin shapeless legs aren't beautiful at all; I prefer your curves to jutting hip bones. And I have a hope of enjoying one of my favourite past times – good food and wine – with you."

"Stuart, I really don't know what to say. You're almost too much."

His hand leaves the gearshift and he reaches over, takes her hand and brings it to his lips without his eyes ever leaving the road. "I want this to be a wonderful night for you."

The drive goes by quickly and soon they're back at Cairness. At the top of the stairs near their rooms, he turns to her.

"I have some things to tend to", Stuart says, "The stylist, Sylvia, will be at the manor between 6 and 6:15." He kisses her cheek, and walks off, leaving her to fend for herself for the next hour and a half or so.

She sets her alarm and decides to nap; it's going to be a late night and she's exhausted. *Too many late nights, too much whirlwind romance,* she thinks as she drifts off.

Too soon the alarm wakes her from her dreams. Groggy, she starts to undress before she realises that most of her toiletries are in Stuart's bath.

Lily approaches his suite and knocks and hearing nothing, she enters. She begins to cross his bedroom when she hears his voice, distant but angry. "Then I suggest you put more of an effort into it. I'm dismayed at your lack of progress. I expect something more from you next time." She hears something slam down and heavy footsteps in her direction.

The door to his study bursts open and he's standing there, eyes flashing. He sees her and regains his composure. "Can I help you, Lily?" He's all business.

"I'm sorry Stuart; I knocked and didn't hear a response. I came to retrieve my toiletries."

He studies her for a moment then relaxes. "Come then." He leads the way into his study and stops at his desk to close a folder and lock some papers. She walks by and into the bathroom, wondering what had him so upset.

She's packing her toiletries and feels his kiss on her neck. "I'm sorry if you heard my raised voice."

"It sounded as if you were disappointed in someone. Personally, you're not someone I would care to disappoint", she says.

He wraps his arms around her. "There's nothing disappointing about you, Liliana." He kisses her temple and inhales her scent. "How are you feeling?"

"Better. I took a nap. I'm such a slouch to-day", she laughs.

"That's fine. It will be another late night I'm afraid; I hope you're ready."

"I'm ready", she says, unsure if she is. She's apprehensive, but excited.

He nuzzles her neck before giving her a little prod towards the door. "You had better go before I get some ideas."

She spends extra time making sure she is well groomed - shaved and tidied up. She's barely showered and dried before there's a knock. She slips on a robe and answers the summons.

A short forty something woman stands at her door. "I'm Sylvia". Lily can see Mrs. MacDonald hovering in the background, and Lily opens the door wide.

"Come in", she says and steps aside. Sylvia has a bag slung over her shoulder and is carrying a case that looks like a tackle box.

Mrs. MacDonald steps forward and hands a small red shopping bag to Lily. "This is from Mr. Watson", she says, and leaves; her eyes are shining with excitement. *What is it with everyone? I feel like there's something I don't understand going on.*

Lily excuses herself for a moment as Sylvia sets up and goes into the bathroom, closing the door. She fishes around in the bag and her hands brush against some fabric and she pulls it out.

It's a pair of panties and matching strapless bra. They're royal purple and made of see through mesh. A delicate red ribbon lines the waist of the panties and ends in a small bow over the left hip. There are no tags, and they smell freshly laundered. *Attention to detail.*

She slips the panties on and can sense moisture building between her thighs. It's been a long time since anyone bought her lingerie, sexy or otherwise. She's flattered by Stuart's attentions and can feel the change in her. *Your mind following your body's lead,* smirks her inner voice. Lily almost doesn't care anymore.

She puts her robe back on and enters the room. Sylvia has placed a chair in front of the vanity table in the corner and an impressive assortment of hair and makeup implements are on display. Her dress is out of the garment bag and hanging on the hook near the door.

"I wanted to see the dress so I could get some ideas, although I do have a few instructions from Mr. Watson. It's a stunning dress." Lily can almost hear the wistfulness in her voice.

"Thank you", she says. "What were the instructions from Mr. Watson?"

"Well one major one, really. That he wanted your hair up."

Sylvia is good at what she does, not least of all because she is terrific at putting others at ease. Lily, not used to this type of attention, is obviously nervous but after ten minutes or so she feels relaxed in Sylvia's capable hands.

Lily has never really liked her hair; it's quite fine and very soft, so she's never had a traditional hairstyle per se. Sylvia manages to curl it and bunch it into a tousled and incredibly sexy tangle of locks that she then pulls back and fastens at the base of Lily's head, just above her neck. A few stray strands give the appearance of wildness, rather than a planned style. Sylvia tucks a few bound twigs of heather into the loose jumble at Lily's nape.

Sylvia is deft with the makeup brush and plays to Lily's green eyes and sensual mouth. *Wow, what a difference a professional makes,* she thinks as she gazes into the mirror. She thought she wasn't really beautiful, perhaps only slightly above average because of her mouth and unusual eye colour, but she's stunned by her reflection. She could have just walked out of the pages of a fashion magazine; the transformation seems miraculous.

Lily gets into her thigh high stockings and heels while Sylvia begins to pack her gear. "Can you help me with the dress when you get a moment?"

It's nearly 7 and her stomach is full of butterflies. Sylvia holds the dress as Lily steps into it. "I'm afraid we'll need a bit more help here", she says, and Mrs. MacDonald is summoned.

Between the two of them, they cinch Lily into the dress and lace it up. Mrs. MacDonald is almost crying she's so overjoyed.

"Are you alright?", Lily asks, stroking the woman's arm, trying to comfort her.

"Tis nice to see Mr. Watson so happy and relaxed; you having saved his life and all… and beautiful to boot!" Then the tears do come, and Mrs. MacDonald's earnestness makes Lily's eyes water. She hugs Mrs. M, who turns away slightly embarrassed and makes for the door.

Sylvia touches up powder and stands to appraise her work. "If you don't mind, I'd like to take some photographs for my portfolio", she says. "In this room", she looks at the dark wood and Georgian features, "the effect will be striking."

"I generally don't take that great photos", Lily says, "but perhaps they'll turn out alright for you." The dress and attentions have altered Lily subtly somehow; she feels more confident and self-assured.

Sylvia poses Lily and takes several shots. "These will be perfect", she says. "Thank you."

Lily puts a few essentials into her clutch and grabs her wrap. "I hope you have a really nice time to-night, Lily; it's been a real pleasure. If I ever need a model, I hope I can call you."

"Sure", Lily says, "Although I'm not here often. And thank you Sylvia; you've practically transformed me into a princess."

There's a knock on the door, it opens and there's Mrs. M. "Mr. Watson would like to know if Miss Sylvia is done. She can go down, if so. I'm to escort you in a few moments, Miss Batchelor."

Lily gives a quick hug to Sylvia as she heads out the door. She's so nervous she wonders how she'll be able to eat at the restaurant. *It's like graduation but worse.* She remembers how anxious she was then.

Mrs. MacDonald looks at her watch impatiently. "All set then?" She says and motions in front of her. Lily throws the wrap over the crook of her arms, snags her purse and makes her way to the stairs.

She thinks of the wedding tradition of the groom not seeing his bride before the ceremony. *Don't even THINK that word,* her voice warns.

She turns at the landing and can see Stuart's back; she can tell he's dressed in a tuxedo. *And I remember how wonderful he looks in that.*

He can hear the clip of Lily's heels on the wood of the staircase but waits to look, prolonging the expectation for as long as he can. Finally he hears the sound of her feet on the tile, and slowly turns.

She's a vision of loveliness, like a goddess descended from Olympus. She's wearing a strapless dress, the rich purple making her look like royalty, the drape at her waist accentuating her hips. The slit goes half way up her thigh, and the bodice is decorated with shimmering crystals.

He steps forward and she smiles, her shy disarming smile that takes his breath away. The moment is magical; they both feel it and bask in it silently for a moment.

"You look simply unbelievable." He says and reaches a hand to caress her cheek, adoration in his eyes. She feels warm affection swell up in her; what an amazing man and wow, she's starting to believe – to LET herself believe – that this is all real.

She can see George just standing off to the side out of view. Stuart turns to him and beckons.

"I think we just need a little something more to make it perfect", Stuart says and kisses her cheek.

George opens a large velvet box and Lily's eyes grow wide. Lying on the soft cushions inside is a delicate diamond choker about an inch and a half high.

Stuart picks it up. "I let it from a jeweler in town, hoping it would do you justice." He steps behind her and clips it around her throat, her hand automatically moving to feel the stones beneath her fingers. The pattern on the choker is one row of small solitaire diamonds with rows of larger solitaires above and below, and the bottom row dangling teardrops.

He steps in front of her. "You could be a queen, Liliana. Helen, perhaps, with men to fight over your beauty." He kisses her hand and she's so overcome with emotion it's difficult to keep her tears in check. He's made her feel so special; unique and irreplaceable.

"You'll need to remove those", he says, pointing to her earrings, and George opens another box, this one flat, that contains a pair of teardrop earrings and a thick rope bracelet, the silvery strands of interleaved white gold studded with tiny diamonds.

"Stuart… you're really the only adornment I need." She says quietly, so it is private between them. He smiles brightly at that, and pulls her to him, his mouth near her ear.

"You take my breath away, Liliana." His hand brushes her back as he steps away. He looks at her suspiciously for a moment. "Turn around."

She rotates slowly, and she can hear the low gasp as the lacing comes into view.

"How sexy…", he says, and she can feel his fingers as they run down the back of her bodice.

She turns so she faces him, removes her earrings and hands them to George. She puts in the proffered diamonds, and Stuart fastens the clasp of her bracelet. She can hear the quieted sob of Mrs. MacDonald.

"Is she not beautiful?" Stuart says and steps back. Lily blushes. He rests an arm around her waist and turns, as Mrs. M takes several pictures.

"We'll be late if we tarry further", he says, and George holds a long dark coat that Stuart shrugs into. He offers Lily his arm, and they follow George outside.

The Rover has been replaced with a Bentley, and for a moment she does feel like royalty as she's helped into the rear of the car.

It's barely dusk - the pale blue of day is giving way to the dark blue of evening. A low ribbon of crimson lines the horizon; distant hillocks make silhouettes of purple against the sky's changing palette.

There's little talk; Stuart holds her hand, periodically bringing it to his mouth and kissing her fingers. She feels like a young lover in a Jane Austen novel, her amazement at the circumstances causing her to break out into a light laugh. Stuart looks absolutely stunning, his eyes bright and fierce with passion, and the attraction between them flows through their clutched hands like the give and take of the tides.

It's nearly dark by the time they approach Aberdeen, the lights of the city a contrast to the dark countryside they have just been driving through. It's Friday evening and the city is bustling with life; throngs of people cross the streets and cars jostle for all too limited space at the kerb.

George pulls up in front of a low dark paneled building. Inside Lily can see the warmth of candle light through half closed red curtains.

Lily waits for Stuart to walk to her side and he opens the door and offers a hand to help her out. She steps onto the sidewalk beside him and he kisses her hand before tucking it into his arm.

An usher opens the door and they enter the foyer of the restaurant. Quiet strains of classical music are just audible, and Lily spies a string quartet to the left. The interior reminds her of pictures she has seen of old French farmhouses, but with far finer furnishings. Most ladies are dressed in evening gowns and the men almost uniformly are wearing tuxedos.

"There's not a more handsome man than you here", Lily whispers to him and squeezes his arm.

He leans and kisses her forehead. "Thank you, my dear, but I think you are the star tonight."

They make a beautiful couple, and quite a few heads turn and murmur as they stand in front of Pierre, the Maitre 'd. Lily is fairly glowing with contentment - she practically exudes it from her pores - and Stuart's pride in his lovely companion is evident.

"Mr. Watson, Miss Batchelor, welcome." Pierre bows. "I will personally escort you to your table." Lily obediently follows Pierre to a table near the middle of the restaurant. It still has a view of the string quartet, but it is nestled in the crook of a wall. Stuart nods in approval as Pierre holds out Lily's seat and then Stuart's. He hands them menus.

"Sofie will help you this evening. Enjoy your supper", he says, bows and departs. The seats are more like armchairs, large and inviting, with brocaded fabric. The table is laid with a crisp floral cloth and ecru napkins; above their table hangs a small wrought metal chandelier with tea lights.

"This place is lovely, Stuart", Lily says. He's sitting immediately to her left, and he places a hand over hers. It's warm and strong and the emotion communicated through that touch makes her legs weak.

"There are several nice golf clubs nearby. The restaurant opened a few years back to cater to the upscale clientele." He explains.

Just then a server brings by San Pellegrino and demi-baguettes. She smiles charmingly at Stuart, nods at Lily and leaves.

For the first time since she met him, she feels a strong pang of jealousy. *He is gorgeous.* This new sensation must mean that Lily is beginning to feel as if they are an item, as if she is entitled to him.

Lily takes a baguette and tears it in half; it's still slightly warm, and the yeasty, wholesome smell of it makes her realise how hungry she is.

She runs her knife in the shape of a cross on her bread and splits it open and begins to butter it. Stuart watches intently. "Why do you do that?"

"Do what?"

"Cross your bread."

"My dad used to do it."

"Tell me about your dad", says Stuart softly.

They're interrupted by the sommelier, who places a wine bucket on a stand next to Stuart, removes the bottle and pours. "Drouhin, Le Montrachet. If you are in need of assistance Mr. Watson, I am Claude, and at your service." He bows and is gone.

Another server just behind him places a plate in front of each of them. "Amuse Bouche. Egg scrambled in shell with herbs and topped with crème fraiche and caviar. Seared scallop with autumn greens and carrot coulis. Enjoy." He quietly slips away.

Stuart lifts his glass. "To many more suppers with you." He says and they both sip.

"Oh good Lord", Lily sighs into her glass.

Stuart smiles. "Wonderful, isn't it? Now I'd love to hear about your father", he says and reaches for a fork.

"It's difficult to talk about even now", she says.

Stuart nods. He read about her father in the dossier he had compiled, but he wants to hear it from her.

She looks at Stuart and considers it a minute. "Usually this is scare off territory for potential suitors." She says. "I feel strongly about things; I can be… emotional." *Alternately clingy and distant too.*

"You're passionate and feel things deeply", Stuart says. "I enjoy that about you."

"Thank you." She takes another sip and plunges in. "My father was killed when I was 8 years old – in a car accident."

"I'm sorry Lily", he takes her hand and she somehow manages to stave off tears.

"My younger brother Nick was a little sickly from the time he was born – he was 5 then – and my father had taken a day off from work to go to the doctor with him and then spend the afternoon together.

"They were hit by some kid joyriding while his parents were on vacation. My dad died at the hospital, and my brother was hurt. Things were never the same."

He thinks about when Lily saved his life; how she had said it was instinct.

He grabs her hand and brings her palm to his lips and kisses it, the bristle of his Van Dyke tickling her skin. "My poor Liliana. I'm so sorry." It was difficult to read on the dossier, thinking about a heartbroken blonde haired girl, but it is far more painful to see her now, a beautiful, smart woman who never had a father to guide her in life - and a father who never got to see what an amazing person his daughter would become.

Their server Sofie appears and Lily is grateful; she doesn't know how much longer she would have been able to contain her emotions.

They place their orders and resume with the Amuse Bouche and wine. "What happened afterwards?" Lily's had a moment to compose herself.

"My mother didn't deal with it well. She and my father had been having problems… I don't understand everything that was going on at the time. But she sent Nick and me to live with my father's brother and his wife, and my mom moved to New Mexico. She wanted to get in touch with nature and paint."

The bitterness in her voice gives Stuart some idea as to why she is 'estranged' from her mother. The dossier had merely guessed at the reasons.

He pushes his empty plate away and tops off Lily's wine glass.

"Are you sure you want to hear this, Stuart? We're in a nice restaurant; this isn't a very cheery topic."

"I know it's difficult to share, but I want to understand you, Liliana. If you're willing to tell me, I'd like to hear. In fact, I want to know everything about you."

She looks at her surroundings; they are about as far removed from the pain of her childhood as you could get. The lush smells, Stuart's kind eyes, the comfortable environment has a soothing effect. Perhaps this is the only place she could really talk about these things to him.

She sighs. "My brother Nick died a year later. The accident weakened him more and he was frankly heartbroken that my mom had left. She saw him once before he died. My aunt and uncle – Tom and Mona - raised me; my mom met some screenwriter in Taos and remarried and they have a daughter, Juliette."

Sofie approaches with two low flat plates. "Tuna poached in olive oil, saffron broth, heirloom cherry tomatoes." She finishes pouring the wine into their glasses and removes the ice bucket.

"This just smells divine", says Lily as she closes her eyes and inhales the aromas.

Stuart watches her. "I like to see you enjoying yourself, in every sense of the word." He switches his fork to his left hand and places his right one on her thigh and squeezes.

His touch seems to ignite every erotic fibre in her body. "Mmm", she says her eyes still closed, enjoying the weight of his hand. "How do you do that?"

He gives her leg another squeeze and picks up his fish knife. "Do what?"

"Your touch just has this effect on me." Lily says and spears a piece of fish and tomato.

"I'm glad to hear that", Stuart says and tries the fish. "Delicious."

They chat and in the back of Stuart's mind a clearer idea of who Lily is forms. She feels abandoned by her mother after the early death of her father, she's someone with strong emotions and is clearly a loyal person to those deserving of it – the way she proudly says, 'my aunt and uncle' being one such example. Her comment about exes not reacting well to her emotional intensity also begins to clear away the rubble and indicate why she has been hesitant to fully engage with Stuart.

This relationship matters and having had so many failed ones, she's walking a tightrope between getting something she wants and getting too involved and eventually hurt.

Just as they finish their plates, Lily notices a figure walking towards them. "Stuart, is that Henri Arton?"

He looks up in time to see Arton at their table. "My friend", he says and sticks a hand out towards Stuart, who stands and shakes it.

"Henri, this is Lily."

"Yes… your beautiful saviour, your guardian angel." She stands to take his offered hand but he brings it to his lips and kisses it ardently. "Were I to have a guardian angel such as her, my friend… well, I would find trouble as often as I can."

"What brings you to Aberdeen, Henri?" There's a bit of tension there; it's barely noticeable but Lily senses it.

"What brings most to Aberdeen? Golf of course!", he says, clearly hoping for an invitation to sit with them, as he eyes the empty seat next to Lily.

"I hope you enjoy it, and the weather co-operates."

"Are you and Lily not here to play golf?" He pronounces it 'Lee-lee' and his frequent gazes begin to make her a little self-conscious.

"No. Lily is on vacation and I offered to show her around."

"Yes, yes, I would too, you know?" He looks over at her again.

Sofie pops her head from behind Henri's broad shoulders. "May I clear your plates?"

Henri takes this opportunity to plant himself in the empty seat by Lily, and she and Stuart reluctantly sit themselves, realising it won't be so easy to get rid of Arton.

"I must congratulate you on your award, my friend. I would have said so that night but you, well, seemed to disappear. Poof!", he laughs. "I can understand why now."

Arton's constant references to her are beginning to grate on both Stuart and Lily, especially as Henri seems to speak about her almost as if she isn't present. She decides this is a good time to excuse herself. They both stand and Stuart steps aside to allow her egress.

Every eye in the restaurant watches Lily as she walks across the dining room, head held high, choker gleaming on her neck, tendrils of hair sensuously brushing the ribbons that zig zag across her back.

"I assume you have laid your claim, my friend. If not, I would enjoy entertaining the lady myself." Henri watches Lily lasciviously.

"We have an understanding", says Stuart, leaving things purposefully vague, reluctant to even share that tiny bit of his private life with Arton.

"Well, leave poor Henri in the dark then! If she becomes available…"

Chapter 15

Lily returns to the table after freshening up to find Henri standing.

"Thank you for stopping by, Henri", says Stuart perfunctorily.

Arton grabs Lily's hand, kisses it and then holds it. "It has been my incredible honour to make your acquaintance, Lily. Should Stuart here bore you, please, feel free to call and I will be happy to entertain you for the remainder of your vacation." He takes her hand again, lingering over it, wrapping his lips around her knuckles and slowly kissing it before slipping a card into her hands.

"Thank you for your kind offer, it was good of you to stop by."

He finally releases her hand, nods to Stuart and leaves.

Stuart helps her to her chair and then sits himself, glaring at the back of Arton as he disappears into the far corner of the dining room. She can sense Stuart's displeasure as she tucks the card into her clutch.

"Did I do anything wrong, Stuart?", Lily asks hesitantly.

"No", he turns to her and his frown is replaced by a smile. "Why would you think that? He was rather… forward about being interested in you, knowing full well that you're here with me. It was quite rude."

"I thought you were friends."

Sofie appears with their main courses and Stuart waits for her to recede. Lily notices that there is a new bottle of wine on the table and two full glasses.

"You are so incredibly beautiful tonight, Liliana. I'm having a hard time concentrating on my meal." He says and places his hand on her thigh.

Her laughter is rich and melodic. "You are charming beyond belief, Stuart, and so attentive. You've really made me feel beautiful tonight. Thank you."

She samples the duck, and it's wonderful. "Tell me about Henri."

"We're competitors. We're polite to one another, but we each know that the other is the biggest competition our companies have. We're not great friends, we're not bitter enemies, although I don't really trust him, but that's another matter."

The intimate mood restored between them, they enjoy their fill of the duck and the wine, which is an Oregon Pinot.

Plates cleared, Stuart moves closer and leans into Lily, his finger meandering along her back.

"I love this choker on you", he says, his eyes filled with wine and lust. "You have a beautiful, long neck."

"It's a gorgeous piece of jewelry. Thank you so much for renting it for me; this has all made me feel quite special. I really appreciate it."

"You deserve to feel special Liliana", he kisses her shoulder and electric current shoots through her body.

"Stuart, you're an amazing man."

"But…", he says.

"No, really."

"Tell me."

She pauses only briefly. "This… thing between us is so intense. It's almost overwhelming. I'm a bit lost." The wine and lovely food have loosened her tongue.

He kisses her shoulder again. She thinks of how good his lips feel on her body and finds it hard to focus.

"It's difficult to concentrate when you do that; your lips feel so nice", she admits out loud.

"Your skin feels so lovely." He places a hand on her leg, and she knows she's wet.

"Stuart, we went through this… really personal, intimate experience together, where we could have been well, killed. So then we develop a relationship based on meeting under those circumstances. Sex, birth, death, they're the most intimate experiences a person has." Stuart's hand traces the skin at the top of her stocking as she speaks. "It's a bit heady."

He leans over to whisper in her ear while his hand moves up her leg. "Liliana, I want you", he says it as a whisper, his accent lending force to his words. "I want to take you home and unlace you from this dress and make passionate love to your body." She closes her eyes and sighs. "I want to be inside of you, feel you underneath me, make you come until you're so spent you beg me to stop."

"Stuart…", she whispers, her voice needy.

His hand moves up her skirt, pushing it out of the way until he's nearly at her hip. "I want to possess you, beautiful, frightened Liliana - completely. I want you to give yourself over to me, surrender to me." Her breath catches in her throat, his words turning her on like no other words have before.

He pulls back from her and looks into her face to judge the force of his declaration. Her eyes are full of barely contained emotion; her lips are slightly parted, her breath fast and shallow.

Sofie deposits a platter of charcuterie, cheese, fruit and crackers on their table along with some port. "Sir, will you need anything else?"

"The cheque, when you have a moment", he says and she leaves.

Stuart removes his hand from her leg and helps himself to some farmhouse chevre. She's practically panting from desire, and manages to spread some brie on a cracker; her hand is shaking.

"Why do you enjoy tormenting me?", she asks.

"I'm not tormenting you." He watches her place the cheese into her perfect mouth and feels his cock twitch. "Doesn't it turn you on?"

"Yes. It turns me on, just being around you… that's the tormenting part."

His hand moves to her thigh again and he slips his finger across the crotch of her panties.

"Delicious", he says before removing his hand.

"How are you so composed?" Lily gasps. "I don't seem to have any effect on you."

He takes her hand and slides it under the table to the hard bulge in his pants. "You do have an effect on me." He says and releases her hand as Sofie approaches the table.

He reviews the bill and hands over a credit card.

"It's a long ride back, Liliana." He says patiently. She groans.

"You have an amazing amount of self control Stuart. If I hadn't felt that…"

"I like being in control; it's one of the reasons why I'm good at what I do."

Sofie is back with the receipt. "It's been a pleasure serving you", she says, with perhaps too much emphasis on the word serving. Stuart smiles one of his brilliant smiles at her and she reluctantly leaves the table; Lily frowns.

"Are you a jealous person, Liliana?" He looks amused.

"Sort of. Yes. I guess." She hates admitting it "Are you?"

"Yes." He pulls out his phone and asks George to bring the car around, then gets up and helps Liliana to her feet. Nearly two bottles of wine between them and a port with the cheese, and Lily's feeling her alcohol, even though it's been spread over several hours.

The restaurant crowd has thinned out considerably and they wait in the foyer for George, as it's begun to rain outside. Stuart stands behind and to the side of Lily, his arm protectively around her. It's cool and she shivers with only a wrap, and Stuart places his long coat over her shoulders and begins to nuzzle her neck.

"I like the sprig of heather in your hair", he says as he kisses her cheek. "I can't wait to get you home, Liliana and take you to my bed." His voice is sultry and she feels weak, so Stuart steadies her elbow.

"I thought you said… I'm not ready." She whispers.

"Are you ready? Do you want me to take you into my bed? To claim you?"

"Yes, Stuart", her answer is a throaty whisper, a plea.

He tightens his arm around her, and moves them towards the door. George is walking towards the entrance, holding an umbrella.

They clamber into the back seat; it's raining heavily outside, and the air is cool. The car is warm and inviting, and Lily rests back on the seat. Her heart is pounding at the thought of finally making love with Stuart, she yearns for him.

Lily looks over at him as he moves closer on the seat. He pushes his coat open and exposes her chest above the bodice, and then runs the back of his hand over her bare skin there. She leans back, her eyes watching him warily; worried about the control he has over her body. "Are you on the pill?", he asks and she nods. "I am safe, so you know", he adds.

He flips his hand over and his fingers move to the choker around her neck. He lightly traces the diamonds on it, and runs his finger along the top edge, causing Lily to arch her neck; she closes her eyes.

His fingers explore her throat, and she can feel his breath against her skin. His hand continues up, cupping the side of her face, his fingers stroking her jaw. Stuart's thumb moves to her lips and he places the tip inside her mouth as she feels a kiss on the top of her chest.

Lily moans and nips at his finger and then flicks her tongue at it, urging it farther into her mouth. He slips it in up to the knuckle and she twirls her tongue around it and sucks. His other hand slides under the jacket and around her waist, and she can feel his hard cock pressing against her through the fabric of her dress. His mouth is still kissing her just above her breasts, along the scalloped edge of the bodice, slowly working its way across her body. His hand is now at her back, his fingers slipping in between the laces to touch her skin.

His lips move to her collarbone, and he mouths it, following the shape to her shoulder. She's so overcome by desire that she's oblivious to George, to the rain thrumming on the roof of the car as it slides through the inky blackness of night.

Stuart moves his hand from the lacing and pulls the coat in back so her shoulders are exposed.

He moves his mouth to her chin; the sharpness of his goatee a contrast to the softness of his lips. He runs his parted mouth along the bottom of Lily's jaw slowly, drowning in her scent as he does so.

"You should always wear a collar like this", he says so low she barely hears him; her pulse is pounding in her ears.

He pulls his thumb from her mouth and runs it along her lips and she slips her tongue out, flicking it as he traces her swollen mouth. "God Liliana, you are so beautiful and so sexy when you're turned on like this. You're going to be mine from now on." His voice is a husky whisper, and she squirms at his words.

His left hand moves to just underneath her abdomen and works its way up slowly until it's cupping her covered breast. He pinches her through the fabric and she whimpers softly as his hand continues to massage her.

His mouth is hovering over hers; she can almost taste him. His hand moves to the side of her face, caressing it, stroking it, and she leans up to him but he doesn't kiss her yet, just continues to trace her cheek and touch her breast.

She's so wet she can hardly stand it; she's desperate for release. Finally he lowers his mouth to hers and kisses her bottom lip and top lip, then traces them with the tip of his tongue. Her mouth parts slightly, inviting him in, craving his touch and then he kisses her, his tongue slipping between her lips, claiming her mouth.

She unbuttons his jacket and slides her hands against his shirt to his back, pressing him against her. His mouth teases hers, pulling away, then kissing or nibbling on her lower lip.

He loves the taste of her; how he can tease her and her body is so responsive to what he does. He can smell her arousal and it encourages him, makes him wonder how far he can take this, how long he can sustain the seduction. His cock is throbbing madly with desire, but he can restrain himself if it means stringing her on longer, prolonging her pleasure.

"Nearly there, sir", comes George's voice. Stuart plants one more kiss on her lips before pulling away and straightening her coat.

Lily rouses herself and looks outside. The rain has turned the dark night into blackness. Just up ahead she sees the yellow lights of the estate, the only sign of civilization around.

George comes around with the umbrella and escorts them to the front door. "Good night, sir, ma'am", he says as they enter, and Stuart closes the door behind them. She can hear the Bentley's tyres against the gravel as it drives off.

Stuart turns to her and grabs her face in his hands and pulls her to him, the force of his passion nearly knocking her off her feet. He pushes her against the wall opposite the fireplace and buries his face in her neck and she tilts her head back as he slides his mouth underneath her jaw. Her hands tangle in his hair and his arm around her is so tight it almost squeezes the breath from Lily.

He pulls back from her and the look in his eyes is primal, all instinct. He grabs her hand and pulls her to the stairs and once again he grabs her in an embrace, one that picks her up off the floor. He backs her up the stairs, holding her, kissing her, running his hands over the curves of her body, until she can feel the top step behind her feet. She steps up onto the floor, still holding his head, their lips locked in a passionate kiss.

Stuart backs her up and she feels a door knob against her spine; he reaches around and opens it and they tumble inside and he locks it behind them.

He takes the coat from Lily and tosses it on the chair. There's a roaring fire in the fireplace; it's the only light in the room and it makes him look wild, like an animal.

He strips off his tuxedo coat and tie and reaches for Lily; her arms encircle his body, tracing the muscles in his back through his shirt.

He turns her around, and pushes her towards a tall chair, and she grabs the back of it for support.

"Keep your hands there", he growls, and he steps close behind her and runs his hands up and down her body. She loves his power and control, his strength. His fingers reach to the top of the laces and she feels the tug as he pulls on the bow. He runs his fingers against the ribbons and undoes the lacing from the first set of eyelets. He repeats it again and again, until she can feel the bodice is quite loose. Stuart slips his hands underneath and slides them to the front of her body and he cups her breasts, tugging and pinching them while his body is pressed against hers and his panting breath is in her ear.

He removes his left hand and gathers her skirt, sliding his hand up under the slit while his right hand still pulls on her breast. She's moaning and pushing against him as his left hand moves to the front of her panties, grabs her lips there and tugs. She bucks against him, and his mouth is on her neck, licking and biting at her shoulder and she cries out, her clit so engorged and needy it feels ready to burst. He teases her like that for a while, tugging and kneading but never letting her come. Then he moves his left hand from under her skirt to the laces at the back and undoes them quickly, unzips her skirt and lets her dress drop to the floor.

Stuart's hand is still tormenting her breast, her nipples erect and plump. His left hand starts massaging her arse cheek, and she leans back into him, a pleading moan on her lips.

"Stay like that", he commands hoarsely and removes his hands, and Lily is left feeling exposed, her body a quivering mess of desire, waiting for his touch.

She can hear the rustle of fabric, shoes dropping, the unzipping of his pants, and then he's pressed against her again, and she can feel his cock hard against the crack of her bottom. His hands move up her legs to her panties, and he slides his right hand in between her lips, grazing her clit. His left hand slides to her buttocks and pushes her panties down slightly and he slips past her rosebud to her cunt and pushes a finger up inside.

She nearly comes from the double stimulation, and bears down on his hand inside her.

"Oh no, sweetheart", he says and pulls his hands away, only to strip the panties off her. "By God I have to have you", and there's a throatiness in his voice she's never heard before.

"I'm yours, Stuart", she pants.

He turns her around and kisses her and backs her to the bed, her legs wobbly on her high heels. She moves to take them off and he shakes his head and pushes her onto the foot of the bed. He places his knee at the foot board, lifts her and adjusts her up farther on the mattress and then like a panther, slowly moves his way up her body.

"You should wear jewels to bed more often." He runs a hand down her body, across her abdomen and up the other side and to her neck. "You're the sexiest thing I've ever seen, dressed like this."

He opens her legs and moves in between them, his sculpted body pressed against her soft curves, taking her breath away.

"Please Stuart…", Lily begs; she can feel the wetness dripping between her legs.

"Always in a hurry", Stuart says playfully, before covering her mouth with his. His left hand slips to between her thighs and he inserts his finger in her again.

Her hands dig into his back and she begins to ride his finger, and he inserts another, his tongue fucking her mouth while his fingers take her below.

She begins to moan hard against his lips and he pulls his fingers out of her and slips off his boxers. She spreads her legs more, and she can feel the tip of his cock against her opening, and suddenly his mouth is on hers again, but this time it's more sensual, erotic tongue play. She feels his head enter and she lifts her hips to him, inviting him further in.

He pushes in more and she groans, his width stretching her, forcing her channel open. He thrusts again, and his mouth is there to cover her moan, his thick shaft making her feel blissfully full and sore at the same time. Stuart leans into Lily again and she cries out as he completely fills her, stretching her so it makes her whimper.

She opens her eyes to look into his face and Stuart's are heavy lidded, drunk on the sensation of being inside of her, and she runs her hands along his back, learning his rhythm as he thrusts inside of her, and matching it with the rocking of her hips. His tongue is twisting in her mouth as their bodies move as one, and she grabs onto his back as she spreads her legs wider, welcoming the feeling of his cock buried deep in her.

Stuart slips an arm around her back and moves his right hand to the slit between her legs. His finger moves lazily to her clit and tickles it and her body responds, desirous of release. He moves his finger and continues to thrust against her as she matches his movements, and then his finger is at her button again, and this time he lets her get a little closer before pulling it away. His mouth is clamped firmly on hers so she can hardly breathe and she wants to scream, to beg him to make her come, but she can't.

Lily can feel his thrusts become more forceful, as if he's trying to split her in two, and she's moaning from frustration. He moves his hand to her bud and flicks it and her orgasm explodes all around her. She's crying out into him, and he pushes hard against her as she's clenching down and then he releases, his seed pouring into her, his body spasming as her orgasm slowly abates.

Stuart begins to kiss her tenderly as she tries to regain her breath; he's ensconced in her, his seed trickling out. He rests his weight on his forearms and his hands stroke the side of her face and he kisses her so softly that it sends shivers down Lily's spine.

She feels like crying, the relief is so absolute, but she just contents herself with closing her eyes and feeling his lips on her face and him hard, still inside of her. She sighs as he begins to kiss her neck and she runs her fingers through his thick hair, now tinged with sweat. The scent of their arousal mingling is delicious; his exotic spiciness with her citrus sensuality.

"Mmm", she sighs as she feels his fingers at her lips and she kisses them lightly. He parts her mouth and slides a finger inside, and her tongue curls around it, running over its length. She's aware of stirrings in her belly again, a spreading warmth in her loins. *How is this possible?*

He slides another finger into her mouth and she groans as his mouth finds her left breast and he grazes his teeth over her sensitive nipple. She can feel herself tighten, his ministrations causing her to get wet again.

He can feel it too. "That's it", he coaxes in his irresistible voice, as she continues to lick his fingers.

He takes her nipple in his mouth and sucks as his other hand finds her right breast and he tugs and grabs it with his strong hands. Lily moves a hand to his ass and scrapes her nails across the sensitive flesh and she can feel him twitch inside her.

He moans, his mouth full of her breast; she licks his fingers, her tongue darting between them before her teeth nip at his pads.

Stuart starts to rock his hips slowly, pulling out slightly then pushing inside her again. She can feel him move and looks up into his eyes, alight with renewed desire. He slips his hand from her breast and down her leg to her knee and he hooks it under his arm. He lifts her leg and suddenly his thrusts are much deeper and she groans, his fingers still claiming her mouth.

He begins to move faster, his cock so deep inside of her it makes her catch her breath every time he pushes into her. She's in a lust fueled daze, the rhythm of their bodies meeting hypnotic.

He places her heel to rest on his shoulder and he penetrates farther, which seems impossible, and her back arches and she cries out, his fingers in her mouth now moving with the same rhythm as his body.

His left hand now free, he slides it down her leg, to the wetness between her thighs. *Oh my God, not another.* Lily shakes her head and tries to mouth the word no, but he whispers in a voice dripping with sex, "Yes."

Stuart's fingers are expertly exploring her mouth, sliding in, twisting as they pull out, pushing back in between her partly closed lips. She is so turned on by him taking her this way, pretending it's his cock in her mouth all the while it's inside her channel, pumping hard into her.

She cries out as his fingers find her clit, horribly sensitive, swollen and exposed. He gently strokes it, so slowly she can barely feel it, then harder as his thrusts become more insistent. Suddenly it's building faster and faster and she moans loudly, his fingers still forcing themselves into her mouth. Lily comes and this time she does cry, the orgasm exploding around her, her body no longer her own but shaking with pleasure, her nails digging into his back. He groans loudly and with one final thrust he's coming inside her again and she can feel his warmth fill her up. His moan is primal, that of an animal finally sated, and he takes his fingers from her mouth as her leg slides off his shoulder to rest beside him. He collapses on top of her; she is utterly spent.

Chapter 16

Stuart pulls out and rolls to lie beside her. She feels empty now, missing him; their bodies together felt so perfect, made for one another. He leans up on an elbow and looks at her.

"Are you okay, Liliana?" He rests his left hand on her belly and the touch makes her quiver.

"Yes", she says, barely finding her voice. "Just so intense." She should stand, go to the bathroom, clean herself up, but she feels so weak, "Like all my strength has been sapped."

He kisses her on the mouth, longingly. "Mmm. That was perfect; YOU are perfect. I loved being inside you. You were so tight, so hot."

She blushes at his directness while trying to manage the deep feelings for him this intimacy has uncovered.

"I should get cleaned up", she says, and slowly rises, her legs wobbly. She looks at the comforter and the pool of moisture on it. "Sorry about that…"

"Well worth it." He says. "I'll take care of it."

She makes her way to the bathroom and stares at herself for a moment in the full length mirror. *I feel different.* Lily feels more alive, more feminine, her sensuality kicked into overdrive.

She's quite a sight, naked except for her stockings, heels and the jewelry Stuart loaned for her. *Very sexy, if a little tarty.*

She grabs a washcloth, wets it and cleans herself up. Her makeup is smudged and she tidies it up as best as she can and opens the door to the bedroom.

Stuart's lying in bed propped up, watching her. The comforter is folded on the floor, a fresh quilt is on the bed and he's obviously tended the fire. His left knee is raised and a crimson sheet is pulled up just enough to cover his crotch. His arm is balanced on his upright knee, and in his hand is what looks like a glass of scotch.

He takes a sharp intake of breath that hisses through his teeth. "God, Liliana, I could take you again, right now", he says. Her sex stirs at the words.

She stands there a moment, unsure of what to do, the firelight bathing her in an ethereal glow, its heat nice against her bare skin.

She walks to the empty side of the bed and sits down, planning to take her heels off. "You look so incredibly sexy like this", he says and she feels him move on the bed behind her, and his hand runs up and down her arm slowly.

"My God, Stuart, you are insatiable." She says, but instinctively leans her head back against his shoulder. His mouth is on her neck, his right hand comes around to cup her breast.

"How do you feel?", he asks, his voice hungry.

"A little sore…" she says, his fingers trailing circles around her areola. "But you felt so good."

He slides his open mouth along her shoulder and moves his hand from her arm and pulls her body to sit between his legs; she feels him hard against her, and gasps.

"Yes", he says. "It doesn't seem like I can get enough of you."

His left hand slips down between her legs and feels the growing moisture there. "And it seems as if you can't get enough of me either."

Stuart moves his right hand from her breast to her neck and arches it back and moves her head to the side, baring the left side of her throat.

His touch is so erotic, the thrill of arousal mesmerizing, it overwhelms all other feelings. She runs her hands along his thighs - the corded muscles there feel so powerful. His body is so strong, his will so overpowering, that her desire for restful sleep is pushed aside, and her one thought is pleasing him while being pleasured by him.

She gasps as he begins to lick and suck her neck, his right hand still under her chin holding her head aside, his left hand between her legs, tugging on her lips, slipping in and out of her wetness.

"You make my mouth water", he growls into her ear and pushes his teeth into the skin at her shoulder, making her cry out. He's a little rough, demanding. *How does he know this is what turns me on more than anything?* "I want to taste you", he says and pulls her back on the bed, moving her so Lily's head is on a pillow.

"Grab the headboard", he commands, and she does so, her fingers wrapping around the posts, the thought of disobeying never entering her mind. Lily looks at him nervously.

He slides down to her legs, arousal wafting from between her thighs. "Don't let go", he orders her, and kisses her mound, and she begins to squirm.

"Spread your legs", and again she obeys, his commands turning her on, making her juices flow.

Stuart lies down between her knees and places each of his hands at the back of one of her thighs and pushes them up, so her legs are lifted off the bed along with her bottom.

"Oh!" She feels totally exposed, her entrance and nether hole open. He moves his mouth towards the cleft between her thighs and she's shaking in anticipation; she can't take her eyes off of him. Lily feels his hot breath against her sensitive lips and then he starts kissing her engorged mound, the very tip of his tongue occasionally sliding in between her lips, causing her hips to buck.

Then he slips his tongue in and she yells loudly, the soft heat of that muscle exploring her crevices, licking around her increasingly large clit. Lily hangs onto the headboard with all her might, her body straining against his arms that hold her open and exposed.

He moves his tongue down to her entrance and tenses, plunging the wet muscle into her hole, fucking her with his tongue, his goatee scratching the sensitive and overused skin and making her writhe in ecstasy.

Stuart slides his tongue out of her and slips it deeply between her lips and laps her clit mercilessly until she comes screaming, her voice hoarse and her body jerking as he licks her juices.

He pushes her legs back farther, so her knees are almost to her chest and watches as he slides himself into her, the penetration deeper than ever and she cries out, sensitive after another orgasm, the pressure of his cock against her g-spot threatening her all over again.

He pumps into her, the lingering taste of her in his mouth pushing him so close to the brink that he needs little time to build before he climaxes, thrusting hard into her, loud moans escaping his lips, the warmth of his ejaculation filling her once again.

Stuart lets her legs down gradually and they tingle from being upright for so long. "You can let go", he reminds her and she releases the rungs, her hands cramped from gripping so hard.

He pulls out of her slowly and moves to the end of the bed and stands. "I need to rinse off. Care to join me?"

She nods and he pads off into the bathroom. "Just give me a minute", he adds and she relaxes her limbs, aware of just how sore her body is. *As enjoyable as that was, another round will probably kill me.*

Lily can't believe what's just happened; mind blowing sex with someone who has to be one of the Pacific Northwest's most eligible bachelors, and who also happens to be a brilliant leader in her chosen field. *I'm never this lucky,* she thinks as she slips her shoes and stockings off.

The door opens and Lily hops out of bed and makes her way to the bathroom. Stuart has the shower running, the stall is filling with steam, and she can't help but smile wryly, remembering what happened there last night.

"Can you help me with this?" She says, lifting her hand to the jeweled choker.

"It looks lovely around your neck, but I don't suppose you can sleep in it", he sighs theatrically and breaks into a smile.

He unclasps it as she removes the earrings and bracelet and hands them to him.

"Thank you Stuart, these were so fun to wear", she says and stands on tip toe to kiss his cheek.

Lily takes the sprigs of heather out carefully and lets her hair down and it tumbles in waves around her shoulders.

Stuart watches, entranced. "Perhaps we should go to supper again to-morrow…", he says and enters the stall.

The shower is relatively uneventful. Except for a few caresses and kisses, it's rather chaste.

"You'll sleep here with me tonight", says Stuart, a matter of fact declaration.

"If you'd like", she says, drying off.

"I would".

"I just need to run and grab some things from my suitcase", she says, and grabs his bathrobe before heading to her room, grabbing her contact lens gear and moisturizer and returning.

Stuart's in bed, lying back on his pillows, waiting for her. The room looks so cozy and intimate with the fire crackling and the red walls and dark wood.

She hops into bed. "It's been a while since I've slept with someone… I hope I don't keep you awake or kick you or something." She slides under the sheet, which is incredibly soft. *Insane thread count I bet.*

"I'm sure you'll be fine", he laughs. "Good night, Liliana". He sounds contented.

"Good night Stuart", Lily says and closes her eyes, and with the fire dancing over her body, she falls into restful sleep.

Chapter 17

Lily wakes and the first thing she notices is that she's cold. Stuart's not in bed next to her and all that remains of the fire are ashes. *Did I dream last night?*

But no - it wasn't a dream. Her arms are sore as are her hips, *to say nothing of other places.*

What did it mean? *Does it have to mean anything?* Of course it does. She's gone from single to dating, *we are dating, right?,* in just a few days. Leave Woodinville, Washington, single - come back dating or, could it be, in love?

Let's not get hasty. Your falling in love has always ended disastrously before.

It's true; she tends to fall quickly and hard, which is why she tried to keep Stuart at a bit of a distance at first. *Well, that's worked out well, hasn't it? He's pursued you devotedly.*

She hears a muffled voice. "Stuart?" Lily says tentatively. She spies the bathrobe she used last night and throws it on and walks towards the door to his study.

She pushes the partly open door aside and enters.

He's sitting at his desk, staring into a screen, and he's got a headset on. She pauses a second and then feels uncomfortable about being there, and turns to go. The scene seems odd, his actions furtive. She hears his voice behind her say 'Talk with you later', and she closes the door just as he calls her name.

She peeks her head back in the door. "Yes?"

Stuart looks angry. "How long have you been there?" His voice is sharp, unpleasant.

"I just got here. I heard a muffled voice." *What's going on?*

He gets up and stalks to the door, his eyes hard. "What did you hear?", he demands. The look on his face is almost frightening.

"Nothing.", she says, as he grabs her arm, his fingers like a vise, painful. This isn't like Stuart; or is it, and he's just been hiding it, charming her. *But why? I'm nobody.*

His eyes soften their edge just a little. "Nothing?"

"No", she says, now angry herself. "I heard a muffled voice, called your name and got no answer, so I didn't know what to think and came to see what was going on." She looks at where he's grabbing her arm. "Do you mind?" she says and shrugs out of his grasp; she feels foolish. Just moments ago she had been nearly misty eyed over finding him; then he turns rough and angry over nothing. She didn't recognise the ardent lover in the person she saw just moments ago.

"Sorry Lily", he regains his composure. "There are just some sensitive items…"

"No need to apologise; this is your house, I'm sorry I barged in." She turns to go, but he takes her arm again.

"Please Lily, don't be mad. I'm sorry I was cross."

"Let go of my arm, Stuart."

"Don't storm out like this." He leans down to kiss her and she pulls away; his eyes flash.

"I'm going to go dress and all that. I'll see you in a bit."

He lets go of her arm and she walks off. Her contacts are in his bathroom, but she'll just put in the spare set she always has and retrieve that pair later.

Lily grabs her dress from his room and makes her way to the bedroom that she slept in the first night there. She locks the door and hangs up the gown; it wasn't a big deal, was it, that he was so sensitive about that call on his computer, right? But no, it was a big deal; he had been so mysterious at the start of things, and she thought once he'd revealed his identity the biggest mystery was solved. *More fool I.*

It was his house; he had a right to expect privacy, but he knew she was sleeping just a room away and he didn't need to snap at her like that. Plus, her arm still ached where he grabbed it. *Perhaps what I have been seeing up until now is the act, and that's the real Stuart; annoyed, on edge, suspicious.*

As she is brushing her teeth and picking out her clothes, she decides on a plan of action. As quickly as she can, she dresses, and after listening at the door and hearing nothing, she tiptoes downstairs.

She finds Thomas easily enough. He's watering one of the plants in the entry. "Miss?", he says as he sees her approach.

"Thomas. I believe Stuart – er, Mr. Watson – mentioned I might be needing a car… for errands."

"Well, in a manner, yes. He said that you were to be given every accommodation, any assistance that you might need. Told George and I that, he did."

"Well, I'd like to borrow a car, while Mr. Watson is taking care of business this morning. Where would I get the keys?"

"Will you be needing to go over some difficult ground perhaps? Do you know how to drive a manual shifter?"

"Yes to both."

"I'll fetch you the keys to the Rover you arrived in from Edinburgh. One moment."

She hopes this won't get Thomas into trouble, but Stuart DID tell them she should be accommodated, and that's just what she is asking for.

Thomas is back. "Here you go, miss. The cars are parked on the west side, in the carriage house. Have a lovely trip. Where are you heading to?"

"Just a few places." She tosses over her shoulder as she makes her way to the front door.

She begins walking towards the carriage house and does a mental inventoy. Purse, including licence and credit cards – check. Raincoat, camera and cellphone? Yep. Map she bought in Edinburgh? She pats her pocket.

The doors to the garage are open and she gets in the Rover. Phew. *No George.* All she needs to do is get off the estate proper and onto a road and she can pull over and plan her day.

It's odd driving a stick from the wrong hand side of the car but she manages it, and makes her way down the road to the gate; it seems to take forever to open. Finally she can pass through and turns left, remembering a car park a few miles down the road where she can pull out the map and consult her Blackberry.

She makes it to the car park and starts scanning the web for suggestions on nearby attractions. *Stupid to let someone else dictate MY vacation.* She's annoyed with herself for getting so caught up in romance. *I never take a holiday, I should be enjoying myself.*

She finds a good candidate- New Slains Castle - desolate, rocky and ruined. She's about to shift to drive when her phone rings. Unlisted number. She answers it.

"Where are you, Liliana?" Stuart's voice is cold with fury.

"I'm driving Stuart; you said I should get whatever I need as a guest."

"Yes, but…"

"I shouldn't talk and drive, I'll chat with you later." She hangs up, knowing it's perhaps a bit childish, but then his behaviour was out of line. He expects trust and honesty from her, 'surrender' even, and then gets angry over something she doesn't even understand; pretty rich of him to preach trust and lecture her about giving in and not fighting feelings, while still being so damn mysterious.

She puts her Bluetooth earphone in and connects it to the phone and pulls out of the car park. *No need for him to know I have this.* But just in case he calls later, or she hits trouble…

And then she realises the number was unlisted; she can't even call him back if she needed to. *Oh well.*

Her phone rings again; unlisted caller. She decides to not answer it and mutes the ringer. *I don't want to play this game, just enjoy my day.*

After a few wrong turns, she makes it to New Slains Castle, and it's just as dramatic as she thought it would be. The sky is overcast again to-day, and the red stones of the castle set on the fiery cliffs seem so vibrant against the stormy blue-grey sky - *sort of like Stuart's eyes.* She shakes off the image.

Lily takes pictures and roams the ruins, which are absent of any visitor but her. It's a beautiful place, and the winds whip off the water here violently and meander through the long abandoned doorways and halls - sometimes whistling eerily, sometimes moaning. It's an amazing sight, and she spends quite some time there, finding the solitude and beauty difficult to leave.

As she walks back to the car, she realises she's famished. She had her phone on quiet mode and there were five missed calls while she was wandering the ruins. *Could be calls from the states and it's not picking up the number*, she muses; doubtful they're all from Stuart.

She decides on the Glendronach distillery next and stops on the way for lunch. She finds a local pastry shop and gets a small beef pasty, then heads into the pub next door and grabs a beer. It isn't much, but takes the edge off.

She likes Glendronach immediately, especially the old grey stones of the building. She takes in the tour and parks herself in the bar and samples the whiskey. It's excellent, and she orders a plate of gravlax to snack on. At 4:30 the closing bell sounds, and she reluctantly leaves. *Another nice stop*, she muses.

Now that it's the end of the day, she is dreading going back to Cairness. *I should never have agreed to stay there.* Since Lily has slept with him, the attachment she feared is complete and the situation has changed. *If I just hadn't spent the night in his bed, this wouldn't have happened - but it's better to know now, right?* She's feeling quite low; something so promising has had a wrench thrown in it, and she's not quite sure what to believe. She loves being with Stuart - loves the sexual tension and the intelligent conversation, but him snapping at her so hard this morning stirs up the coals of apprehension that were cooling in her heart. The mind feeds what it fears.

She picks up her purchases – two bottles of scotch – and heads for the Rover. She packs them in back with her purse, shuts the door and is just about to climb in when she feels a tap on her shoulder.

"You look like you could use some company to-night." She turns around and it's one of the men from the Glendronach bar - she noticed that he kept looking at her; he reeks of whiskey.

"I'm fine, thank you."

"Yes you are", he says and licks his lips. "Mighty fine. Which is why you shouldn't be alone.

"Les go to the Jolly Roger down the cor'nr." He puts his hand on her arm. He's drunk, and a little taller than her. She's kicking herself for not taking a better looks around the car park. She's normally cautious and had made a quick sweep, but it obviously hadn't been thorough enough; he must have been waiting for her.

"I'm not interested, but thank you." She doesn't want to anger him and hopes she can just brush him off.

"No, but I think ya are. Saw you giving me the eye. Don't be shy." He pushes his face towards hers.

Lily shoves him away and gets a foot into the car before she is yanked out of it. She stumbles and falls, and feels a weight drop on her back. The open door is facing away from the distillery, in the shadows of a beautiful tree; she's now cursing the choice.

She gets out the beginning of a yell before a hand is clamped over her mouth. "None of that, now." She tries to push herself up, but his dead weight is too much. *You pulled Stuart out of a smashed car; don't be a wimp now.*

With a heave she pushes up off the ground and he tumbles off her. "HELP!" she yells at the top of her lungs, before her attacker punches her in the jaw; luckily it's a glancing blow. She hears voices and he tries to dart off but she grabs his coat and yells again. Now she hears running.

It's two distillery workers. *Thank God.* One of them holds the thug against the car while the other calls the police. In a few minutes they arrive at the scene, and Lily is questioned. They insist she go to hospital, as there's a bleeding cut on her hand from when she fell. *Great - just my bad luck, always such a klutz.*

It's 7:30 when she leaves the clinic and heads for Cairness. Lily is starving, tired and a little shaken. That could have ended differently, but it could have happened anywhere; she's been pestered by drunks in Pioneer Square and elsewhere often enough to know that.

It's after 8 when she pulls up to the gates. *Shit, I don't know the code.* Lily was hoping she could just sneak in, but no dice. She presses the call button and after a moment hears George's voice.

"George, its Lily."

There are several minutes of silence. She's about to consider turning around and finding a B&B when the gates slowly begin to open.

Her heart is pounding as she makes her way up the drive. In front of the house is Stuart, standing like a sentry. She pulls past him to the carriage house and parks the Rover in its bay, retrieves her purchases and turns. Stuart blocks the exit.

"Where the FUCK have you been?"

"Stuart, you said I could borrow a car…"

"Enough with that horse shit. You and I both know why you took that car without telling me." He starts to walk towards her.

"I wasn't aware I needed your permission to leave. Am I a prisoner?"

"For fuck's sake Lily, what the bloody hell happened to your hand?"

He closes the distance quickly, stands in front of her and grabs her bandaged left hand.

She knew there would be no way around it when they wrapped it, but they'd had to pluck some gravel from it, put in a few stitches and it hurt like hell. *Thank God the light's not better or he'd see the scrape on my chin.*

"I fell", which was mostly true, and she tries to snatch her hand from Stuart but his grip is like iron.

"I'd like to go and bathe and eat, if there's anything around. Let go of my hand."

"Don't EVER storm out like that."

"Am I a prisoner?"

"Don't give me any ideas", he sounds half serious. "You startled me this morning."

"Most people don't react like that when startled. Look Stuart, you're one to go about telling me I need to give in and surrender to feelings and be honest and all that when you're keeping secrets that I have no idea about. A dozen mistresses on two continents?" She thought about this speech during the day, but it's not quite coming out how she planned.

His eyes flash with anger. "Stop."

"You bit my fucking head off when I accidentally interrupted you on the computer. I decided to go out and try to enjoy my vacation, which I rarely take. Get off my case." She rips her hand from his grasp, which makes it start to throb all over again, and she makes her way to the house carefully, hiding her limp.

She can hear his voice coming after her. "Don't do this, Liliana."

Chapter 18

She's almost weak from hunger and pain, but she makes a beeline for her room and locks the door. She puts her bag from Glendronach on the chair and lights the arranged logs in her fireplace, sits down in front of the fire and starts to cry. How could this have gone downhill so quickly? Last night was pure euphoria.

It was only an argument – one argument. But his reaction this morning was alarming and come on… this could be a deal breaker, couldn't it? A blowup is not an auspicious sign, right?

She makes her way to the bathroom, wondering how she is going to wash off without her hand getting wet; she'll have to take a bath.

She digs around and finds the first aid kit she always takes on trips, and one of the plastic bags she always packs for laundry. She trims the bag then covers her hand with it and tapes it shut with first aid tape as the water is running in the tub. She wants to take one of the pills to dull the pain, but she's had nothing to eat. *Who fucking cares,* she thinks, and swallows one with a bit of chaser from a sherry bottle on the charger in her room. *Thank God for the Scots and their traditions.*

She feels like a fool getting in the tub with mitten hand, but there's nothing much she can do. There is a radio in her room and she sets it on the bathroom window sill, plugs it in and finds a symphony broadcast. *Beethoven's Pathetique, how appropriate.* The soft strains wafting through the bathroom help soothe her.

The mixture of pills, sherry, music and a warm bath are starting to have an effect. She feels decidedly relaxed, almost dopey, and the throbbing in her hand has abated somewhat. She washes her hair one handed, closes her eyes and reclines.

She starts - was she sleeping? That sounded like the bathroom door. Lily opens her eyes and Stuart is standing above her, a mixture of anger and concern on his face. She forgot how sexy he looks, even when he's mad – well, perhaps even more so then.

"Why did you lie to me?"

"About what?"

"You were attacked."

FUCK. It's her turn to be stunned. "How did you find out?"

He crouches by the tub. "You brought in a Glendronach bag. I thought about it and made a few phone calls."

Shit. Too fucking observant.

"A man tried to fucking rape you", he's furious. Stuart has cursed more in the past hour than he has in the past few days.

"He attacked me, that's all. He was drunk, I doubt…"

"And you lied."

"First off Stuart", she's feeling her pill and alcohol and it emboldens her, "spare me the bullshit lecture on honesty; I think I covered that hypocrisy a little in the carriage house.

"Secondly, I didn't lie to you. I did trip and fall. He pulled me out of the Rover and I tripped and fell when he did that, which is how I tore my hand; I just omitted the 'he pulled me' portion of the equation. It was glass and gravel; luckily I'm right handed."

He motions to her hand covered in plastic. "What is the damage?"

"A cut, four stitches." Lily glares at him. "Can I finish my bath in peace now, and how the hell did you get in anyway?"

"It's my home, I have keys to all the rooms, and I was concerned. But… this bathroom used to be shared with my bedroom – you forgot to lock that door." He points to the second entry right near the bathtub.

He looks at her closely. "Your eyes… are you on something?"

"I took a pain pill; my hand throbs like hell. Any more questions?"

"How are you going to get out of the tub?"

"One foot at a time, Stuart. Any intelligent questions? I should have been more specific."

"You're trying all my patience, Liliana", his voice is stern, but her insolence is also a turn on somehow.

"Welcome to my world. Now, I'd like to get out of the tub and try to relax before turning in for the night, so if you don't mind, you can leave now."

He stands up and in one quick move, jerks Lily up out of the tub and places her on the bathmat.

"Jesus Christ, Stuart!"

"I should spank you, Liliana, but I'm too fucking glad that you weren't hurt worse."

He grabs a towel and begins to dry her off. "You are mine now, and this is not fucking okay. You don't go running off."

"I can take care of myself", she snaps. One look at Stuart's face and she drops it.

He dries her off in silence, but is gentle about it. Normally she would have enjoyed the attention, but she's tired, hungry and a little shaken up. She's tall and generally pretty tough; she doesn't think the attacker would have had too much success, especially since he was drunk and unsteady, but that doesn't mean she couldn't have gotten hurt worse in the scuffle. A LOT worse, now that she thinks about it.

"Thanks", she looks at the floor and her tone is surly as she unwraps the tape at her wrist.

His hand touches the back her head and he kisses her forehead. "Christ, if anything had happened to you…"

She's not quite ready to deal with the Stuart anger thing, so she says nothing and makes her way to the bedroom door. She hopes Stuart doesn't notice that she's…

"Why are you limping?"

She sighs. "I broke my leg near my ankle a few years ago, see?" She points to a scar on her lower leg. I wrenched it today during the… at the distillery. It's gotten stiff now."

Stuart's beside her immediately and scoops her up in his arms. "Put your arms around my neck", he says, and she obeys reluctantly. *Don't let him fool you again,* her inner voice chides.

He feels so good under her - strong and constant. *I'm NOT a damsel in distress.*

He places her gently on the bed and looks at her. "This was more than just a minor incident."

"No, it was, really. It was quick; it's just bad luck I landed on some glass in the car park, and anyone can stumble and strain an old injury. I just want to rest and go to bed."

He reaches for the house phone. "Mrs. MacDonald? No, she's alright. I will, I'll tell her. Can you bring something up? Tomato soup and a BLT. Right." He hangs up.

"Oh."

Stuart realises that if Lily ever finds out about the dossier –which includes things like her love for tomato soup and BLTs at Mert's Diner near work – she'll be furious. No, that won't even begin to scratch the surface of her reaction. He knows the comfort food will help her unwind, however.

"Mrs. M is glad you're alright. I can get you some sweatpants…"

"No, I have my silk pyjamas." She tries to get up but Stuart is there pushing her back down on the bed.

"Liliana, please. Just put it aside for now and let me take care of you."

She glares at him but stays seated. He follows her eyes and sees the pyjamas folded on the hope chest at the foot of the bed, and takes them to her.

She slips on the shirt and then the drawstring pants, tying them. The sight of her beautiful hand wrapped in gauze makes him so angry he nearly sees red. It is fortunate for her attacker that he is being detained, or Stuart would have… had to have a talk with him.

But Lily's getting up and he moves to her. "I'm just going to the fire", she says and Stuart watches as she slowly makes her way there, impatient that she is refusing his help.

"I've never met anyone as stubborn as you, Liliana."

"You must not look in the mirror much." He smiles at the comment; *she's right of course.* He moves a footstool up for her foot and receives a curt "Thanks."

Stuart pulls up a chair close to Lily and sits down facing her.

"I… have some things that are developing at work. Sensitive things. You startled me this morning and I reacted… a bit unnecessarily."

"Oh, am I an industrial spy, come to seduce Stuart Watson and steal his secrets?", there's a sardonic edge to her tone.

If she only knew, thinks Stuart; it's one of the reasons that dossier was started on her.

"Don't jump to conclusions, Lily."

There's a knock on the door, and Stuart jumps to answer it. It's Mrs. MacDonald with a tray. The food smells divine, and Lily realises how one meat pasty and a little gravlax haven't gotten her far, considering she skipped breakfast and spent hours tromping around old ruins.

Mrs. M places a stand in front of Lily and on it a tray with a steaming bowl of creamy tomato soup and a crisp BLT.

"This looks so good, Mrs. MacDonald. Thank you."

She touches Lily's head affectionately. "We were worried about you, not coming home and all." She casts a look at Stuart, then turns and leaves.

Lily looks at Stuart. Worried? He didn't seem that worried, more like angry. She takes a spoonful of soup; it's just want she needs. The sandwich is perfect; a little excess of mayo and the bacon is crispy.

"What happened?" Stuart says quietly, watching her. She's obviously hungry. "Where did you go to-day?"

"I went to New Slains and then Glendronach."

"And…?"

She finishes chewing. "There's not much to tell", she says, and relates the details. She can see his fists clench and unclench several times during the narration.

"When you go out to-morrow – IF you go out to-morrow – someone will be with you at all times. Either myself or George."

She sighs. "That's absurd, Stuart. It won't be repeated."

"That's for damn sure. We're lovers - you're mine now, part of my life; I want you safe."

Lily bites her tongue. The whole day she's been wondering if getting involved with Stuart was a good idea. She still doesn't know a lot about him, and she has no idea what this difficult situation of his is, and the attack has certainly brought out a possessive streak.

She finishes her sandwich and soup and pushes the stand away. "That was nice. Please tell Mrs. M that was excellent." She's hoping Stuart gets the hint.

But he's watching her. "I'm serious Lily. No solitary excursions, no more sneaking off to get a car whilst I'm busy; in fact, I'll just tell Thomas and George you're not to get keys."

"I am not your ward, so I must be a prisoner, is that it?"

"Liliana, I just want you to be safe."

"There's no target on my back! This is just an unfortunate coincidence, and there was a happy ending. I'm on vacation for the love of God." His tone is making her agitated.

"I'll be back in a minute, Lily. I'll take this tray down and then we'll talk. Think about what I said."

He takes the stand and tray and leaves. *He thinks if he leaves me alone I'll consider it and agree with him!*

Lily hobbles over to the door and locks it. Even if he can open it with a key, maybe he won't and more importantly, maybe he'll get the message that she wants to be left alone.

She's tired, and all she can think about is sleep - glorious sleep, a reprieve from all this craziness.

Stuart is delayed downstairs, and it's twenty minutes later by the time he makes his way back upstairs. He goes to open Lily's door and it's locked.

"Lily?", he calls softly before unlocking the door.

She's in bed, in her pyjamas, sound asleep. Stuart watches her chest softly rise with each breath, her bandaged left hand outside the covers, and he notices a scratch on her cheek. Just last night she was draped in jewels and finery, laughing with him over supper, flirting; then they made passionate love and it was the most intense sex he had ever had which frankly, was saying quite a bit.

To-day had been a disaster, and she had been hurt. No, it won't happen again; she is his now, and that means her safety is his responsibility.

He pulls the covers back slowly and slides his arms underneath her. She stirs a little, but remains sleeping; she's probably more drowsy than normal thanks to the pills.

He lifts her off the mattress and carries her to his suite and gently places her in his bed. He strips down to his boxers, crawls in next to her, and falls asleep.

Chapter 19

Lily wakes up and is disoriented. *What? Where am I?*

She's lying on her stomach, her arm outstretched. It takes her a moment to realise that she's not in her room; she sits up.

"Good, you're awake. How do you feel?"

She turns around and cocks a bleary eye at Stuart. "What am I doing here?"

He's sitting up in bed, reading a book; she can't see the title. He has no shirt on, and the sheet is draped over his lap; tightly defined muscles and tousled bed hair flip a switch between her legs. *Not now.*

"I was concerned about you, so I brought you in here."

"The locked door not give you a subtle hint?"

"Lily, I'm… crazy about you. I was worried you'd have a bad night, and well, feeling a little guilty. I'd like to explain to you, but I can't."

"Arggh." She flops down on her back and stares at the canopy above her.

"I can see you're feeling better", Stuart chuckles. "Come on, brekkie."

"Why are you in such a good mood?" She says as she watches him get up. He's wearing drawstring pants that are almost too low; they show the line of hair that leads down to his crotch and are barely staying put on his hips. She grinds her teeth in frustration; last night, angry. To-day somewhat angry but quite horny.

"Because I woke up with you in my bed and I'm glad you're okay. I was hoping we'd go someplace together, wherever you want; I'll play chauffer."

"I was actually looking forward to my vacation, partly because I would be alone. I wanted to do some thinking, figure stuff out." He's being awfully presumptuous.

"What sort of 'stuff?", he stands in the doorway to the study.

"Just… things, Stuart. Where I want to go, what I want my life to look like, am I happy with the way things are. I'm working on my Masters, what after that?" A lot of things were unsaid; should she reconcile with her mother who has been calling, applying at Watson & Dickson is now out of the question, so she will have to look elsewhere meaning relocation, and then the thing she HADN'T expected, what to do about Stuart?

"I have a feeling you're omitting something", he says.

"Stuart, I'm going to get ready for the day. I'll see you downstairs in a little while."

Lily enters her room, closes the door, locks it and places a chair under the handle.

Forty minutes later, she's ready to join the world for the most part. Putting her bra on with her bandaged hand had been a pain – in every sense of the word - and her ankle was a little tender but other than that, she felt pretty good.

She is really having second thoughts about her intimacy with Stuart. She feels overwhelmed by how he has insinuated himself into things. *Type A to the Type A personality; and the woman he cares about was attacked, so he wants to fix things,* her inner voice chimes in with a rare note of empathy. *Aren't you still looking for a reason to end this because it complicates things further for you and scares you?*

She makes her way downstairs to the smell of Mrs. M browning griddle cakes. Lily threads her way to the breakfast room and Stuart is there, dressed smartly in his ubiquitous 501's and a navy sweater.

She plops down and manages a small smile at Stuart while Mrs. M putters around preparing a plate for Lily. She places the food in front of Lily and greets her with a kindly, 'good morning, dear', before leaving the room.

"Talk to me Liliana."

"What are we doing… you and me? I mean, what's going on?"

He puts his hand on her wrist, below the bandage. "Isn't it obvious?"

"Stuart, I told you, I'm not really good at this stuff."

"I've… fallen quite hard for you, I'm afraid. Isn't it straightforward then? I've seen it in your eyes; you have similar feelings for me."

"Hormones?"

His eyes darken. "Don't cheapen it."

"How do I know that's not what it is, Stuart? Do I really know you well enough to have… you know…"

"What?", he raises an eyebrow.

"Developed strong feelings for you."

"I think you know the answer to that."

She feels a pang in her gut. *You were drawn to him when you first saw him in the car, then at the hospital, and when he walked across the room at the conference.* Physical attraction, and yet something more. The most intense sex, this incredible pull he exerts…

"As for what we're doing, I also thought that was pretty obvious. We're lovers - dating, going out, whatever vernacular you choose."

She runs her fingers absently across her lips, thinking. The sex bit… that alarms her a little, how easily she loses control, how irresistible he is.

Stuart growls low; he's staring at her mouth and her fingers. "Don't do that unless you want to get me more wound up."

She yanks her hand away from her lips. "Sorry."

"What do you want to do to-day? More ruins, or I have a suggestion – Crathes Castle. It's a lovely structure with wonderful gardens."

She brightens at the idea. "I love botanical gardens." She's still concerned a bit that he's tagging along… it's difficult to think around him.

"Well then, since we're both done with breakfast, let's head out."

Crathes is a lovely place; the castle itself looks like something out of a fairy tale book, and the gardens are sumptuous and very relaxing. Her ankle flares up a few times so they find a place to sit near the impeccably tended grounds and just enjoy the sights and scents of the gardens.

On the way back home they stop at Macallan, which might be her favourite distillery. Stuart pays for them to go on a VIP tour, with a special sampling flight and snacks at the end.

By the end of the day he's worn her down somewhat and her wariness about him has lessened but not completely evapourated. Her mind has put aside the miasma of Stuart to a small degree and is churning on various issues related to dating him. She works for a competitor, (technically), even though they're not in the same league; he's got a bit of a control-freak streak that she worries about as well.

But by the time they get back to the Rover and pile in, she's relatively relaxed from the beautiful day and the samples of scotch that are now warming her belly.

On the way back they find a gastropub, The Thistle, and enjoy a great meal washed down with pints of Belhaven Ale. The place is packed and has a great vibe and Lily remembers what it's like to lose herself in a crowd, to be part of a large group participating in gestalt energy while at the same time being anonymous.

Stuart has been increasingly affectionate all day and Lily, who is normally a very affectionate person herself, is both grateful for it and wary of it. He talked of them being an item that morning over breakfast and she didn't dissuade him, so it's not really right for her to act otherwise. She has never really wanted just random flings, and here is a man who wants a relationship. It's so odd that her mind is the problem here.

He's a bit possessive, putting his arm around her when another man looks at her, but she thinks that's also probably because she was attacked. *Two nights ago Stuart did admit he is a jealous person… but then so am I.*

He's pulled his chair close to hers and put his arm around her shoulders, stroking the sleeve of her shirt. There's a band playing at the end of the pub and they're enjoying the music and energy. His hand periodically brushes against her bare skin and it gives her goose bumps. When he begins to touch her, resistance weakens. *Does he know this?*

As if sensing her thoughts, he leans over and kisses her hair, smelling her fragrance, luxuriating in the silkiness of her tresses. She notices her hand has moved of its own accord to his thigh.

He excuses himself and leaves the table to get a few more pints. He's been gone perhaps a minute when she hears a voice.

"Pardon me miss… Is this seat taken?" The Scottish accent is thick but rolls along. She looks up.

A smart looking thirty something man in a dark coat and plaid scarf stands there. He has a hand on the chair next to her that Stuart was so recently occupying.

"Actually it is", she says.

"Tis a shame. My name is Jack; and who might you be?"

She's not quite sure what to do; how does she shoo him away without being rude? Stuart will be back any second, and she's having a nice evening and worried he'll be jealous.

"My name is Lily. Sorry there's no place for you to sit in the pub…" She looks around and all the seats are taken.

"Might this seat be taken by one of your lady friends, or are you here with someone?"

"She's here with someone." Stuart's voice is hard and absolute.

"Well met." He puts out a hand to Stuart, who refuses to put the beers down and shake. "Well I'll leave you to it then", he says and tips his head at Lily. "Miss".

Stuart sits down and places a beer in front of her. "I'm gone for two minutes…"

"He was just looking for a place to sit. The pub is packed."

"I know I can't be the only man to appreciate how beautiful you are, but…" Stuart makes a fist and puts it on the table.

"Have women come up and spoken with you, regardless of whether or not you're with someone?" She's thinking of their waitress Sofie, who couldn't spare a glance for Lily as she only had eyes for Stuart.

"Perhaps."

"I'm not encouraging it, but if someone speaks to me I'm polite."

She is encouraging it, Stuart thinks, she just doesn't know it - it's her innate sensuality. Men want to flock around it like moths to a candle. Lily doesn't understand this is why she's had many interested men, even if the relationships eventually fizzle.

They finish their pints and decide to head out. It's nearly 9 o'clock and been a busy day. In some ways she'll be glad when her vacation is over and she is in more familiar surroundings and a bit more autonomous.

There's a light drizzle falling as they step back into the Rover for the ride back to Cairness. They're barely on the road when Stuart takes a call and she decides to check her Blackberry. For the most part, Lily has ignored much of her email, regardless of whether it was work related or personal. She pauses when she sees an email with the title, 'Thought you should know abt this…' from Jenna, a co-worker who Lily is friendly with.

> Lil-
>
> Hope you're having a great trip! I've always wanted to go to Scotland as you know.
>
> I thought I should tell you about something weird. I had someone approach me early Friday and ask me about you; I think it's happened to a few other people, too. He said he just wanted to know what kind of person you were. He said it was confidential, about some kind of grant or opportunity that you might be eligible for, and they were interviewing friends of the nominated parties so they could make an appropriate decision. Sounded fishy, so I told them you kill houseplatns. (har har). Told them that you were a great person and if anyone deserves something good it's you. They told me not to say anything as it's supposed to be discreet. Is something exciting going on that you're not sharing? Will never forgive you if that's true!

Take care and come back soon,

J

The words she threw at Stuart last night fall back into her mind. *'Am I an industrial spy, come to seduce Stuart Watson?'*

There's no way…

She looks over at Stuart; he's winding up his phone call.

"Everything okay?", he frowns when he sees the look on her face.

"Oh, I just got an interesting piece of email."

"How's that?"

She watches his profile closely. "Someone has been interviewing people at my job, asking about me." He doesn't flinch, which doesn't necessarily mean anything. He's a top notch executive used to dealing with pressure situations and tough negotiations.

"And?"

"So, I just wonder who would do that?"

"Perhaps it's some head hunters."

He seems too blasé about it. "Stuart, have you hired people to nose around in my life?"

He rolls down the window and punches the code for the gate.

"Stuart…" She's beginning to get a sick feeling in her stomach.

"Why would you think that?" He says and drives through the gate.

"That's not an answer."

He pulls the Rover into the bay.

"Don't you think it's a ridiculous question, especially since you've made your mind up?" He's usually so direct, this is NOT good. They both get out of the car and she walks over to confront him. Lily is surprised how steady her voice is.

"All right, Stuart. Tomorrow I am going to take my things and leave here. I would leave tonight but it is late and I've had too many pints."

He grabs her arm and she rears back her other hand but he grabs it before she can slap him. He pulls her close to him and tries to kiss her but she turns her head.

"Don't do this, Liliana." His voice is low, threatening.

"You're a fucking scoundrel, Stuart. You've sent people to my work to spy on me!" She struggles against his grip.

He pulls the knit scarf from around his neck. "You're irrational; you won't listen to reason, will you?" He takes both her hands and holds them tightly in his right one, wraps the scarf around her wrists snugly and ties a knot before she can wrench away.

"Let me go!", she yells and tries to pull away but he hoists her over his shoulder. She begins to kick and he grabs her ankles and presses them hard against his chest.

She's twisting and turning but can't free herself and he walks to the front door. He slides her feet to the ground and wraps an arm around her torso.

He enters the foyer and heads for the main corridor and the staircase, dragging Lily along.

"You're just looking for an excuse to leave, aren't you?", he asks as he pulls Lily up the stairs. He releases her arms for a moment, blocking escape with his body, undoes the door to his suite and pushes her inside, locking the door behind him.

"Lily, there are things you don't understand…"

"You're right. I don't understand spying on people you supposedly care about." She's yelling as loud as she can. Then she realises Stuart mentioned that morning how this was the staff night off. They won't be back until late, most likely.

He pushes her farther into the room. "Will you listen to reason?"

"More charming lies?" She can see the anger in his eyes at that comment.

"I'm not a liar." He grabs her around the waist and pulls her to him. His other hand is at the back of her neck and he holds her head still as he brings his lips to hers and begins to kiss her. She's struggling against him, and it makes him more aroused.

"You're terrified aren't you Lily? Terrified of what has happened between us, how badly you want me."

"Stop trying to change the topic." She says. "I'm not!"

"I can see it in your eyes Lily. You don't even want me to explain, because that's not your point. You found your cause and it's given you an out, and it's shabby."

"Talk about shabby!" She is hurling out all her fear and uncertainty from the last few weeks at Stuart. Fighting her desire, her concerns about what to do about her unhappy job situation, her hopes that he would turn out to be someone she could connect with… all the angst in her life comes flooding out.

"Are you interested in hearing what I have to say?"

"There's nothing that you can say…"

"Nothing I can say?" He grabs her and pushes her against the wall. "How about show you, hmm? Remind you."

He roughly slips her coat from her shoulders, tangles it at her wrists and holds it with his left hand. "Remember that night when we had supper, Lily? I could feel the tension between our bodies; I can still feel it now, and I know you can too."

It is true; even now her body is brimming with lust. "That's beside the point." She squirms.

"It's not." He brings his right hands to her face and holds her cheek. "Meeting you has changed everything."

She starts twisting her body, trying to get away. "You're just saying that."

"I'm not." He brings his lips to hers and it still sends electric shocks throughout Lily, despite her anger at him.

"This isn't a good idea", she pants after he pulls his mouth away.

"I think it's a fine idea", he says as he covers her mouth with his again. This time there's less resistance.

His kisses turn from tender to passionate, and she can't help but sigh. His tongue enters her mouth, teasing her. Her body strains from desire even as she wants to push him away.

"You've been so bad though, Liliana - you need to be taught a bit of a lesson."

Her hands still bound, he pulls her towards the bed, and motions for her to sit. She does, and tries to untangle her hands, while Stuart pulls his sweater and shirt over his head.

Her hands are free now, but Stuart is blocking the path to the door. She's confused, having blown through her angst, and now set adrift on a sea of conflicting emotions.

Stuart's shirt is off, his muscular chest giving way to a ripped abdomen and the tattered fringe at the top of his 501's. He walks to a small dresser set near the bed, takes something from a drawer and turns around without her seeing what it is.

"Why does this matter to you? Why don't you just find someone else?"

"Because I don't WANT anyone else, Liliana. You wanted someone in your life and here I am, and now that things have gotten quite… intense, you've tried to wriggle out."

"We've gotten off base here", she stands up, the anger flooding through her again as she points at his impeccable chest. "You hired people to spy on me."

He grabs her outstretched hand and quickly loops a rope around her wrist. She stares in shock at it and tries to pull away but isn't quick enough, and he grabs her other wrist and binds it to the first.

"And yet, Liliana, in all your supposed anger about it, you didn't show much interest in finding out what was going on; why I might have done it, if those were indeed people I hired and what the fallout might be. You didn't think that the president of one of the world's largest materials firms might care to be a little cautious when it comes to a new lover - when that woman is in the same field - especially considering a failed hostile takeover last year."

She looks at her hands and Stuart adds. "That should make things a little more interesting, yes?" He grabs her face in both his hands and brings her mouth to his and kisses her hard, almost violently, and her retort is knocked from her lips.

Her hands are resting on his bare chest, bound, the bitter ends of the rope dangling between them and she can feel his heart beating fast underneath her finger tips.

She finds herself kissing him, just a little at first, and then…

She pushes herself off his chest. "Not a good idea."

"Very good idea" he says and takes a step forward. He's exuding so much animalistic sensuality it's practically flooding the room.

The back of her knees hit the bed and she sits down abruptly. Stuart lifts her leg and pulls her shoe and sock off of first one foot than the other.

"Don't…", she manages to squeak out, albeit quietly.

"You don't want me inside you? Kissing you? Touching you?"

His hand delicately traces her face as he looks into her eyes. She opens her mouth but can't find the words. This is wrong, but the memory of them making love is so powerful. "You want me, Liliana, as much as I want you. I can smell the arousal on your skin, I can see the fire in your eyes, and the fear. You remember Friday night, don't you?"

Her tongue involuntarily wets her lips at the thought. "Yes, Liliana, you remember… how hard you came as I fucked your mouth and your cunt; how my cock felt inside of you." His recital is making her so hot for him, his words making the button between her legs pulse.

Stuart pushes her back on the bed and straddles her, pulling the rope and her hands above her head. His mouth descends on hers again, tugging on her lips, and he runs his mouth down her throat, licking and kissing her skin.

He moves his free hand to her waist and slides it underneath her shirt and pulls her bra cup so it sits underneath her breast. His lips are still caressing her neck, and the fingers at her breast start tracing her nipple in slow circles.

"Feel it, Liliana." She knows she's getting terribly aroused, knows he can sense it and she's powerless to do anything. Even if she protested he is stronger than she is, *and besides he's right.*

His mouth hovers over her lips and his hand begins to pinch and twist her nipple until she opens her mouth to cry out, and then he slips his lips over hers, sliding his tongue into her mouth and pressing his body hard against hers.

Lily is doomed and she knows it. His physical strength, the force of his will are no match for her. She has to resist, though, has to make an effort, even if everything he says is true.

He slides her shirt over her head and pushes it to her wrists, her chest exposed, her bra half askew. He starts anew, kissing the skin below her collarbone, running his tongue over the tops of her breasts. He kisses the nipple of her exposed breast before his tongue begins to lap at it, slightly rough, which makes her squirm.

Stuart reaches around and unclips her bra before pushing it up to join the shirt around her bound wrists. He pushes her breasts together and takes both nipples in his mouth, sucking hard, making her cry out in a mix of pleasure and pain.

He kicks off his shoes and pulls her up on the bed with him, towards the headboard. He takes the free ends of the rope and ties them to one of the rungs in his bedpost, so her hands are stretched above her head.

She starts squirming again, moving up towards the headboard, but he pulls her legs back down and unzips her pants before stripping them off.

Stuart puts his hands between her legs. "Christ, you're wet." He can feel the moisture through her thin, flesh coloured panties.

With an iron grip he takes her thighs and pries them apart and he kisses her mound, pushing his tongue at her slit, tasting the arousal on the fabric. She can't help herself; she bucks and moans when he touches her.

He yanks her panties off and then she's naked, panting, tied to Stuart's bed.

He stands up and off to the side of the bed, slowly stripping his pants off as he looks at her. "You're so fucking sexy tied up", he growls. He slips his 501's and boxers off and his erect cock springs to attention, its tip already wet with precum.

"At least you're quiet now", he says.

"You're just a fucking bastard." *What are you doing!? He'll do other… things, or is that what you want?*

"Liliana, you just sealed your fate." He flips her over so she is on her stomach. He lifts her pelvis and slides an extra pillow under her lower abdomen.

She can hear him walk to the dressers, but can't flip over on her back. Underneath her bound arms she sees him pull something from the dresser and as Stuart turns he conceals it behind his back.

She's never really looked and studied his cock, but now she has a good view. It's long and thick, arching up slightly at the base, the flare at the crown thick and pronounced. It's beautiful in its own way - the physical manifestation of Stuart's intense virility.

He climbs on the bed, and he's now out of Lily's line of sight; she becomes nervous.

"What are you going to do to me?", she whispers, ashamed at how wet she is.

"Well, Liliana, I'm going to teach you a lesson", his voice is authoritative, precise. "Then I'm going to fuck you harder than you've ever been fucked before. I'm going to pound my cock into you until you cry for mercy."

She gasps loudly, his words both frightening and arousing.

She can feel his hands at her buttocks; he's rubbing them, massaging the large muscles with deliberation. He pulls her cheeks apart and looks at her bud, making her squirm.

"I can tie your feet too, Liliana, if you become too rowdy", he warns. "In fact, maybe that's a good idea." She can feel rope being wrapped around her ankles and then tightened. She's never felt more helpless.

Without a warning, Stuart raises his hand and slaps her buttocks.

"Ow!", she cries out, more from surprise than pain. He rubs her cheeks again before letting go with another swat, this one a bit harder.

He alternates his rubs with increasingly hard swats, and Lily can feel the heat rising in her buttocks.

"This is what happens, Liliana when you misbehave." He swats her again then rubs her bottom. "You were rude, not permitting me explain." He hits her again, and Lily can hear something jangle.

"Stuart…"

"Shh, or I'll gag you. You need to take this." He rubs her ass almost tenderly and then she feels another impact, this time with what must be a belt.

"OH!" that one hurt a little, coming as it did on her already pink and spanked bottom, but in an oddly delicious way; it was thoroughly arousing.

"And we're not going to have any more of these little incidents." He swats her again with the belt, and it issues a melodious sound as it makes contact with her sore flesh. "No more lies about how you were injured." He swats her and she cries out involuntarily.

"No more attempts to run away from me", this swat has even more power behind it, and it licks at the delicate low curve of her bottom and Lily can feel the vibrations in her clit. This time it's a low moan that escapes her lips. She's feeling lightheaded, sort of as if she's had a bit of alcohol on an empty stomach. It's a wonderful, lazy feeling, and an unbelievable contrast to the hard physical contact of the belt.

"You will give in", he swats, "you will surrender", another slap of the belt, "to your desires." He rubs her cheeks, which by now are a lovely red colour - a few welts here and there beginning to form.

"Do you understand, Liliana?" When she doesn't answer he swats her with his hand.

She mumbles something, but he can't hear her and hits her again with the palm of his hand. He can feel her body respond under him - at the same time arching towards his hand while trying to twist away. She's perfect, Stuart thinks, just perfect.

"I can't hear you, Liliana." He spanks her again, this time with the belt, and her body shudders. "You have such a beautiful arse, and I'm enjoying myself. I can do this for a long, long time."

He swats her again, the sound of the thick leather on her soft flesh like music to him. "Do you understand?"

"All right!" The concession is wrenched from her as a yell.

Stuart slaps her bottom again with the belt, this time holding it looser so the end of it licks out and stings. Lily moans and squirms.

"That wasn't a very polite or respectful answer. One more time, before I start swatting in earnest. Do you understand, Liliana?" He's massaging her ass cheeks hard, causing them to feel incredibly sore.

"Yes. I understand Stuart."

He sighs. "That's too bad. I was really enjoying this." He continues to rub her bottom vigourously and he slips his other hand into the small gap between her tightly closed legs.

"Liliana", he's impressed. "By God, you're soaking wet. Mmm. One might think you liked it – that you liked it very much in fact." He pushes a finger into her and she clenches around it and sighs deeply.

"Did you like it, Liliana? Did it arouse you?" He's rubbing her bottom in circles with one hand, while his finger is sliding in and out of her delicious wet cleft. When she doesn't answer, he swats her bottom again.

"I thought there was going to be no more of this nonsense. Do I need to spank you again, hmm?" He leans over and nibbles on the bottom curve of her cheek and she yelps.

"You said surrender, not answers", comes her flippant reply.

"Oh, now I think I have an answer to both of my questions – yes, you enjoyed it, and yes, I need to spank you again."

He pulls his fingers out and she gasps, desperate to have him touch her that way again.

He takes her ankles and pushes them towards the head board, so she has no choice but to kneel, her ass in the air, her face buried in pillows. Her cunt is exposed in this position, her legs are still tied and she feels vulnerable.

She can feel Stuart move on the bed, and then the soft, hot muscle of his tongue stabs through the swollen folds of her cleft and she groans, grinding into him, all semblance of decency lost in her desire to climax. He slips two fingers in her this time and she moans and then it comes - the delicious smack of the belt on her reddened ass as his fingers probe her.

"I wish you could see how gorgeous you are right now", Stuart's voice is stretched tight from pent up desire. The belt hits her again, and it seems that Lily's senses are enhanced - that she can smell the leather warmed by its contact with her ass, hear the slap reverberating longer than she should. She is totally in the moment, in touch with her body and sensations in a way she never has been before and it's completely immersive.

"Please Stuart." He swats her and she moans. "I want your cock in me." She is utterly transported by the regular slapping of the belt like a metronome, the thrusting of Stuart's fingers into her, the stinging in her sore ass.

"What do you want?" The belt is singing as it hits her flesh.

"I want your cock inside of me. I want you to come in me. Please, Stuart."

The belt hits her again. "I'm enjoying myself now, but your little cunt is quite hot, quite juicy, quite ready to be claimed, I think."

"Oh yes, please", Lily's moaning and rhythmically thrusting against his fingers. "You've mastered me, now take me." She is utterly swept up in this submission to Stuart, in surrendering to all the myriad feelings and her body has never felt so good.

His fingers are still pumping away inside her as she feels the bounds around her ankles loosen.

“Open yourself to me”, he commands, his fingers still pulling out, twisting back into her, and her pelvis is moving of its own accord, fucking his fingers, trying to pry every last bit of sensation out of them.

He pulls them out of her and she cries out as they are immediately supplanted by his hard cock. She can feel every bit of it; every pleat, every ridge of each vein that runs along his magnificent shaft.

Her head down in supplication, she moans with every thrust of his firm length inside of her, every rub of his crown against her tender spot, every sensation of his large balls slapping against her.

Stuart reaches one hand around and slips it inside her thoroughly engorged nether lips, easily finding her aching clit. He thrusts so forcefully into her that she slides forward on the bed, her hips sore from his relentless pounding.

“Now, Liliana”, he growls and she sighs a yes as her body tightens in its final knot under his onslaught and then releases. Her climax hits her so hard her voice comes in sobs, and she’s crying Stuart’s name as she feels him continue to pound into her. Then he too is coming, his hot seed filling her as his hips still slip his shaft in and out of her, prolonging both their orgasms.

She feels his cheek on her shoulder; her knees are so weak they are shaking uncontrollably, and his cock is still hard inside of her. He kisses her back, and her body feels lightened somehow, her rosy and sore bottom somehow rooting her in the present.

Stuart leans back and pushes her left leg up, so it’s doubled almost underneath her chest and then pushes hard into her again. This time it seems his cock has slid in so deeply it feels as if it’s in her chest and she’s groaning with each earnest thrust of his, his persistence and stamina wearing away the last tiny shred of her resolve. Lily knows in this moment that she has never been so thoroughly possessed or so dominated by another’s will. It frightens her and releases her; it’s a tie that binds and yet it somehow frees her to feel everything without hindrance.

Stuart places both his hands on her cheeks and begins to pinch and lightly slap her welts as he begins to pick up the pace of his rhythm, and she feels her arousal start to tick upwards again. She pushes her pelvis out to meet his thrusts, his throbbing cock filling her, pulsing against her like a heartbeat, his head stroking the deepest places of her womb.

She feels that tingling flush course through her, his relentless pounding constantly reinforcing that Stuart is in control of her body and will do with it as he sees fit. This revelation makes her moan, and she abandons all decorum and begins to frantically push her hips against him, determined that his next orgasm in her body will shatter him.

Lily realises this fuck is for him, his pleasure, and he leans into her, moving his hands from her roughly used ass cheeks. He slides his left hand to her breast and tugs on it hard, and an open mouthed moan escapes her lips. His right hand moves between her legs and pulls on her labia, pinching them closed so that the juices flow from between them.

"You're a little hussy now, aren't you, grinding your hips into me?" Stuart pants into her ear, his hot breath sending shivers down her spine.

"I love your cock inside me", the admission breaks through and it's true. The sensation of his thick shaft piercing her, the feeling of being mounted so thoroughly by this incredibly virile man -that he's picked her, claimed her, and has spent himself inside of her is the sexiest thing she can imagine.

"That's where it belongs", he's rough now, all instinct and animalistic passion. "My cock belongs buried inside of you. Don't forget that." He bites her shoulder and she arches her back harder into him, and is rewarded when his fingers slip into her cleft and begin to tease her.

She's still weak from her last orgasm. "Oh, no", she moans.

"Don't tell me what I can't do. I'll do whatever I like with your body", he says, and slides his left hand from her breast to her open mouth, slipping two fingers in between her wet lips.

She moans and instantly begins sucking on them and cries out against them when his right hand begins to flick at her swollen clit.

"You are so fucking hot, Liliana. I could fuck you all day, in every hole, and want to do it again the following day."

In acknowledgement she hums against the fingers in her mouth, trying to concentrate on sucking on them as she would his cock but she's finding it difficult to do. The sensation of Stuart pounding into her so hard is almost trance inducing, while his adroit fingers at her clit have her body practically dancing around them.

He slides a third finger into her mouth and she slips her tongue in between them, his fingers fucking her mouth, filling her on one end as his cock is filling her pussy on the other.

She feels almost raw, like a nerve ready to be plucked one more time before it explodes in sensation. The bottom of her ass cheeks are abraded by his body slapping against them, and her clit feels as if it's going to burst, it's almost over stimulated.

There's the tell tale tightening in her belly, the irrepressible tingling in her extremities, and she moans against the fingers that fill her mouth.

"Hold onto it, beautiful one", Stuart whispers. "Until it consumes you."

Lily tries to stave it off, keep the pleasure at bay but all at once she's immersed in it, plunged deep into her climax and she's bucking against Stuart as he thrusts into her and comes, calling out her name. She can feel his warmth flow into her, his essence filling her as she clasps around his twitching cock.

He pulls the fingers from her mouth, and Lily realises she had bitten down on them. His hand moves from her throbbing clit and he kisses her back softly. All at once her knees give out, and she falls down onto the bed, crying softly.

Chapter 20

Everything has changed. Lily had to let go last night, had to explore the heights of physical pleasure Stuart could bring her to while at the same time admitting the incredible connexion they had. After fucking her hard he had untied her and held her as she wept, unable to control the flood of emotions that broke through the gates.

He needed no explanation, was just content to be her anchor as she worked on letting go of some of her tightly held fears. Afterwards he pulled her close to him and nuzzled her neck and they slept, their bodies physically and emotionally sated for the time being.

Lily wakes the next morning and feels a flush of shame over her weakness. She let someone she respects and thinks highly of see her emotions spill so uncontrollably, yet Stuart seems able to maintain perfect control. Oddly enough, she feels relieved in a way, like she did when he announced to the conference that she had saved his life. It was cathartic, and yet she still nurses a deep rooted fear that her emotions will drive him away; that she is somehow broken, and he will eventually find out.

She lies in bed for a while, curled on her side, enjoying the silence. Cairness is good for the soul; isolated and old, with good bones and lovely detail. It's so removed from the frenzy of modern life - she can understand why Stuart would like spending time here. She can almost imagine him transported back in time as the master of the estate when it was first built - sitting on a horse and exuding raw sexuality as he oversees construction with the keen efficiency he has. She sighs softly at the image, the memory of her body and his together stoking her arousal.

The arm around her tightens, and pulls her closer. "Mmm, you're awake." Stuart rumbles, his voice even lower and sexier in the morning. She can now feel his hard cock pressing against her leg.

"And I can feel you're awake too." She murmurs and presses back into him. One of the things Lily missed most about not being in a relationship was the intimacy; the private moments with another human being which they alone share.

Stuart leans in and kisses her cheek, and she closes her eyes, relishing the contact, drinking in the spicy scents of his body, savouring the tingle in her spine as his Van Dyke roughly brushes her soft skin.

"Lily…", Stuart breathes her name huskily into her hair. "Your body just calls to me, I can't resist."

She tries to turn over in his arms so she can touch him, feel his face, but he stops her, and instead pushes her so she partly lies on her stomach.

He folds himself over her, and pushes her left leg up as he had last night, and she can feel his thick cock brushing against the tangle of hair between her legs. She relaxes and enjoys the weight of his body pressed against her, like a barrier against the outside world.

He slips his hand between her body and the bed, to the top of her slit, and slides a finger in between her nether lips, groaning at the wetness he finds there.

Stuart positions his body so the tip of his shaft is at her entrance and Lily's body arches into his, betraying how much she wants him inside of her.

His breath is in her ear. "Hungry this morning, aren't we?", he teases and her pulse begins to race as his fingers languidly explore her.

"Always for you, Stuart", she gasps, enjoying the feeling of being trapped, enveloped by him, the primal strength of his body overwhelming her.

He slides the head of his cock into her and she moans and pushes against him, the arousal from his skin assailing her senses. His breath is warm against her neck, tickling her throat, his lips brushing sensually along the sensitive skin of her jaw.

Pinned by him like this, where she can't touch his face, see his eyes, tangle her fingers in his hair or lick the arousal from his skin is driving her mad.

"God Stuart, I want to touch you."

"Mmm, you feel too good like this, sweetheart", he pushes into her more and she moans. Leaning on his right arm, he uses his hand to brush the hair away from her neck.

"More", she says and grinds her hips into his pelvis, which elicits a grunt.

"You want some more of my cock?", his tongue flicks out and touches her ear, which makes her shiver.

"Yes", she pleads and he nudges into her again and she cries out as he stretches her, the pressure of his head hitting inside her womb causing a delicious mix of pleasure and fullness.

It takes her a moment to catch her breath; the feeling of him is nearly indescribable, delicious. "Fuck, Stuart", she finally gasps, adjusting to his size.

"Mmm, that's what I intend to do", and he lazily pulls most of his length out and with a shimmy of his hips, plunges into her again, causing her to yell.

"You like this, my little minx, hmm?", he says as he slowly withdraws again and thrusts, which earns another pleading cry from her lips.

"Oh my God, yes", her breath is husky with desire. "You feel so big, it's overwhelming."

Stuart's mostly stilled hand at her clit begins to tease it - now swollen and exposed - sensitive and ready for him.

He brushes against the nubbin between her lips, while his hips continue their languid dance and she's powerless to do anything to stop the inexorable march to climax that Stuart is in control of.

"You feel so good Liliana - made for me, so sexy", the last words come out almost like a prayer.

She can feel her climax build, familiar and yet each time slightly different. Her body begins to tense; Stuart's fingers torment her clit with lazy strokes, his cock hard and deep inside of her, claiming her sex as only he can. Lily hears her breath as gasps and it's almost otherworldly, as belonging to someone else, so full of desire and desperation.

"Stuart", she pants, the rhythm of his thrusts hypnotic, the feel of his cock inside of her so pleasurable she's reluctant to come, to surrender the blissful feeling of anticipation being fucked by him arouses.

"Liliana", he acknowledges as he gasps out her name; his lips tease her throat, sending shivers up and down her spine.

He loves the feeling of her body under his hands, wrapped around his cock; the way she writhes as he fondles her, pushing her hips into him greedily, wanting more of him. He loves the scent of Lily's skin when she's aroused, the way her voice becomes breathy and the husky way she says his name when she's close to coming.

Stuart slides his fingers unabashedly over her clit and she has nowhere to escape, his deft touch pushing her towards her orgasm and she rocks into him in response, his cock thrusting harder into her as a result.

She's falling apart under him and surrendering to the pleasure, unable to do anything else. He thrusts deeply into her, wanting to consume her and own her completely - leave no doubt that she is his, utterly.

Her breath is a series of sharp gasps and he strokes her exposed clit and then she cries out as her orgasm can't be contained any longer and erupts inside of her. Stuart feels her clench tight around him and it pushes him over the edge. He lets out a low groan as he continues his thrusts, his seed pumping into her, tremors racking his body. The noises from his mouth are of primal satiety, of a deep seated lust being satisfied.

They lie there together, Stuart's body still pinning her, both of them panting and enjoying the dwindling glow of their pleasure. He kisses her temple and ear, causing her body to begin to shake.

"If I had my way…", Stuart begins, his voice still throaty, "I would keep you in my bed all day." He nuzzles her neck and she sighs as he kisses her throat. "And I would alternately fuck you and make love to you until we were exhausted."

"Mmmm…"

"Then, Liliana", he turns her head slightly, and his lips pause over hers, "we would sleep - my cock still inside you - leaving no doubt for you, even in your dreams, that you are mine."

She gasps at how forward his words are, how even now they make the warmth between her legs grow. She lifts her lids and looks into Stuart's face. His eyes are wild, filled with unquenched desire and wicked thoughts.

"After we slept - and drank and ate perhaps – I would take you again, and again, and make you come until you beg me for mercy." Then his lips are on hers, and his cock, still inside her, begins to throb against her g-spot, making her moan.

"You would tire of me", she manages breathily, in between his lust filled kisses.

"Never." His certainty is absolute. "So you are fortunate that this is your vacation, not mine."

"What makes you think", she says as his hand delicately strokes her neck, "that I wouldn't want what you described?"

"Mmmm", he mouths her exposed shoulder where it meets her neck. "Don't tempt me, or you'll not see the outside of this bedroom for the remainder of your trip."

She raises her head and her eyes glow green in the morning light. "Is it… like this a lot?"

He chuckles, running a hand down her cheek. "You mean, is it usually like this when I've had other lovers?" She nods.

"No, Liliana. Never." She dips her head down again and kisses his chest and sighs. "You?" She shakes her head at Stuart's question.

"Isn't this about the right time for you to tell me how right I was?" He runs his left hand down her back to her bottom and squeezes tightly.

"Er, no…?", she hazards. Stuart laughs.

"No? The correct answer is: 'Stuart, you were right. We have amazing chemistry and mind blowing sex, and you knew we would all along'."

She looks at him under half closed lids. "That's what I'm supposed to say? What good would that do?"

"You shouldn't doubt me", he says, and kisses the side of her forehead.

She averts her eyes and pouts. "Fine. You were right."

"Come; let's tidy up, lest we tarry in bed all day."

Chapter 21

"No, Stuart! I'm serious." They're standing in the gift shoppe at King's College, Aberdeen. Lily is trying to offer her credit card to the cashier, while Stuart holds it at arm's length and offers his. The cashier is watching the exchange with some amusement.

"I enjoy buying things for you, Liliana", he says and kisses her cheek.

"I work hard for my money, Stuart, and I want to spend some." He looks at her exasperated for a moment and then releases her hand.

"Thank you", Lily smiles at him, and waits until the cashier looks down before sticking her tongue out at him.

Stuart raises an eyebrow. "THAT will get you into trouble."

The cashier hands Lily her card back and begins to wrap the purchase. It's a lovely print of the College Chapel, hand tinted and framed.

"I have one similar from the time I went to London", she explains. "That one is of St. Paul's cathedral." Stuart takes her hand, pulls her to him and kisses her tenderly on the lips.

"You are the most stubborn person I have ever met." He takes the proffered bag from the cashier and carries it for Lily as they turn and head outside.

Stuart is so pleased to find that their compatibility in the bedroom is mirrored by how well they get along spending time together outside of it. He enjoys seeing Lily's reaction to things and watches her as she interacts with people. A ready smile is always tugging at her mouth, a compliment or word of gratitude sure to follow soon. When she is at ease, Stuart can't imagine a better companion to have by his side. Her mixture of inquisitiveness and humour is infectious, and he finds that he's enjoying himself more than he has for years – if ever.

It's a partly sunny autumn day in Scotland. Streamers of sunlight break through the clouds and dot the verdant countryside like bright confetti. There's a slightly crisp chill in the air as they walk back to the Range Rover.

Stuart walks around the Rover and holds the door open for her. She favours him with a shy glance, which belies their intimate knowledge of one another's bodies. She wonders whether she'll ever tire of these small gestures; of the polite manners he shows to her when they're out and about. Lily enjoys them immensely, and finds him utterly charming.

He places her package in the rear seat and climbs into the driver's side and smiles at her. There's an unspoken tenderness between them - a sweetness about their manners that reveals the burgeoning feelings that are developing between them.

Stuart starts the engine and chances a glance at her. The brisk wind has put some pink colour on her cheeks, and her tousled hair lends Lily a rough and ready look. Her smile is disarming - genuine and full of life - making both his heart and cock stir at the sight of her.

"Shall we grab a bite?", he asks. It's mid afternoon.

"I'm famished", she admits. "Wherever you would like."

He nods and pulls out, driving only a few blocks before pulling into a spot near the kerb.

No sign announces the name of the establishment that they enter; Stuart merely walks up to a door and pulls it open before ushering her inside.

She looks at him curiously as he closes the door behind them. It's an old building; the room is close around them, with dark wood paneling and matching beams.

He catches the curious and amused look on her face and smiles. "I spend sufficient time here that I know good locations", he says, and after an encouraging nod from the hostess, selects a seat near a stone surround fireplace.

"Can I help ye'?", a young lady inquires. The words are all run together and Lily has a hard time parsing them.

"Menus and water, please", Stuart says. As she leaves he grabs Lily's hand under the table.

She loves how ardent he is, how affectionate. If she were to design her perfect man, he would have Stuart's high cheekbones and strong jaw, neatly trimmed Van Dyke and propensity for displays of affection. She privately smiles at how close a match to her ideal he is; perhaps that's why she resisted him so, innately knowing the danger he possessed.

Claire, their waitress, dutifully drops off menus and water before tactfully leaving. Stuart slides his chair close to Lily's and strokes her hair back behind her ear to give him a clearer view of her face.

"I'll order for us, if you don't mind", he says as Lily cracks the menu open. She looks at him briefly before closing it and pushing it aside.

"Okay Stuart", she says simply and smiles her slightly crooked smile at him. How could she be everything he ever wanted?

"I wanted to ask you something about this morning."

She pauses a moment and her lips part and eyes grow wide before she regains her composure. Her emotions are so close to the surface all the time it's difficult for her to be deceptive; it's one of the many things he likes about her - Stuart finds her openness and honesty refreshing.

"What is it?", she asks breathless.

"I was lying next to you, waiting for you to wake up", he says, and she looks down a moment, remembering what happened. "You sighed. What were you thinking of?"

Claire spares Lily for only a minute as she approaches, takes their orders and departs. Lily waits a second before answering, taking in the rich smells of cooking food along with the faint aroma of old dried timbers and oiled floors.

She looks at Stuart's intense gaze a moment. She can see the flicker of curiosity in those azure depths, as well as the ever present strength and intensity of his personality. She wonders if she will ever get used to him, or his insatiable curiosity to know what she's thinking.

Her mind races back to her thoughts that morning and as she recalls her rather indecent musings, her lips tighten.

She looks at him briefly before turning her eyes to her hands, which are twisting in her lap. "I was… thinking of you, as you could have been, when Cairness was built." She steals a brief look at his scorching blue irises before turning her eyes back to her lap. "I could almost see you, astride a horse, surveying the construction, your keen eyes taking it all in. How… in command of it all I could picture you being." *How sexy he would be, his cock barely contained by his breeches…*

He looks pleased and intrigued for a moment. "I like the images you have of me", he says, the hand around her shoulders stroking her hair. "They interest me and amuse me", he says and gives her a look that makes her nether regions warm.

Claire returns with two glasses of wine and gives Stuart a wistful smile. He's impossibly handsome, his long sculpted body draped in a dark blue woolen sweater and slightly torn 501's. His body is just screaming 'sex machine' to Lily; his powerful legs wrapped in soft denim and his strong arms caressed by wool. The juxtaposition between the power of his body and the soft fabrics that cover it is something she finds difficult to ignore.

He catches her longing gaze and flashes a look at her, full of indecent intimations and it makes her flush.

"Don't be shy Lily, or ashamed of anything. You're the sexiest women I've ever seen…", he says as he kisses her neck.

She can instantly feel her body react to his touch; his kiss makes her moist between her legs, her pulse beats faster. *How can he think I'm the sexiest woman he's met?*

Claire returns with their entrees; mustard seed encrusted salmon, wilted spinach and pilaf. Stuart sits so close to her that the miasma of his sensuality spills over into her space, embracing her, enticing her to touch him. Being around him is so heady; she's well acquainted with his ample talents, his proficiency at arousing her and coaxing the most intense of orgasms out of her.

"Did you send someone to spy on me, Stuart?" She asks it quietly, and for a moment she thinks perhaps he hasn't heard. She hears the clack of his fork as he lays it on his plate and turns to look at him - he's staring at her intently, studying her.

"I did, initially", he admits. "I knew nothing about you, wanted to be sure your presence there wasn't… coincidental."

She pauses for a moment to absorb the information.

"Liliana, it has been a… difficult few years for my company and me. I thought it was a prudent measure."

"So the email I got from Jenna about someone asking around…"

"Wasn't me. After I had spent some time with you I called it off. Also, my investigator was VERY discreet; I made sure of that."

Lily's stomach feels filled with lead. As much as she didn't want Stuart to have spied on her, the thought that some unnamed person was doing so was more alarming. If she considered it, Stuart's caution made a bit of sense.

Stuart can see the concern on her face. "I know, Liliana. I thought of it when I verified this morning that it wasn't my agent."

Her fear changes to annoyance. "Were you going to tell me?"

"Yes, I was. But I wanted to give it a day or so, hopefully give you a reprieve."

"There IS no reprieve Stuart…"

"What's going on is thousands of miles away", he says as a matter of fact. "I just wanted you to have a nice day."

She looks at him warily; the last bit is probably true but she's still uneasy. Claire checks on their progress and they eat a moment in silence.

"I'm afraid Lily that I'll have to insist on a bodyguard for you at all times. I usually travel with someone; when you're not with me, someone will be watching over you."

She puts her fork down; the salmon is delicious; the spinach wilted with bacon divine, the pilaf delicately seasoned. She can't believe she's having this conversation with him, when so much of the rest of to-day has seemed so perfect.

"Stuart", she says pleadingly, but his face is impassive.

"I'm sorry, Liliana, I wish there was some other way."

"But, I just want… PLEASE Stuart."

He looks at her... those bright intelligent eyes that bewitch him so - her soft skin and full mouth and her body... yes, her beautiful curvy body that is the source of so much pleasure. No. However she might beg, it's for her own good.

He puts his fork down once more and takes her hands in his, careful to not crush her bandaged left palm. "Sweetheart, you are irreplaceable. Someone is curious about you; I don't know why. It's the prudent thing to do."

Her eyes are pleading with him, almost desperate. "I'm nobody Stuart, it's all a misunderstanding. You'll see."

He shakes his head. "You are too precious to me. I can't take that risk; if something was to happen to you again, and it could have been in my power to prevent it…" The thought makes him shudder; he'd have a difficult time living with himself.

She looks at his face and drops her hands; she knows better than to argue when he has that look in his eyes.

Disappointment is etched on her face. "I don't UNDERSTAND", she says, picking up her fork once more.

In that moment Stuart gets a glimpse of Lily as a young girl, and it makes his heart ache acutely. He can almost see her as an eight year old, with blonde hair and precocious emerald eyes, wondering why her mom would abandon her and her brother right after her father's death. It's that same innocence he sees now in front of him - a desire to understand what she did that was so wrong as to warrant someone causing trouble for her at her place of work.

The realisation brings him some understanding of why Lily was so fearful and reticent; she fears loss, abandonment - being close to someone who lets her down.

He doesn't fight the urge to comfort her, and puts his lips against her hair and drinks in her scent. "Liliana, my sweet Liliana - it will be all right, my dear. I promise." As strong as she is, Stuart is caught up in the desire to be her knight in armour - protecting her from the pangs of the world, and shielding her from harm. His emotions for her are so fierce - it's like nothing he's ever felt before.

She smiles weakly and turns back to her food. He's cross that this intrusion has cast a pall over the day - perhaps it can yet be rescued.

"Are you still interested in going to Islay or Skye?", he asks, shoving his near empty plate from him, and reclining back in his seat.

Lily turns to answer and pauses a moment to drink him in. He is so at ease in his skin. His right leg is bent, while his left one is stretched out in front of him. His hips are thrust forward in the chair, one arm draped along the back of his seat while his other hand is wrapped around his pint glass. She can see hints of his muscular thighs beneath the faded indigo of his jeans and she feels her chest tighten and her core clench. He is just so unbelievably beautiful, so completely arousing even in a non-descript setting like a restaurant in the middle of wind swept Scotland.

He catches the look on her face and his eyes widen. "Liliana…", he says softly, like a caress. She feels her face get hot under his intense gaze.

"I'm sorry Stuart", unbidden, it rushes out of her breathlessly. "Sometimes I just can't believe how gorgeous you are."

He smiles his devastating smile at her and cocks his eyebrow; the combination is breathtaking. "I can't tell you how pleased I am that I meet with your approval."

She looks down at herself, bemused.

"Don't", he warns, and the tone of his voice makes Lily look up. His eyes are stormy.

"But…"

"Don't second guess, Liliana. There is a part of me that is only alive with you. There's nothing I can do for it."

She gasps, her heart pounding so hard in her chest she thinks Stuart must be able to hear it. "Don't say that if you don't mean it." She feels lightheaded.

"I mean it, absolutely", he says and leans forward towards her. The simple act of touching her arm makes her quiver and she closes her eyes and takes a few deep breaths. *So fast; all of it so fast.*

She feels his hand on her face and nestles her cheek into his palm. "Sweetheart, what is it?"

She opens her eyes to his; deep blue luminous pools of tenderness. Her whole self yearns for him - for his touch, his presence inside of her, his body next to her, his breath, his scent, his sexy voice. It makes her ache with an indescribable loneliness when his hands aren't on her body, when his breath isn't hot in her ear.

She's afraid to answer, but she does. "Just that after so long it's… very hard to grock this, take it all in. It seems so fast – intense – and after all this time…" She lets it hang; so long wanting something like this, so long waiting for someone who felt strongly about her, who obviously cared deeply for her. Finding Stuart feels like running into a brick wall, a shock to the system.

He chuckles, even as he strokes her face with incredible gentleness. "You've thrown my life into a bit of a tangle, make no mistake, Liliana. I've never met anyone quite like you." A curious look passes across her face and he answers her unasked query. "And it's a GOOD thing." He touches his lips to hers.

He pulls away and observes; her eyes are lusty, her swollen lips slightly parted. His pants tighten around his cock as it expands. He feels a strong rush of arousal sweep through his body like fire.

Stuart leans forward and places his lips next to her ear. "It's all I can do, Liliana, to keep from throwing you on this table, stripping you bare and fucking you until this restaurant is filled with your screams of pleasure." His words make her catch her breath and warmth stir between her legs.

He pulls away, triumphant at the effect his words have on her. He can sense even the most subtle changes in her body that tell him when she is aroused, and he knows that Lily is generally on the cusp of arousal constantly.

Stuart's shocking words thrust her excitement into overdrive, and he can see it in her eyes, smell it as it wafts off her skin deliciously. He enjoys the control he has over her body's response -that a touch or handful of words can prepare her for him, regardless of whether she consciously wills it or not. Lily's body wants him - is in a near constant state of being ready for him; exists for him to take and merely requires a signal from him to be ready for his cock and his mouth. It has the effect of making him almost always horny, knowing he has that kind of effect on her.

Stuart knows that she finds it disquieting – that it's alarming what kind of power he has over her body. He hopes she finds it freeing somehow, and enables her to let go and let him see her, bare and unvarnished.

"You didn't answer my question", he asks, still so close to her that Lily can feel the energy emanating from his body.

"I'd love to go somewhere in the Hebrides", she says, her voice still hoarse from arousal.

Claire comes to clear their plates and Stuart asks for the bill before focusing back on Lily. "When is your flight out?"

"Thursday evening", she replies and fills him in on the flight details.

Stuart considers it for a moment before pulling out his phone and dialing a number.

"George, yes. Can you arrange accommodation for us in the Hebrides? Yes… It's a bit of a drive, so I'd say two. Lily leaves Thursday evening to return to the states. No, we'll keep departure on Wednesday, I have my meetings Thursday & Friday evenings. Yes. Thank you." Stuart hangs up and turns to Lily.

"May I have your phone?", he asks.

Lily is surprised but hands it over. "Of course, Stuart."

He's busy a moment pressing buttons and then hands her Blackberry back to her. "I've programmed my home, cell and business numbers into your phone", he says. "It seems sort of silly after all that's happened between us that you don't have them."

Stuart's phone rings and he answers, and after a few words with George he hangs up. Claire has returned with Stuart's card and receipt and is only too happy to tell him what a pleasure it was to serve him. Lily's about ready to growl at her, but Stuart grins and says something kind and she leaves, a smile plastered on her face.

Stuart turns to Lily and the corner of his lip curls in a wry smile. "I love that you're jealous."

"I don't", Lily grumbles as Stuart stands. "Are we leaving?"

"I'm afraid we should. George has secured a cottage for us in the Outer Hebrides. It's rather a long drive to Skye and then the ferry to the Isle of Harris. We'd best have an early night as we'll be leaving sooner than you'd like to-morrow morning." He smiles at her.

Lily narrows her eyes. "I've said it before… I can be a morning person if I need to be", she says, pretending to be annoyed at his subtle ribbing.

Stuart stands; this is probably the most relaxed and at ease she's seen him. She sometimes finds it difficult to remind herself that he's the CEO of a very successful materials engineering company. Then she thinks back to how persistent he was in pursuing her, how determined he was and then maybe it's not so hard to see after all.

He reaches his hand towards her as she rises from her seat. His desire to constantly show they are together romantically is reassuring, yet there's no mistaking the possessiveness about it.

Lily waits until they're in the Rover before asking. "So, what's the agenda for the remainder of the week? You're leaving Wednesday?" She's feeling some inner turmoil over this. Her vacation is coming to a close swiftly, and when it began she had no idea it would be managed by Stuart. Initially she perhaps resented it a little, but now she's come to enjoy it. The news that he is leaving a day early is disappointing. Part of her worries that it is the location – and her interest in his homeland – that has made things so special between them. How will their relationship change when they are both back in Washington State?

"Yes, I'm sorry about that, but it cannot be helped. I have meetings Thursday and Friday that cannot be avoided. You can drive back down to Edinburgh with me on Wednesday afternoon if you'd like."

She thinks for a moment. "I'd like to do that. I wouldn't mind spending Wednesday and Thursday before my flight in Edinburgh."

She watches Stuart for a moment, admiring the sinewy strength that seems to pervade all his movements.

"Stuart…", she doesn't quite know how to begin. He downshifts around a corner and watching his hand on the shifter makes her think of his hands gripping her breasts; she does her best to collect her thoughts.

"Why did you have ropes in your bedroom at Cairness?"

He looks over at her briefly, completely unruffled. "I'm surprised you didn't ask earlier, being as observant as you are."

"I had other things on my mind at the time." He catches her eyes and sees a flash of desire pass through them.

"You had mentioned that one of your exes", Stuart's tone becomes slightly icy as he says the word, "tied you up and the experience was arousing. I tied your hands at the hotel and you came in my mouth." His hand grips the shifter tight at the memory of it. "I wanted to be prepared."

Lily squirms uncomfortably in her seat; she did ask for an explanation after all.

She can feel the sexual tension rise in the car; it's always there between them, like an ember that needs only the tiniest breeze to spring into flame. She enjoys it - loves that feeling of untapped potential that is constantly between them but realises that's not all she wants, as powerful and exciting as it is. She wants Stuart to respect her and enjoy her company outside of the bedroom.

He pulls up in front of Cairness and they enter, Stuart insisting on carrying her packages for her. He follows her to the bedroom she began her stay in.

"I have a few suggestions", he says, still hanging onto her bags. "I'm taking a private jet back; I think your purchases will arrive in better condition if you allow me to take them instead of trusting them to a major carrier."

Lily thinks about it; the print, the china teacup she bought for Janet's collection and other miscellaneous items are fragile. She doesn't see any reason why she should object so she doesn't.

"That's really thoughtful Stuart - thanks." She smiles and he places the bags near her door.

"The other is the schedule; you asked about it in the car, and then distracted me with… other matters." He looks at her so lasciviously she can feel her mouth go dry even as her clit throbs.

"We will head to Skye and then take a ferry. This will take most of to-morrow, so we'll stay on the Isle to-morrow night and Tuesday night and head back early Wednesday. It will be a bit of a stretch, because I will be departing Wednesday night. Pack your main luggage, because George will meet us in Edinburgh with our suitcases. We won't be coming back here."

For some reason, that makes Lily sad and she looks away. She loves Cairness; the wooden treads on the stairs that squeak, the tapestries and art and Mrs. MacDonald, with her kind and gentle face.

Stuart steps to her and takes her face in his hands. "We won't be coming back here again this trip." He corrects softly, kissing her forehead. "Do you like Cairness, darling?"

He asks it so tenderly it makes her heart ache. "Yes", she whispers quietly. Her eyes close as Stuart softly fondles her face. His sweetness towards her makes Lily's heart want to burst with happiness. She wraps her arms around him and clutches him to her fiercely.

"Then we should make sure you come and spend more time here."

She lets out a wistful laugh. "Stuart, you are too kind to me, really."

"Anything for you – everything for you, my dear." He says and tilts her face up towards his. He brushes his lips against hers softly, the contained passion and emotion in them makes her want to cry. He was so strong and determined last night, taking control, giving her no quarter. The contrast with the kindliness and concern towards her over the past few days have touched her heart so profoundly that she knows she is falling head over heels for him, and there's nothing she can do to stop it.

Will things change when they get back?

"Mmm…", he says, enjoying her warmth and affection. "You are nearly too much for me Liliana." His eyes sparkle for a moment. "Nearly. Now, we need to pack." He kisses her forehead, steps to the door to retrieve her packages and then is gone.

Chapter 22

Lily is aware of a slight shaking of the bed, an irregular movement.

"Earthquake?", she mumbles through a drowsy haze.

A masculine voice with a Scots accent laughs nearby. "No, darling. Time to rise."

Lily opens one bleary eye to find Stuart's two gem like ones staring at her with obvious amusement. "So is this your 'I can be a morning person if I need to be' act?", he says, laughing.

"Be careful", Lily cautions as she partly stifles a yawn. "Once roused I'm quite dangerous."

She doesn't clearly remember Stuart coming to bed last night. He'd had to stay up for a late conference call, and when she woke up around 3 AM to use the loo she found him sprawled next to her, one of his arms draped over her body.

"What time is it?", she asks, trying hard to push the last webs of sleep away.

"It's early, regrettably", he says, his eyes staring hotly at her. "When you're tousled and sleepy like this you're practically irresistible, but we have a long day ahead of us."

She sits up in bed and nods, the bedclothes slipping from her and pooling in her lap. Stuart growls hungrily before leaning over and kissing her on the mouth, his right hand cupping her breast.

"Very regrettable." His boxers now contain a growing erection. "The day is now going to feel even longer."

Lily looks at him lustily, her dawning wakefulness leading her to growing arousal - his strong sinewy body on display pushes all her buttons.

With great effort, Stuart turns away. "You'll be the ruin of me, Liliana", he says, and moves to the open suitcase on his side of the bed.

"Do I have time for a shower?" she slips her feet from under the cover and dangles her legs over the side of the bed.

"Yes, barely. I've already showered, thank God. I couldn't restrain myself if I had to take one with you."

An idea begins to take form in Lily's mind as she considers his words.

"I won't be long", she says, and walks towards the door connecting to Stuart's study and the bathroom.

As she surmised, he looks up from packing to watch her make her way to the door. She's naked, and the warm rays from the morning light coming through the windows bathe her body in a golden glow. Stuart can feel himself stiffen, his cock now painfully hard.

Lily pauses in the doorway a moment, allowing him a view of her back and ass before turning towards him. She rests one hand on each side of the doorway, her body on full display for him. "How long of a drive do we have?", she says in as sleepy a voice as she can manage.

She can see the ropes of muscles in his neck tighten and his cock pulse against the cloth. "Just over five hours, perhaps as much as six." His voice is stretched tight.

"Huh", she says, shifting her weight, so that her hips rock seductively. "That's interesting."

Stuart's eyes grow dark and stormy, his voice is almost desperate. "Don't, Liliana."

"I don't know WHAT you're talking about", she says before turning and walking through the door.

She showers quickly and packs her toiletries, considering her plan. Stuart enjoyed teasing her, tormenting her right from the get-go. His subtle caresses and rough words are enough to get her drenched; in his suite the night of the awards dinner he had her begging for his touch. Lily now realises she has some power of seduction over him, and she is ready to find out how deeply it goes.

He always seems ready; he's incredibly virile, always erect with incredible stamina and self control, yet he could break down Lily's resistances so easily. What would it take to do the same to him? To cause a kink in that self control to split wide open and make him fall apart, consumed by his lust for her?

She has at least five hours to find out. Lily feels confident now; Stuart's attentions, persistence and worship of her body have made her feel more sexy than she has ever before.

Lily slips into the bedroom; Stuart isn't there and neither is his suitcase and she hurries to dress. She is sitting on a chair tying her chukkas when he returns with George closely on his heels.

"Is the suitcase for Edinburgh packed?", he asks. She nods towards the corner where it stands zipped. George takes it and leaves, pulling to door to behind him as Stuart stands looking down at her.

"Why do I have a feeling you're going to be trouble for me to-day, Liliana?", he says.

"I don't know what you mean, Stuart", she says and leans forward and wraps her arms around his legs, clutches his ass cheeks in her hands and mouths his crotch. The rivets of his jeans are cool and hard under her lips.

"Fucking Christ, Liliana." She can feel him begin to harden even through the denim, and he places his hands on her head.

She stands up and slips her arms up his back and curls her hands over his shoulders. She leans into him and kisses the top of his chest that is exposed by an open button. Lily opens her mouth and moves up his throat, her tongue flicking at his neck until she plants a ferocious open mouthed kiss on his chin, his goatee stinging her tongue.

She looks up into his eyes, and they are wild; almost unrecognisable. The heat from his lust almost makes her fearful that she's unleashed a beast she won't be able to contend with.

"Caution, Liliana", he says, his erection threatening to undo the buttons of his fly, his hands tightly gripping her back. "You did this on purpose, didn't you? Waited until we're clothed, ready to go and then you did this."

"I'm just exploring my sensuality", she says in as coy as way as she can.

"I don't think you understand… what you do to me."

She nuzzles his neck and nips at it, a guttural groan coming from his lips. "I'm learning", she says.

There's a knock on the door. "Mr. Watson – all is ready."

With a searing look at Lily, Stuart tears himself away and grabs her rucksack and slings it over his shoulder before grabbing her hand. "Come", he says.

Mrs. M is teary and Lily hugs her warmly, thanking her profusely for her kindness, before shaking hands with Thomas and Mr. MacDonald.

George assures them that the bags will be delivered to the Balmoral Hotel in Edinburgh prior to Stuart's departure time.

They make their way outside; it's raining softly, and Lily takes a long, forlorn glance at the manor. It's been the location of the happiest – as well as the most perplexing – times of her life recently, and she is reticent to leave. Stuart watches her, notices the desire to belong to someplace on her face, hoping he can bridge that gulf somehow.

They climb into the Rover and wave goodbye to the staff, who are lined up to bid them goodbye. Lily turns her face away, her wanton teasing of Stuart replaced by a genuine feeling of loss.

For his part Stuart is silent; he appreciates Lily's capacity for emotion while at the same time is sad to see her so cut up at leaving. It's the one quality about her that he loves and hates; her almost infinite capacity to love and experience happiness while at the same time it's paired with almost equal faculty to experience loss and regret. He knows that when Lily loves it is unequivocal and without reservation and that same ability leaves a huge potential for disappointment and hurt. So while he steers the Rover down the drive towards the gate he says nothing but grabs her right hand and squeezes it tightly, which elicits a muffled sob from her. For all her strength and posturing, her emotions are unadulterated and true. He's touched to the core that her time at one of his favourite places in the world has meant so much that it is painful to leave.

Stuart shares her feelings; but under his practiced and professional façade he is able to protect himself. For some reason Lily lacks this defensive shell, and her emotions are raw, laid bare. When he listens to her gasp between sobs he hears the tearing of his own heart at leaving some place dear to him; it nearly gives him permission to feel the intensity of his emotions and he wonders how she can function – and thrive – in a world that must feel so rough and cruel.

The farther away from Cairness they are, the less harsh the reminders and Lily manages to regain a measure of her composure. She is grateful for Stuart's silence and his support, communicated through his strong fingers intertwined with hers.

Eventually he can sense the tension in her body ease, and a small sigh of relief escapes her. Lily has become so precious to him; as important as anything else in his life, and although Stuart doesn't fully understand why, he doesn't care. She is sexually enthralled by him and his attentions have given Lily permission to be herself; in her he senses something so unique and special that he will do anything to keep her. Stuart has never felt so alive, so vital, so empowered as he has since he met her.

The scant habitation gives way to more open roads; Stuart decides on a less traveled route, and traffic is sparse. He doesn't say anything, ruminating on his new found discovery and wondering what he needs to do in order for Lily to feel safe and break free from her past.

Eventually she speaks, and her voice is as soft as a pleasant dream and wistful as a spring day. "I love this open country."

"As do I", he says quietly. Desperate to ease her melancholy, he adds, "You know me so well, Liliana; I don't think you even realise it."

She places their still entwined fingers on the shifter, untangles her hand and reaches over to place it on the upper part of his thigh. "You read me so easily, Stuart", she says, and steals her fingers over to his crotch, running her nails over the tightly drawn denim.

He lets out an open mouthed sigh at her touch, the sharpness of her nails cutting through the fabric, igniting the embers of arousal that always burn in his loins.

On the nearly deserted road, with tinted windows on either side, Lily decides to take a chance, grabbing the growing hardness in her hand and squeezing.

"Liliana, this is NOT fair", Stuart pants, doing his best to keep his eyes on the road.

"Do you think it's fair, Stuart, the influence you have over me? We both know it, so I'll admit it." She nearly sounds resigned. "You pretty much just snap your fingers and I'm undone."

He smiles inwardly at this truth, knowing how difficult it must be for her to confess it.

"So", she continues, "as you said to me once and I'll paraphrase; 'Think about this; what it means about us and about what I want and you want.'"

His eyes narrow at the thought that his own words could be used against him.

Lily's hands loosen the buttons on his jeans and in no time her hand has rooted into his boxers and her fingers are wrapped around his cock.

"You were hard before I had you in hand", she observes and watches Stuart. His jaw is set, the veins in his throat throb as his whole body reacts to her touch.

"Do you think I want you more or less than you want me?", she asks quietly, and she tightens her grip on his penis, making him gasp.

"Liliana…", he says, his voice a mixture of awe and caution.

She takes a quick look around before unbuckling her seat belt and leaning over the console. Her face is in his lap, her mouth watering as she eyes his throbbing cock. "This is going to be harder for you than for me", she says in a slight mocking tone, before extending her tongue to lick the precum off his shaft.

The moist contact is almost more than he can bear and he shivers at her touch. "How is the great Stuart Watson now? How easy is it for him to keep his composure?" Her hand grabs the base of his shaft as she lowers her waiting mouth over the head of his cock and hollows her cheeks, sucking on his head. He lets out a loud yell, and the car jerks slightly, but he manages to keep the Rover fairly straight on the road.

"God, you taste so good", she murmurs between licks, as her hand strokes his shaft and her tongue licks the circumference of his head. "You've utterly seduced me…", she says and grazes his tip with her teeth, "…ruined me for anyone else…", she flattens her tongue and gives his head a languorous lick, "… so that all I want is you." Her hand tightens around the base, and his moans fill the car.

Stuart doesn't know how he is staying on the road. Mercifully, there are almost no drivers and it requires all his resolve to focus on keeping the Rover between the lines as her mouth alternately fucks and makes love to his cock. He doesn't want to give her the satisfaction of coming – he doesn't want her to win – but shortly it becomes obvious that the conclusion is undeniable. Lily seals her lips around his penis just behind the crown and quickly flicks his tip while pumping his base and with a loud scream of her name he pours himself into her.

She nearly gags as she tries to take it in, the huge spurt of his seed filling her throat as his cock twitches in her mouth. She lovingly licks it clean, her murmurs of satisfaction keeping him aroused even as he recovers from the most wanton orgasm of his life.

She trails kisses along the length of his shaft before tucking his still hard cock back into his pants somehow and buttoning them up.

Lily sits back into her seat and sighs. *Never has pleasing a man been so fulfilling, so satisfactory.* It's also thoroughly aroused her, and her panties are soaking wet.

She puts her seat back down as far as it will go so she is reclining, her body invisible behind the wall of the door. "See what you've done to me, Stuart?", she says as she undoes the button of her pants and unzips her jeans. "I'm no better than a slut now."

Lily moves her hand inside her jeans. "No, Liliana, don't", Stuart pleads, his mouth hungry for her, the hard on still raging in his pants. He wants to fuck her hard and teach her a lesson, but he knows pulling over is one sure way of getting the attention of the police. "You've made your point."

“Have I?”, she says. “You’ve unleashed my sexual side…”, she says as she slides her right hand down the front of her panties. “I think you need to understand what that means.”

Her finger makes contact with her clit; it’s nearly bursting with arousal, her pussy the wettest she’s ever felt it. She sighs as she strokes the swollen tissue, her labia full and pressing against her fingers.

“Jesus Christ Liliana”, he says and his voice is hoarse. It’s almost impossible for him to concentrate on the road; he can see her out of the corner of his eye.

She moans and bucks as her fingers coax her button towards climax. “Oh my God, oh my God…”, she pants as her strokes find a rhythm. “Oh, Stuart!” she screams as her body tightens and her eyes clench before she lets out a sensual sigh and her body ripples with the force of her orgasm. She continues to stroke, milking her clit until she can’t stand it and she yanks her hand out of her pants to rest on her leg.

Stuart grabs her hand and pulls it to his mouth, sucking on her fingers, the rivets in his pants painfully pushing on his hard shaft. He licks the juices off her fingers, and just the scent of her makes him want to come again and he yearns to be inside of her, the ache to take her almost consuming him.

Chapter 23

It's nearly four hours into their drive when Stuart pulls off the motorway. He can still taste Lily in his mouth, and it's been driving him mad all morning; her brazen teasing was the ultimate turn on for him.

He locates a small pub and they park around the corner and emerge under the gray, storm filled sky. His erection has hardly abated over the past several hours, and has become a painful ache. He grabs Lily's hand fiercely and before they turn the corner he brings her fingers to his mouth and licks the dried arousal from between them. Lily is flushed with her new found power and exudes even more sensuality, if that is possible.

"I don't know if you realise what you've done, Liliana." He says softly, as he opens the door to the pub.

It's dark and intimate, the smell of frying food mixing with the creosote from burning wood. They manage to find an unoccupied table in the back of the pub, a corner booth with carved wood surround and a sturdy wooden table accompanying it.

A bar maven approaches them almost the instant they take their seats and plops down menus. Stuart orders two beers and she turns and makes her way back to the bar cheerfully.

Stuart holds onto Lily's left hand under the table and flips his menu open. He can smell the arousal still lingering on her fingers and her scent is pouring off her body. The fact that he can't have her for several hours is driving him insane and it just continues to feed on itself. She truly has no idea what manner of door she has opened.

Lily tries to remove her hand from his grasp but he clings to it. He is almost mad at her for making so obvious the deep seated and undeniable need he has to possess her.

She leans towards him and puts her lips near his ear. "I wish your cock was inside of me."

His left hand grasps the edge of the table, his knuckles white. She continues. "I hope you want what you've got Stuart, because you've unchained me; I can't get enough of you. All I can think about is when you take me, how you feel inside of me, what your skin tastes like."

She hasn't had anything to drink yet to-day but is thoroughly intoxicated on Stuart's pheromones, his sensuality, so that it blocks out anything else. Their waitress returns with their beers and takes their order for two BLTs before casting a wistful glance at Stuart and leaving. He is doing everything he can to maintain a casual look on his face. Lily is relentless.

"Liliana… DON'T." He doesn't want to hurt her bandaged hand, but he squeezes it hard, trying to inoculate against how aroused her words get him.

"You're like my fucking air now", she says. "I love the way I feel when I'm with you - sexual and powerful."

Their waitress returns with their sandwiches and after getting an order for two more pints, she departs.

"So help me Liliana… if I let go of your hand will you behave?"

"Yes", she says, and he releases her hand tentatively and grabs a half of the sandwich in both hands and takes a bite. "We have close to another three hours before we get to the cottage."

"I know", she says.

Their waitress returns with refills, and sensing the sexual tension, departs.

"If you're trying to wind me up… you've succeeded. My cock hasn't gone down since you started sucking it off. All I can think about is plunging it inside of you."

"That's all I can think about."

Stuart tries to steer the rest of the lunch conversation to other topics, with some success. Lily insists on picking up the tab, and finally wears Stuart down on that front.

They depart the pub, a little tight from the two beers and constant sexual arousal. When they round the corner, Stuart grabs Lily and pushes her up against the wall and presses his body against hers, his hard member straining against the denim of his jeans.

Stuart kisses Lily so hard he's worried he'll hurt her, but she only moans under his onslaught, hungry for more. Instead of relieving the longing he has it makes it more pronounced, feeding it.

He pulls away, gasping. "Christ, Liliana, what have you done to me?" His attraction to Lily was previously otherworldly, but her raw sexual abandon on this car ride has awakened some animalistic need in him that he doesn't recognise.

"The same thing you've done to me", and she nips at his throat, her own primal awakening now dawning on him.

"I don't know how I'm going to make it until we reach Harris", he groans

Lily grabs the back of his head with her hand and pulls it to her, stroking his tongue with hers. Stuart grabs her hips and pulls them against his pelvis, his hard cock pressing against her belly.

"You see what you do to me?", he breathes into her mouth hungrily. "It's not going to go well for you to-night." He lets her go and with supreme effort backs away and turns to the car, unlocking it. Lily walks around to the passenger side, her gait unsteady as she climbs in.

She's feeling a little guilty about teasing Stuart as they meander their way towards the departure point on Skye that will take them to Harris; Stuart seems almost petulant and withdrawn.

When they finally arrive at the Isle, Stuart tracks down a grocery store and they head inside.

"I'm cooking supper", he says simply. "Would you mind terribly hunting down a couple bottles of good wine? One should be a chianti."

"Okay", Lily says, surprised at the request. She had anticipated cooking supper, but Stuart is insistent.

She wanders off and finally finds the wine section and pulls on her limited knowledge of Italian wines and web access on her Blackberry to locate a promising bottle.

She feels Stuart before she sees him; the hairs on her neck prickle and her skin begins to form goose bumps. Almost immediately he is at her elbow, his perpetually sexy voice in her ear.

"Find something?" She turns and places her two selections in the cart and glances over the contents.

"Spaghetti Bolognese? I had no idea you could cook." she asks, as Stuart reaches around her and plucks another bottle off the shelf.

"I enjoy cooking; it's relaxing. You?"

"I love to cook; I was anticipating cooking for you tonight."

"Well, we'll just have to rain cheque that." Stuart replies, a sly smile playing across his face for a moment before it's replaced by a mask of impassivity.

They head to the checkout and in no time are loading groceries into the Rover.

The grey from afternoon rain makes the day darken early. It's half an hour to the site, where they retrieve keys to the cottage.

The building is quaint, standing on a small bluff with the tip of the roiling Atlantic spread below them. Rocks tumble down to the coast of the island, where waves smash into boulders with such force that giant geysers of spray erupt in front of them. It's cold and lonely, and the tingle of salty mist on Lily's face is invigorating.

She unpacks groceries from the Rover while Stuart gets the lay of the kitchen. Lily searches until she finds their bedroom upstairs. Its medium size, with a king size bed covered in a homey looking quilt. Logs are already stacked in the wood stove in the corner, and she lights the kindling.

She makes her way back downstairs to the main living space to find Stuart in full prep mode. He pauses for a moment to throw her a grin and then continues chopping celery. Lily hunts around, finds a wood carrier and fills it up with logs located under the overhang outside and takes them upstairs, filling the log holder in the bedroom.

The room is beginning to heat up now; the chill of autumn is being taken out of the room. Lily decides to head downstairs to see if Stuart needs any help.

The smell of browned vegetables assails her nostrils. Decadent spaghetti Bolognese on a chilled night like to-night sounds heavenly; the fact that Stuart is actually cooking it is charming.

"Why don't you start your shower, Liliana? I've got it under control", Stuart advises. He seems perfectly at ease, almost in his element.

"I hadn't planned on taking a shower…"

"It's been a long drive, Lily. I would think you'd want to relax."

"Hmm…", she considers it a moment. "Alright. I'll see you in a bit."

She drags her bag upstairs and lays it down on a chair near the wall. The glow from the logs in the wood stove bathes the room in amber light and she shuts off all other sources of illumination except for one lamp. After removing her shoes and digging out her toiletries, she finally makes her way to the bathroom.

Old white hexagonal tile covers the floor; the walls are bead board to about four feet in height, then topped by a chair rail. Above the rail the walls are a cheery yellow and are a marked contrast to the stormy seas and dark sky that she can see outside the split pane window.

The large claw foot tub also serves as the shower. The very back of the tub abuts a partition wall, and shelves there are lined with bath salts and knick-knacks. A huge fixture is attached above and curtains hang from the oval track in the ceiling and follow the contours of the tub.

She starts the water and undresses, the shower head sprays straight down and makes it appear as if it is raining in the tub. After checking that towels are handy, she eases into the tub carefully, her shower necessities bundled in her arms.

The shower is luxurious, and as Stuart had suggested, it relaxes her. Her hair is brushed and face moisturized when she opens the door into the bedroom, her hand rubbing a towel against the still damp ends of her hair.

She stops only a step in, surprised at what she finds. Stuart is sitting in the chair near the door, which is closed. The fire is stoked and now provides the primary illumination for the room, along with a few candles. His shirt is off, and the firelight plays along the definition of his muscles. The top button of his jeans is undone, the bulge of his erection obvious. His feet are bare, and there is a glass of what looks like scotch in his hand.

The look he gives Lily when he sets his eyes on her is indecent, and her hand moves the towel from her head to her chest, in an effort to cover her nakedness.

"Ah, Liliana…", he says, his voice dripping with sex. She feels trapped, and nervous. The virility of his body is potent, making her feel nearly faint under the onslaught.

In one graceful move he puts his drink down and is on his feet, covering the distance between them quickly.

He stands in front of her and pulls the towel out of her grip and tosses it towards the bench near the bed. "Nowhere to go my beauty, and the time of reckoning is at hand." She visibly gulps.

"I tried to warn you Lily", he continues almost regretfully. "But instead you tortured me to-day, teased me."

"You are constantly tormenting me", she whispers as the knuckles of his hand softly stroke her cheek. The sexual menace in his voice is unmistakable.

His left hand moves to her naked bottom and he caresses it, pulling her closer to him as he does so. She casts a glance at the door and realises it is locked; she remembers Sunday and the thorough fucking she got and realises that this will be so much more intense. She's not sure if she can handle it.

"Stuart…", her mouth is dry and damn her body, but she can feel the quiver in her clit as it awakens, and the stirring in her belly.

He thrusts his lips over hers so violently it knocks the breath out of her. His hand on her ass tightens so hard she parts her lips to yell, and Stuart pushes his tongue into her mouth, greedily stroking hers.

Her hands are on his forearms and she tries to push away; she can feel where this is going, she senses a tempest of raw carnality building in his body and it makes her quiver alternately with excitement and fear.

His right arm encircles her tightly while his left massages her arse; there is no escape. Lily feels her body begin to betray her; her mouth opens wantonly and her hands cling to his sinewy forearms instead of pushing away.

His kissing is forceful and relentless, claiming her mouth, giving her no reprieve. He turns her so that she faces away from the bed and begins backing her towards it.

"Supper", she manages to breathlessly ask.

"Simmering", he answers before covering her mouth again with his. She can feel the edge of the bed behind her knees. Her bottom is swollen from his strong kneading and she had yet to regain her breath from his ravishing kisses.

He leans into her until she falls back onto the bed. Stuart grabs her hips and slides her so she is lying on the bed with her head on one of the pillows. He's on top of her quickly, pinning her to the bed with his body. He begins to kiss her lazily, his tongue slowly exploring her mouth while his hands stroke her body, her face.

She involuntarily moans into him; he tastes so good, and the scent from his skin is delicious. Lily reaches her hands up and runs her fingers through his thick, short hair, relishing the feeling of having him on top of her, taking control.

He slips her right hand out of his hair and holds it up above her head; she stretches underneath him, the slight roughness of his denim against her nakedness arousing.

His mouth is hard against her, his body crowding her and she squirms underneath him, basking in the force of his will, the power in his body.

Her eyes shoot open as she feels something against her wrist; Stuart's mouth is still trapping hers, and she can't move underneath him. He reaches and grabs her left wrist from the nape of his neck and pushes it above her head as she confirms her suspicion; he's binding her arms to the bed.

She tugs but can't free them, and then she realises he must have planned this while she was in the shower, prepared the bed. He probably has been scheming for a good part of the day; Bolognese only becomes more rich when it simmers, so supper is no problem. There is plenty of time for whatever he has planned.

Lily gulps and tries to buck underneath him. His mouth is still bruising her lips, his fingertips lightly trailing the tender, inside skin of her arms; it sends shivers all over her body.

Stuart breaks the kiss and sits up, impossibly gorgeous with his slightly tousled hair and partly unbuttoned 501's. His chest is heaving, his eyes slightly wild with passion.

"Isn't this what you wanted, Liliana?", he says looking down at her as a panther might eye its prey. His sinewy and lithe body seems taut with sexual tension, desperate for release.

Lily, lying below him and now helpless, looks lovely. Her damp hair spreads out around her face like a gold filigreed veil, her beautifully round and ample breasts sway with her deep breaths, and her lips are red and aroused from his hard kisses. There is a slight fear in her eyes that is partly obscured by her overriding curiosity and arousal.

"Stuart…", she pants; it is both admonishing and seductive.

He slides back and gently touches her leg at the ankle, slowly tracing up her leg. "Liliana, can you come just from penetration?"

The boldness of the question shocks her but also arouses her further. "I… no." His touch is delicate on her leg, so tantalizing, promising more intimate brushes to follow.

He cocks an eyebrow. "Hmm. Is that so?" His right hand has now reached the upper part of her thigh and she sucks her breath in anticipation. He trails up to her abdomen instead, and flicks gently at her belly ring.

"I like this, by the way", he says and leans forward and kisses her stomach, gently tugging on the ring with his teeth. He moves up her body, taking his time, kissing and mouthing her quivering skin.

Stuart moves each of his hands to one of her breasts and starts kneading. She moans softly and he looks at her under lids heavy with desire. "I can't tell you how stunning you look, bound to the bed this way." He pinches her nipples hard and she gasps, squirming under him. She can feel wetness pool dangerously between her legs, her body already demanding satisfaction.

"Don't worry", it's almost as if he can read her mind, "I'm going to fuck you as you've never been before, but I am intent on taking my time."

His voice is dripping with lasciviousness, and it turns Lily on immensely. His mouth is again over hers, his body pressing so hard on her chest that she almost can't breathe, but the sensations are erotic at the same time. Stuart's masculine smell blends with the arousal seeping out of their pores; the slightly sharp, acrid smell from the burning wood and her own soft perfumes from her recent shower meld into a heady aroma and it is completely intoxicating. Lily feels almost transported, the ropes around her arms freeing her from the duty of being shocked, allowing her to sense Stuart and his wants with every part of her being, with no regrets.

She leans into her kiss with him, her entire body wantonly expressing its desire for his. Stuart breaks free and the look in his eyes is dangerous and Lily feels a shadow of nervousness pass through her. He adjusts the pillows under her head so her torso is slightly propped up, her head just shy of the headboard.

He sits back again and trails his fingers down her leg this time. She feels herself straining against the bonds; she wants to touch his skin, bring his face to hers, rake her nails over his back, but she can't and it – this bondage – heightens everything.

Lily watches him wrap his long, strong fingers around her ankle, and he pulls her leg wide, and she sees another rope, a loop already premade and she gasps loudly and struggles again. He slips her leg into the loop and tightens it, and now her left leg is pulled near to the edge of the bed and fastened securely.

With three limbs tied, there is no place for her to go, yet she puts up a token struggle as he slips the loop over her right ankle and secures it.

She is now spread eagled on the bed. Each of her wrists are pulled up and tied tightly; she can look and see the rope as it curls over the edge of the bed, presumably to the legs that support it, and her ankles likewise are pulled to the corners. She is open and exposed and the knots are true; there is no way for her to free herself.

Stuart stands now to examine his handiwork, his erect cock tenting his tight jeans. "Christ, but you are gorgeous when you're helpless, Liliana", he says breathlessly. She can see a slight glisten of sweat as a sheen over his sculpted muscles.

He walks up to the head of the bed and looks into her eyes, checking to make sure she is okay. Lily's eyes are slightly dilated, her breath coming in pants, and her tongue flicks out of her mouth, wetting her lips. He can smell the arousal coming off her body, see the glisten of her juices as they cling to the newly trimmed hair between her legs.

He reaches his left hand to stroke her head, even as his right one moves down and softly pats the short curls at the apex of her thighs. "Mmmm, very nice, Liliana. Thank you." She turns bright red and attempts to turn away but his hand on her forehead stops her.

She is completely out of her depth and she knows it; the command he has over her body so powerful she can think of nothing else but how badly she wants him.

Stuart keeps his palm on Lily's forehead, puts a knee on the bed and looks into her eyes as his hand slowly massages her engorged labia. He can see the flicker of pleasure reflected in her eyes, feel the slight twitch of her body as his index finger slips slowly between her nether lips.

He sits on the edge of the bed to better watch her face. "So very, very wet, dearest. Very good", he says and almost chastely kisses her mouth, even as it's open, begging for his tongue to enter it. He catches her bottom lip in his teeth and tugs, as his right hand grabs between her legs and pulls. She moans, her pubis leaning into his teasing hand, desperate for more contact.

He releases her head and stands up, walking to the end of the bed, where there is a bench. Stuart moves it slightly before laying his torso on the bed between Lily's legs, his thighs resting comfortably on the padded top of the bench.

He languidly kisses the inside of Lily's thighs, sometimes sucking, sometimes biting, as he gradually moves his way up to the wet cleft between her legs. She's groaning under his ministrations, her hips wiggling each time his mouth makes contact with her skin.

He takes her pussy lips and spreads them wide and hears her moan 'no', as he examines her, slipping a finger into her swollen entrance. She feels so helpless and vulnerable; Stuart's lazy exploration of her most private parts is both arousing and humiliating.

"You are so lovely", Stuart says, planting a kiss just shy of her wet mound. "Nothing to be embarrassed about."

He slips a finger into her once again and feels her tighten around his intrusion, her hips bucking shamefully with the desire she feels. "It's going to feel so good to fuck you", he says, slipping a second finger in and eliciting an appreciative moan from Lily. He slides his thumb down and pinches her engorged inner lips at the same time he licks her sensitive clit. Lily moans loudly, her back arches and Stuart begins to massage the inside of her womb with his long, dexterous fingers.

"Mmm, I just love the way you taste", he says, slowly licking her slit and using his left hand to pull apart her lips. She pushes into him, struggling against her bonds, each gasping breath filled with the longing for release.

Stuart hardens the tip of his tongue and flicks it several times across her swollen button, making Lily scream in pleasure. "This is why you have to be bound, you struggle so", he teases, as his tongue again laps around her clit.

He can feel she is close, and he takes a nipping suck of her lips before removing his fingers from her and pulling back.

Lily's frustration is expressed in a primal roar of anguish - her pleasure denied. Stuart wipes his face and hand with Lily's discarded towel. "I love that I can still smell you on my face", he says. Lily whimpers.

Stuart slowly unbuttons his fly and pulls out his cock. His shaft is hard, the veins in relief along it, a glisten of precum on the head. He makes his way up Lily's body, until he is straddling her chest, his knees pushed into her armpits.

He hangs over her, his thick, long cock just inches away. She's desperate to taste him, to get relief for her arousal by pleasing him. Stuart slides his right hand to her cheek and pushes to signal she needs to open her mouth. She parts her lips, and Stuart slides his shaft between them, while keeping eye contact with her.

She'd nearly forgotten how big he is, how his length is too much for her to take in completely as she feels the head of his cock hit the back of her throat. She hollows her cheeks and slides her tongue around his shaft and he lets out a guttural moan, and begins to slowly pull out and thrust into her mouth.

He tastes good - salty and a little spicy, slightly tinged with sweat. Concentrating on pleasing him and making him groan focuses her attention on him instead of her throbbing, unsatisfied clit. She sucks and licks his shaft earnestly, encouraged as he lets out a loud moan and arches his back. His thrusts in her mouth quicken and she struggles to keep up as his body tenses over her.

He reaches back and pinches her left nipple hard as he pushes deeply into her mouth and as she yells in pain she can feel his seed sliding down her throat as he comes explosively in her mouth.

He caresses her face and looks down at her, "Good girl", he says, his right hand still absently toying with her breast behind him. The pulsing in her clit has come back with a vengeance and she moans plaintively and shimmies her hips suggestively.

He pulls his still hard cock out of her mouth. She can feel the dampness increase between her legs; she's desperate to have him inside of her, to have their bodies joined.

Stuart gets up and throws some more wood on the fire. "Please, Stuart", she begs. "Have mercy."

"This is for your own good, my dear", he says and she lets out a frustrated cry. "Don't be impatient."

The flames in the wood stove flare up, making his muscles look like etchings in stone. He turns back to the bed, his hard cock still sticking out of his pants, and it looks fearsome in the firelight. He catches her gaze and holds her eyes as he peels away his jeans and makes his way to the foot of the bed.

"Thank God", she whispers softly, but Stuart lays down between her legs and begins to kiss her thighs again.

"I want you inside of me Stuart. PLEASE", she's nearly ready to cry, her arousal is so sharp.

He ignores her and kisses her pubis, his right hand spreading her lips apart, his index finger finding her channel and slipping inside. She is so slick and aroused that he has no problems slipping in two move fingers as he begins to lick around her clit, only rarely teasing it.

Lily's hips come off the bed, her pelvis gyrating as her body desperately seeks release. Stuart's expert tongue hardly does any work before she is on the verge of coming, at which point he stops his licks and pulls his fingers out.

Lily sobs, "Please", her body racked with uncontrollable tremors of desire. She can feel Stuart's hands at her ankles and they are free. He pulls Lily's legs up, her cleft near his face, and he sucks her labia before sliding her legs down and impaling her on his cock.

Her back arches far off the bed and his shaft feels as if it's splitting her open as he drives into her with determination.

"Come for me Liliana", he commands, his thrusts firm and sure.

"I can't" she sobs, grateful for the feeling of him inside of her, but it has made her arousal more acute than ever.

Stuart tilts her pelvis and continues to thrust hard and deep in her and Lily yells out, the head of his shaft hitting the swollen tissues in her womb. Her face flushes, her body clenches uncomfortably and still he thrusts relentlessly into her, tilting his hips and hers so his cock scrapes against her g-spot, pummeling it.

"Oh!", he can feel her body tense under him as she yells it.

"Come, Liliana", he says in his most commanding voice, laced with his own arousal.

He's pounding hard and fast, and it seems inevitable - her body is tight, so tight, into this point of desire… and then she feels it, the slight tremor as she crosses into climax and Stuart slips his finger onto her clit and then it's a rush, her orgasm fully crashing down around her and she's crying in relief.

Stuart continues to thrust into her and play with her clit, milking her, and he comes again, pushing hard into her.

He drops her hips down and her legs shake; she's weak from the power of the orgasm she had. Stuart leans into Lily, his cock still thick and twitching inside of her and he kisses her passionately on the lips. She can smell the muskiness from her arousal still clinging to his Van Dyke.

"You just need some encouragement, a bit of coaxing, the right kind of attention", he teases her between kisses, as he wipes the drying tears from her cheeks.

"It's not right that you are able to do that", she said shakily.

"Are you complaining?", he says in mock surprise as he covers her mouth, his tongue slipping between her lips and caressing hers.

"We should do more of this", he says, stroking her face, running his mouth over her jaw.

"That was… the best orgasm", she concedes, laughing. Stuart stands up and walks towards the foot of the bed. "Um, my arms?", she asks.

Stuart sits on the bed by her feet. "Not quite yet, I'm afraid", and Lily looks at him, shocked. He lifts her right leg and brings it over his head and holds it in his lap. He moves his right leg to between her thighs, and starts pulling on her lower lips.

Lily closes her eyes and leans back, "Jesus Christ", she says, feeling the desire spreading through her body again, the slit between her legs moistening.

She tries to edge away from Stuart, but he just holds her leg more tightly and slides his fingers up and down her cleft.

"You are so easy to arouse, Liliana. Your body wants mine so badly. I adore that about you." He leans in and plants a kiss on her mound, her hips grinding into his face.

He lifts her leg and slides underneath, and grabs his jeans from the floor and steps into them.

"Stuart, don't leave me like this."

"You look so beautiful there – beautiful and helpless. I won't be gone long", and he walks to the door, unlocks and opens it and leaves. Lily can hear his feet on the creaky stair treads.

She pulls on her ropes, trying to loosen them. She remembers when she was a child playing Cowboys and Indians and how often she was stuck being the captive that needed rescue. The neighbourhood kids tied her to a light pole in an abandoned lot, while they ran around with their cap guns chasing each other.

It had taken her several minutes, but despite the bonds feeling tight and unforgiving at first, she had managed to work them backwards, feeling the loops, threading the bitter end out until she had freed herself. Then SHE had been able to join in the carousing, feeding her untamable tom-boy spirit of adolescence.

But these knots; she tugs, she wiggles and twists and she can't free herself. She can feel Stuart's essence trickle from between her legs, even as her struggles make her wet. She is imprisoned here, bound to Stuart's whims, exposed and naked, waiting for his pleasure. It seems hours have passed until she finally hears his footsteps on the stairs, and then he emerges through the door, closing it behind him. He has a tray with a glass on it, and a bottle of opened wine.

The contrast between his choice to go shirtless and her utter nakedness is not lost on her. She remembers what Stuart said early on; he wanted to own her utterly. She had called it surrender, and Lily was now getting a taste of what it meant to want someone so completely that indeed it was almost surrender.

Stuart places the tray on the bedside stand and pours wine into the glass. He inhales and samples it before taking a generous sip. He sits on the bed near Lily's head and holding the back of her head up with one hand, proffers the wineglass to her lips.

She takes a sip and feels the heat of the alcohol rush through her, the aromas from the grapes filling her head with sensuous smells. Stuart takes another sip before filling the glass again and placing it on the stand.

He runs his hand over her belly slowly. "It's such a turn on to know you are up here, tied to my bed with my seed inside of you, just waiting."

She can feel the blush of arousal in her nipples and her groin at these words. He lifts the wine glass with his other hand, his left palm pressed against her stomach, still rubbing it. She takes a deep sip and lets the wine slide down her throat and begins to lose herself in all of it; the warmth of the fire caressing her externally while her own arousal and the alcohol warm her from within.

"What do you like about it?", she says, feeling brave. His hand moves to the curve of her hip.

"Possessing you; knowing you are mine completely." He stares at her over the glass as he takes a sip.

"You like having control."

"You like giving up control", he counters, and Lily looks away. The hand on her hip tightens. "Why?"

She pauses a minute before answering. "I don't know."

He slips his hand back to her abdomen, so that it's lying near her mound. Arousal seems to course through her body from that point of contact; she can feel it run through her, engorging her clit, plumping her breasts.

"You know, Liliana. Why?"

It's as if he is willing her body to respond - the command is relayed through his touch so it spreads throughout her body, bending it to his will.

"It's… nice to have no choice. To be forced – or given permission – to feel things." She turns her face away, humiliated by this confession.

"And?"

She swallows hard. "I enjoy giving that to you. So I don't have to be this strong person all the time. So I see where you take us."

His hand moves from her belly, and turns her face to his. She has trouble meeting his eyes, but she catches a glimpse of the fierce pride he has in her. He lifts her head up and gives her another drink of wine, before taking another one himself.

She closes her eyes and sighs, resignation seeping into her. Stuart knows her better than anyone ever has before; she has stepped on that path and there is no turning back. Either he will be the love of her life, the saviour for her loneliness or he will utterly destroy her.

She feels his breath on her face an instant before his lips claim hers as only his can - his hands pushing her mouth open, his tongue slipping aside hers, and that burning desire for him flares up swiftly again.

His teases her; he holds her mouth open with his hands while his tongue intimately explores her lips, running over her teeth. She gasps as he traces her bottom lip and bites it, and she can taste the smallest tinge of metal as he draws blood.

His hungry mouth devours her jaw and moves to her neck. She can feel him move, straddling her on the bed, his hard cock pressing against her belly through the rough denim. He scrapes his teeth along her neck and she arches into his mouth; he growls before biting her shoulder, and the sharpness of his teeth mixed with the softness of his lips feels so good.

He slips to her breasts, taking them both in his hands and pressing them together hard so he can suck both nipples into his mouth. She cries and shifts beneath him and he flicks his tongue between the two nubbins, teasing them until they become hard kernels. He flattens his tongue and runs it roughly over them, before taking them again in his mouth.

Her cries are like an aphrodisiac, egging him on to make her moan louder, cry with more fervor. He kneads her breasts in his hands and he trails his mouth over her stomach, watching her belly quiver under his touch.

He lowers her to the bed and pulls his cock out of his pants and thrusts hard into Lily, stroking her clit until her body surrenders and shakes and she clamps tight around him.

He pushes forcefully against her and quickly reaches his own climax, screaming her name as he pours his essence into her, his passions for the moment spent.

Chapter 24

He lies with her a while after that, their tangled sweaty bodies seeming to be not two but one as they watch the fire dance on the ceiling, its warmth soothing their nakedness.

Stuart finally unties Lily; her arms are sore but her body is relaxed and satisfied more than it has ever been. He is tender with her, touching her and stroking her face, and kissing her temples and hair.

Finally he rises and showers and Lily rinses off, his seed trailing out of her when she stands. In a way it's a mark of ownership; Lily is claimed by him, has been taken and pleasured by him and this is a reminder of it.

They dress in flannel pants and t-shirts after the shower and head down to eat. They busy themselves with preparations for supper, talking lightly about the meal ahead.

After they sit down with poured wine and steaming bowls of pasta in front of them, Lily feels comfortable enough to broach a topic.

"So, you were married. What happened?" She twirls some pasta onto her fork.

Stuart pauses a moment to consider Lily's question. "I… realised she was two different people."

"That's cryptic", Lily observes as she slides the fork to her mouth. "Oh my God, Stuart, this is the best Bolognese I've ever had."

His smile is a bit smug. "I did say I like to cook."

"I can see why." She smiles warmly, the affection she has for him obvious.

He relishes it a moment before responding. "When you are successful – or people perceive you are successful – they often change who they are or relate to you differently. A more basic example – a person with a college degree as opposed to someone who dropped out of high school. You make assumptions and treat them differently, or expect different things from them once you know."

"She was opportunistic? A gold digger?"

Stuart purses his lips and considers for a moment. "I guess, in a way", he replies although it bothers him to admit it and of course, there are other things...

"You aren't the first, or unfortunately the last, man to be taken in like that." Lily observes his reply over the rim of her wine glass.

"Don't you treat me differently than you would otherwise?"

"I hope not. I mean, I got mad at you in the car at Cairness, knowing it would make you so angry that you might not want to see me again."

"But part of that was pushing away from me, Liliana."

"Still – your position could have factored into that, but it didn't. I have a great deal of pride in what I've done so far. I graduated years later than most, but it's because I worked full time while going to school. So as much as I admire you and your company, I've worked too hard myself to just brush it all aside and try to piggy back on you."

Stuart looks at her thoughtfully, considering her words. "It's the reason I wanted to get to know you before you realised who I was. Plenty of people can rent a nice suite in a hotel; not many are worth hundreds of millions of dollars or are president of a multi-billion dollar company."

Lily feels her face go white as all the blood drains out of it. She looks at Stuart.

He has a look of surprise on his face. "You really didn't get that about me, did you?"

"I just… didn't think about it, realise… I mean, I knew you were successful. You took over from your dad and W & D was already an established company …" She considers it; how could she not have known? *Hundreds of millions of dollars? But he is nice to people, seems normal, is fun to be around.*

"Hmm. Interesting." Stuart knows she is telling the truth; no one can make their face pale like that on command. She knew he had done well, but had no idea as to the extent of his wealth.

"So your, ahem, ex-wife was interested in your pocket book a bit?"

"She definitely was a different person to people depending on whether I was there or not, that's for certain. It was little things at first - screaming at George when she thought I was gone, calling him 'George darling' when I was around."

Stuart pushes his bowl to the side and leans on the table and looks at her. "But I've had a nice evening so far", he reaches a hand out to stroke her arm, "so I'd prefer to not talk about this right now, if that's alright."

Lily smiles at Stuart, his touch radiating warmth all over her body, making the lips between her legs tingle. Stuart stands up and takes their dishes. "Let's clear up and head to bed." There is a twinkle in his eye as he says it.

****

The next morning comes all too soon. Lily's muscles ache from the long car ride and being tied spread-eagled for so long on the bed the night before. She's a bit slower getting ready for the day, and Stuart refuses to disclose their itinerary.

The only hint is an admonishment to dress warmly, which he adheres to. His thick cotton t-shirt is covered with a moss green woolen sweater and thick canvas coat. Lily eyes his clothing choices and ignores the button down shirt she had laid out and hunts for the baggy cable knit sweater she packed.

Their first stop is at the MacGillivray Centre on the west coast of the island. Stuart is fascinating and knows far more than the placards at the centre, relating interesting historical tidbits about William MacGillivray. After taking in the centre they have an early picnic lunch on the tables outside, the wind blowing up from the nearby shore and tousling Lily's hair about so it look as if she's in a tempest.

Stuart ambles back to the Rover and returns, a piece of twine in his hands. Lily is mystified as she watches him approach, an impish grin on his face.

"Turn forward", he says, and with a smile gently pushes her chin so she is staring straight ahead. He then proceeds to tame her wild hair and begins to braid it.

"One of my sisters is older than I am, and she taught me to braid her hair", Stuart explains. His fingers are deft and confident, and in no time a golden plait hangs down the back of her neck. He places one hand on her nape and with the other tilts

Lily's chin back and kisses her lustily on her lips, the intimacy of the moment making her heart beat wildly.

"Thank you. What other talents do you have that I don't know about?" she says playfully.

Stuart's eyes narrow and he smiles wickedly. "You'll find out."

The extra foodstuffs purchased at the store the night before now make sense. A lovely pesto tortellini salad and cold chicken washed down with wine are followed by some farmhouse cheese, a torn piece from a boule and an apple Stuart slices with a Victorinox he pulls out of the folds of his coat.

Lily watches Stuart as he places his thumb on the skin of the apple and confidently carves off another slice for her. He hands it across the table. "What are you thinking of Liliana?"

She can't help but blush; he's caught her in the midst of introspection. She looks up, and his blue eyes seem somehow more vibrant under the muted gray of the coastal sky.

"Just how much I've enjoyed the trip. How…", she pauses to look down towards the shore and the regular lapping of the water against the rocks there. "… you almost seem – well." She tries to brush it off with a wave of her hand.

Stuart places the knife on the picnic table and reaches across to caress her cheek. It's cold from being buffeted by the wind, and sports an attractive pink glow. "How it's all seemed so perfect?"

She's frustrated with herself for letting too much slip. "Yes."

"It's because I know you Liliana, perhaps better in some ways than you know yourself. It's important to me that you enjoy yourself; I take care of the things I have."

"Well, thank you Stuart", she says feeling closer to him on this remote island than she ever has before; she conveniently ignores the possessiveness of his tone.

They pack up and make their way back to the Rover, and head down south. Lily finally gets the courage to ask about something that's been bothering her.

"What happens when we get back?"

Stuart wrinkles his brow. "What do you mean?"

"What happens between us when we go back to Washington State?"

"We continue to have mind blowing sex, suppers, and spend time together." The furrow in his forehead deepens. "What did you think would happen?"

"I just wanted clarity."

"You thought this was just a holiday affair? No, I'm afraid not, Liliana. What part of, 'you are mine', was unclear? Someone must have hurt you badly indeed for a beautiful, intelligent woman like yourself to be so insecure about relationships."

Lily doesn't answer and just turns to face the window, watching the savage beauty of the landscape as it rolls by.

In a short time, they pull up to a gravel clearing and Stuart parks the Rover. They walk up a short distance to what is clearly an old church. Dozens of headstones at irregular angles dot the soft hill leading up to the chapel, its pale gray and tan stones making it look like a spectre against the angry dark sky.

They exit the Rover and he waits for her, grabbing her hand as she walks to meet him. Together they cross wind tousled grass, his hand tightly gripping hers, until they reach the entrance.

It's a lovely church; the sandy grey of the interior stones make it seem warm and inviting. Alcoves housing three tombs are inside, each of the sarcophagi covered with a carving in dark, hard stone.

"It's beautiful", Lily whispers almost breathlessly, overcome by the majesty and ancient feel of the place.

"It was built nearly five hundred years ago", observes Stuart, as they slowly peruse the interior. "Lovely, isn't it?"

Lily turns and watches him. She can sense the pride in his heritage and again catches a glimpse of him as he might have been centuries ago - still commanding, intense and full of sensuality.

After looking at the standing slabs on display and meandering through the graveyard, Stuart ushers them back to the Rover.

“I’m afraid it’s back to the cottage, my dear”, he says, a hint of regret in his voice. “We need to be up early on the morrow so I can be in Edinburgh for my flight in the afternoon.”

“Ah…”, Lily says, a bit of melancholy touching her voice. “So this is our last evening together.”

“On this trip, yes”, he says, and glances over at Lily, but she’s turned to look out the window.

A soft rain begins to fall, the angry sky finally venting some of its emotion. Gradually it turns into a steady rain, and then the wind begins to pick up. By the time they’ve reached their cottage, the wind is racing over the hillocks before it meets the waves at the shore below, the two forces of nature crashing into one another.

As they exit the Rover, Lily is glad once again for the braid that Stuart made of her hair; the gusts are attempting to whip the tendrils about. The sky is unnaturally dark for this time of day, it being only very early evening.

They are safely inside the cottage, the door is closed and they can feel the wind finding its way into cracks; there are little drafts in some parts of the house. Stuart suggests they bring in more wood, and so they brave the storm once again and by the time they are back inside their cheeks are red and they’re chilled through.

“I’ll start one upstairs if you’ll take care of down here. When you’re done, come up”, says Stuart, hoisting a canvas carrier full of logs over his shoulder. Lily nods and with some coaxing, is able to start a fire in the massive wood stove in the kitchen.

She throws an extra few logs into the firebox and heads for the stairs. She’s sad that it’s the end of her vacation, and she’ll have to go back and face the unhappiness of her job. She’s worried the change in scenery will alter the relationship with Stuart, as they’ll both be distracted with the regular patterns of their lives.

The bedroom is warming up; already the edge of chill is falling out of the air and the firelight – the only illumination in the room – feels so good on her eyes. Every so often she can sense the house vibrate slightly as it is buffeted by the storm but it’s almost a soothing, rocking feeling.

"Liliana?", Stuart is calling to her from the bathroom, over the sound of running water. She steps to the door and opens it.

He's taken the oil lamps and scattered them around the bathroom. A bit of steam rises from the tub, which is being filled with water; she can see the tops of suds.

Stuart is standing shirtless next to the bath, his sculpted body perfection itself, his demeanor casual, relaxed. He beckons for her to enter.

She approaches tentatively, a little shy, which makes Stuart smile. He reaches down and grabs the bottom of her sweater and pulls it over her head, dropping it on the floor. His arms are around Lily, pulling her close to him, and he kisses her head and her hair before pressing his lips softly against hers.

She wraps her arms around Stuart, tracing the muscles on his back, feeling them tighten under her fingertips. His strength is both comforting and arousing.

She slides her hands between them, and starts to unbutton his jeans; this is something she's never done before and it's sexy - feeling a little more of his exposed skin as she undoes a button, her hands alighting on the aching bulge under the soft cotton of his boxers.

Stuart slips his hands up to Lily's back and slowly undoes her bra; their soft kiss becomes more passionate - their mouths open and tongues explore.

He moves his hand to Lily's jeans and unfastens the button and slips the zipper low as her hands push his jeans down his legs along with his boxers. Stuart slips his hands between Lily's panties and her hips and likewise pushes them down.

They're standing there naked, in the sultry warmth of the bathroom, the flickering lamps and candles making the room feel very intimate. Stuart steps to the bath and turns the water off, before reaching out a hand to Lily. She watches him breathlessly, marveling at the graceful, sinewy lines of his body, how every move of his is confident.

Lily takes Stuart's hand as he steps into the tub, helping her in so she stands in front of him, facing him.

"Turn around, and sit down" he says, lowering himself into the tub.

Carefully Lily does as he asks. She's sitting in between Stuart's legs; she can feel the base of his erection at the bottom of her back.

He curves his right arm across her chest and pulls her gently so she is against him, and she leans her head back and left, so it rests on his shoulder.

She closes her eyes. "I must be dreaming", she whispers, hearing the rain slap against the windows.

"Why is that, Liliana?" Stuart brushes stray tendrils from her neck with his left hand and plants a kiss on her right shoulder.

"Because this is too wonderful to be true", she says quietly. The warmth of the water soaks into her chilled body, Stuart's luscious scent works its magic on her and his embrace makes her feel protected.

"Mmmm", Stuart agrees, moving his left hand to her belly and pressing Lily tight against him. He nuzzles her neck, trailing kisses down it as she reclines into him, resting her hands on his corded thighs. "I don't think you appreciate how much my body wants you Liliana; every hour of every day."

She laughs. "I wouldn't be able to walk!"

"You would just stay in my bed all day", Stuart moves his right hand to her breast, and idly plays with her nipple. "No need for walking." His touch gives her that uneasy warmth between her legs, and she can feel her nipple harden under his fingers.

Lily sighs. "You have no right to know how to turn me on the way you do. It's not fair."

"You like the slow seduction, don't you?" His left hand moves from her abdomen to brush over the mound between her legs and down her left thigh.

"Yes", she breathes as his lips trace the curve of her shoulder. "You know I do."

"My incredibly responsive Liliana", Stuart murmurs silkily, "You are just irresistible."

"The water is cooling…" Lily observes reluctantly.

"I know a cure for that", Stuart says as he steadies himself and stands up behind Lily. He steps out first, then gives her a hand for assistance. He offers her a towel and grabs one for himself.

"I like your hair braided; tousled around your face is beautiful, but in a braid makes you seem more the Viking queen." He laughs at his own observation and steps close to Lily. "Plus, I get to enjoy that lovely neck of yours more easily this way."

She gasps in mock shock which suddenly turns to real surprise as Stuart leans down, grabs her and hoists her over his shoulder.

"Stuart!" she yells, half laughing, half admonishing him. In response he turns to kiss her bottom cheek.

He carries her into the bedroom and sets her feet on the floor so she is standing in front of the wood stove. It feels wonderful - warm waves of heat are caressing her skin. The fire undulates dramatically through the glass door, the wind whooshing down the chimney making it dance excitedly.

Stuart looks like a god, naked and bathed in the amber firelight; Apollo come from Olympus to seduce a maiden, his perfection almost unbearable.

Their bodies are separated by inches, and he reaches out gently and touches Lily's face with his right hand. He trails it down slowly, to her shoulder and down her arm. Stuart is mesmerized; her eyes glow like emeralds set in an ancient statue, her body curvy and feminine yet with a strength and resilience to it.

His hand reaches her right one and he curves her palm over his fingers and tugs her the rest of the way towards him, so her breasts touch his skin, the hair on his chest teasing her nipples. She reaches her hand up, her fingers curling over his well formed arms, his soft skin a foil against the sinewy threads underneath.

His right hand cups her cheek and he brings his lips to her face, kissing around her mouth as he moves his left hand to massage her buttocks. Lily sighs contentedly, feeling the strings of his muscles flex under her hands, his body tighten with desire as he touches her. His lips cover hers and he presses her tightly against him, his right hand pulling at the string in her hair until it is freed and he tangles his fingers in it.

Lily's hand moves to his face, feeling the stubble along his strong jaw line, and then she slides up to bury her fingers in his thick, dark hair.

Stuart kisses her languidly, his tongue slowly playing in her mouth as his hands fondle her. His left hand still massages her bottom, pressing her hard against his erect cock between them, while his right hand holds the nape of her neck, then trails and lingers at her collarbone before stroking her face.

She can feel the burning between her legs, his touch a command for her body to waken that it cannot refuse. He scoops her up in his arms, and she twines her fingers around him and her mouth is at his neck, kissing and sucking at his throat and chin.

Stuart lays Lily on the bed and straddles her, cupping her face, stroking her body gently. "You are so beautiful, Liliana."

His gentle touches and caresses are driving her crazy, and she pushes her hips into him as he kisses her deeply.

Lily takes his face in her hands, pulls away from his lips, panting, and leans her forehead against his. "Stuart", she kisses him hard, "I want you inside of me, please." She moves to his neck and licks and nibbles it. She yearns for that completeness she feels when their bodies are one - moving together, reaching climax together.

"You are mine, Liliana", he says and runs his fingers between her cleft, relishing how wet she is.

She is kissing Stuart lovingly, his skin like an intoxicant - it's a transformation, as if she is a statue coming to life under the touch and ministrations of her own Pygmalion.

Stuart pushes her legs apart, moving between them, his lips and hands never leaving her body, his touch at once gentle yet demanding.

His right arm is resting on the bed, next to her shoulder. He reaches his hand and strokes the hair around her face. "You are mine, Liliana", he repeats again, his left arm caressing her thigh as he pushes it open wider. She can feel his cock throbbing at her nether lips, his contained passion making her squirm beneath him.

"Yes, Stuart, I'm yours", she says staring into the endless depths of his blue eyes.

His answer is a kiss; a long, lust filled kiss as he opens her up and slowly thrusts inside of her until he is fully sheathed and her cries and kisses dissolve in his mouth.

The storm outside rages. The wind rattles loose shutters and the rain pelts the cottage with unrelenting force as Stuart makes slow love to Lily - soft and deliberate, so that tears borne of emotion well up in her and overflow.

Tomorrow means leaving the idyll of Scotland and an end to the interlude they have had together but what other wonders could be in store? But for now Liliana is content.

TO BE CONTINUED…

About the Author

Holly Blackstone has been writing stories and poetry since she was seven and has always been an avid reader. She enjoys cooking, painting, reading, blogging, music and gardening, and lives in the Pacific Northwest.

If you've enjoyed Holly's books, ***please*** leave a rating and feedback on whatever site you ordered your ebook from and/or on Goodreads. Reviews mean a lot, especially to writers starting out. Thank you!!

Holly welcomes messages from her readers. You may contact her through her website at http://www.hollyblackstone.com or email: hollyblackstone.author@gmail.com .

Twitter: http://twitter.com/HollyBlackstone

Goodreads: https://www.goodreads.com/HollyBlackstone

Amazon: http://www.amazon.com/-/e/B00C3OO7QE

Facebook: http://www.facebook.com/AuthorHollyBlackstone/

Pinterest: http://www.pinterest.com/hollyblackstone/

Instagram: http://www.instagram.com/hollyblackstone/

Books by Holly

Liliana Batchelor Series (Contemporary Erotica)

An Accidental Affair

Step Across the Rubicon

The Air I Breathe

Banish the Darkness

Step In To the Light

The Void Chronicles (Fantasy Erotica)

A World Away

Rise of the Necromancers

Since Qua Non Cycle (Cyberpunk Erotica)

And Laugh at Digital Butterflies

Standalone Book(s)

Dark Erotica:

Blood and Frost

Coming soon…

The Templars Falter - **Void Chronicles**, book 3

Title tbd **- Sine Qua Non Cycle**, book 2

www.ingramcontent.com/pod-product-compliance
Lightning Source LLC
Chambersburg PA
CBHW030816310726
48980CB00006B/515/J

* 9 7 8 0 9 8 9 1 9 1 2 5 8 *